'A bravura feat of imaginat[...]
characters jostle for spac[...] [...]
Doris Day, John Lennon, Sammy Davis Jnr – as Cogan
traces her dramatic arc from fledgling performer through
VIP glamour to eventual flame-out . . . At considerable
risk, Gordon Burn has turned over the furniture of
modern iconography . . . *Alma Cogan* tears off celebrity's
mask and examines what lurks beneath: not the fear of
being forgotten, but the dread of not being allowed to die'
London Review of Books

'By any standards this is a beautifully written *tour de force*
of a novel: chilling, enthralling and repellent by turns'
Marie Claire

'This is a brilliant but disturbing book . . . Gordon Burn's
boldly imaginative act of resurrection'
Observer

'No other novel has displayed the originality and power of
Gordon Burn's *Alma Cogan*. This is my book of the year
because it is the one I desperately wish I had written'
Hilary Mantel, *Spectator*

'If Gordon Burn had simply risked this much and failed,
you'd have to love this dream memoir for its daring alone.
But to have succeeded so brilliantly makes *Alma Cogan* a
novel to treasure. As a dark meditation on fame and its
undertow, as a dangerous and loving vision of post-war
England, as a ruthless antidote to nostalgia, it's unlike
anything I've ever read'
Michael Herr

'A brilliant, and above all readable, debut'
The Face

'You'd be hard pressed to find a better British novel this
year'
iD

Alma Cogan

Gordon Burn is the author of two highly acclaimed books of non-fiction, *Somebody's Husband, Somebody's Son: The Story of the Yorkshire Ripper* and *Pocket Money: Bad Boys, Business Heads and Boom-time Snooker*. He was born in Newcastle in 1948 and lives in London.

Alma Cogan

A NOVEL

Gordon Burn

Minerva

A Minerva Paperback
ALMA COGAN

First published in Great Britain 1991
by Martin Secker & Warburg Limited
This Minerva edition published 1992
Reprinted 1992 (twice)
by Mandarin Paperbacks
Michelin House, 81 Fulham Road, London SW3 6RB

Minerva is an imprint of Reed Consumer Books Ltd

Copyright © Gordon Burn 1991

A CIP catalogue record for this title
is available from the British Library
ISBN 0 7493 9816 7

The Way You Do The Things You Do
Words and Music
by William 'Smokey' Robinson and Bobby Rogers
© 1964 Jobete Music (UK) Ltd
Lyrics reproduced by permission of Jobete Music (UK) Ltd
35 Gresse Street, London W1P 1PN

The Deadwood Stage (Fain/Webster)
The Way You Look Tonight (Fields/Kern)
The Little Drummer Boy
© Warner Chappell Music Ltd
Reproduced by permission of Warner Chappell Music Ltd

Off The Peg by Louis MacNeice
from *Collected Poems*, Ed. E. R. Dobbs (Faber, 1966)

The quotation from Alan Bennett's diary
reproduced by permission of the *London Review of Books*

The painting of Alma Cogan is by Peter Blake

Printed and bound in Great Britain
by Cox & Wyman Ltd, Reading, Berks

For Tom Baker, 1964–1988

And for Carol Gorner

Q: Did you ever dream of being
   an entertainer when you
         were a child?

A: No. I just had dreams
   about being murdered
         all the time.

– Madonna, interviewed 1990

Alma Cogan
was born in Golders Green, London
on 19 May 1932.
She died on 26 October 1966.

One

I always found having my picture taken with members of the public a frankly grim and, in the end, even a distressing experience.

The terrible conviviality and the unwelcome physical intimacy with total strangers of course was part of it.

Personal hygiene wasn't high on everybody's list of priorities in those days (it couldn't be: we're talking about the early fifties, barely a decade after the war, when plentiful hot water and unclogged fibres were still regarded as luxuries).

The women pressed close smelling of dandruff, candlewick, camphor and powdered milk, thinly disguised by a 'top-note', as the perfume manufacturers put it, of 'Evening in Paris' or Coty 'L'Aimant' or some other cheerful, rapidly evaporating technicolour stink from Woolworth's.

Despite the fact that they were wearing their 'best' clothes, the men gave off stomach-heaving waves of dog and diesel, boot dubbin, battery fluid, pigeon-feed, dried cuttle-fish, cooked breakfasts, rough tobacco, week-old hair oil and belched-back beer. They were odours that I unwillingly but instinctively associated with scenes of domestic mayhem – children scalded, wives abused, small dogs dropped from high windows – and of the time when the scraps of paper being so urgently thrust forward for my signature would be found curled up in the back of some sideboard drawer or dust-lined wallet.

(Starting out, I was given the following advice on how to deal

1

with fan mail by Max Miller: 'Stick them all in a sack until it's full,' he said. He was relieving himself in a handbasin at the time, talking to me over his shoulder. 'It makes a bloody good fire. How many people are you going to offend? Not more than a quarter of a million.')

They weren't monsters. They could be sweet, the fans. But they were ruthless. They wanted to be your best friend. The hands that reached out to take your elbow, or encircle your wrist, or that clamped themselves damply to your waist in order to position you for the viewfinder, said as much. 'Alma this' and 'Alma that'. All that pawing. They were all over you like a cheap suit, if you let them.

What did it for me, though, the thing I found truly unnerving – it used to make me feel vertiginous, bilious – had only a little to do with how they smelled and a lot to do with how they felt. No matter how casual, placid, sober, offhand or unimpressed these people looked, they were all, almost without exception, when you got close to them, men and women, throbbing and pounding and exploding inside; inwardly erupting.

You'd place your hand on a broad shoulder, if only in an effort to stay upright in the scrum, and find that under its cardboard-like jacket the shoulder fluttered like a small bird, quivered like a fish. Chests palpitated and knees knocked as if in some secret spasm of sexual excitement. The most casual contact with head or arm or buttock or thigh revealed a level of activity – flesh jerking and dancing, jitterbugging about, sinews rippling like wind in a curtain – that I could never completely come to terms with. Outwardly, these people appeared as simple and stolid as pillar boxes or lamp standards. Norman and Norma Normal. Inwardly, though, they twanged like tram wires, boiled and bubbled like kitchen geysers.

Not, of course, that I was very much different. Look at those pictures now and what would you see? Not a woman whose sinuses squealed and whose breastbone ached from heaving up, as she always heaved up, before having to go out and sing. But Alma Cogan, the glamorous radio, television and recording personality, surrounded by her adoring public.

The difference was, 'Alma Cogan' was a confection. That was accepted. (At least I thought it was.) Giving autographs and being photographed with fans after a performance was an extension of the job. You were still up. You were still 'on'. I was *expected* to perform; to be at once aloof and accessible; glamorous and homely; to give value.

'Enduring the bizarre projections of others' somebody once said was one of the penalties of fame. But that was okay. I was prepared for that.

What I couldn't handle and, as I've said, eventually came to dread, were those shivering, shaking bodies hanging around waiting to put themselves next to mine out in the dark every night. I was terrorised by the instant access that being well-known seemed to give me to the complexed, mysterious interior lives of complete strangers – people whose settled, unrippled surfaces, their bodies told me, concealed echoing chasms, recesses, sumps, and unpredictable underwater currents; a whole un-charted subaqueous existence.

This was some years before the events in Dallas. And I never really expected a Jack Ruby to step out of the crowd one day and do for me the way he did for Oswald. But I began to speculate on the histories – and futures – of the people I was asked to pose with outside theatres, at civic receptions and during PAs at factories and shops.

You were supposed to evolve a technique for those semi-public situations when you were in that strange limbo-land: half your projected public image and half your private self. The idea was to switch off; glaze over; go through the motions, head up, shoulders back, and don't forget to smile, etcetera. Just corpse it. But I couldn't do that.

Beneath the veneer of professional nonchalance, I was

3

actually extra-alert. Him, for example, the one with the slim-Jim tie and the cap pushed to the back of his head: did he seem a potential GBH-merchant/child-molester/wife-murderer/gang-rapist? And her, the one in the angora sweater and the milky lens in her glasses: did she seem the victim type? Which, if any, of these faces would one day rise to notoriety and have a name put to it? Would this picture – 'Move in a bit closer, Alma, she won't bite' – could this be the one that the hack doorstepping the unfortunates on the receiving end of some as yet unknown outrage or disaster would slip out of the family album and bury in his mackintosh pocket?

What is it they say? 'Fire lies hidden in wood.' Well that's the sort of thing I'm reaching towards here. That puts in a nutshell the sort of potentials, the devious dark energies I began to suspect in people.

Up until the night of the events I am about to describe, however, I hadn't, to the best of my recollection, been the object of or even witnessed any overt act of violence.

I was twenty-two in the summer of 1954 and my success was still new enough to want to get it out and drive it round the block every so often just to gauge the reaction.

I had had my first chart successes earlier that year and would travel to London on several Sundays during my first seaside summer season to record the songs which would turn out to be some of my biggest hits. In the next year and a half I'd register in the high-seventies on the 'reaction index' with the public. That put me up there with the likes of Denis Compton, Gilbert Harding, Archie Andrews, Lady Docker and the younger royals, and way ahead of, for example, Rab Butler and the Home Secretary of the day, David Maxwell-Fyfe (a long way ahead of him).

It was all just starting for me in 1954 and I'd wake up every morning and immediately experience the rich ache of anticipation: what good new thing was going to happen for me today? I

4

felt it as a constriction in the throat, a slow orbital turning of the stomach.

The season had just four more performances, two more nights to run. The leaves were already dropping. It was the end of one of the happiest extended periods I could remember.

Fourteen weeks was a long time to spend bumper-to-bumper with a single group of people. But it had been a friendly company, with no more than the usual quota of drunks and lechers and only the usual run-of-the-mill tantrums, back-biting and bellyaching. I'd rented a comfortable villa close to the town but well off the tourist route and had been given a dressing-room with a window from which there was a sheer drop to the sea.

The theatre was on the end of the North Pier and the dressing-room was in a rear corner of the theatre. We performed every night on a stage which rested on tarred timbers, bearded in green and scabbed with shells, which were apparently sunk into the sea-bed. This was, and remains, a source of mystery to me.

I could hear the sea gurgling and sucking around the timbers every night as I dressed and prepared to go on. Sometimes it did more than that: it blatted and slapped, and pasted gobs of slime against the windows. But I remember it as a mild summer, with nothing very dramatic in the way of weather.

That July, rationing came to an end: housewives burned their ration books in Trafalgar Square and comedians everywhere started scrabbling round for new material. It was the first summer for many years that shop signs and neon lights were turned on. Standing at the window as I changed, I could see lines of coloured lights strung out around the bay and, behind them, the pulses and scribbles of neon from the cafés and arcades. When you stepped backwards into the room, the colours looked kaleidoscopic beyond the salt frosting.

Three months earlier, I'd been hypnotised by all this. But it wasn't the best preparation for going out to sing the jaunty crowd-pleasers and up-beat novelty numbers for which I was

5

becoming famous, and so I canned it. I closed the curtains at the end of the first-house when the sky was starting to reflect pink in the water and kept them closed until it was time to leave.

That next-to-last night, though, which was going to be celebrated with a party in the town afterwards, it seemed appropriate to indulge a mood that went with the yellowed good-luck telegrams that would soon have to be unpinned from the wall, and the outpouring of sentiment which was the traditional accompaniment to these occasions. That night, we'd all write things like 'It's been fabulous knowing you' and 'Great to have worked with you again!!' and 'From one hobo to another – hope to see you around again sometime somewhere', knowing that the likely destination of these messages, though no doubt heartfelt at the time, was the toilet bowl and the incinerator.

In order to get into the mood, I turned down the sound monitor which kept me in touch with what was happening on- stage – although by this time I hardly needed it: 'It wasn't a question of keeping the wolf away from the door so much as getting the bloody thing out of the house,' the second-spot comic was saying as I put my finger on the button, meaning it was about ten to nine – and drew back the curtains to have a look at the view.

It was still there. And, together with the sea, whose surface that night looked as if it had been gone over with a varnishing comb – there were eddies gathered like knots on the flat surface and long, grainy striations – it was still powerfully melancholic. But, like a song that used to blow you away and now merely sets your fingers tapping, it no longer struck me as anything to write home about. The old bone-chilling thrill was gone. It was a view which already belonged to nostalgia rather than the present.

Stan, one of the band boys (he later became my MD and

accompanist), had volunteered to walk me to the party. We waited until after eleven and then stepped outside to brave the usual suspects and what had turned into a gusty, autumnal night.

I hesitated on the top step under the bare lightbulb to give them an eyeful – I was wearing a fitted suit ('figure-hugging', as the tame pen performers for the papers who'd already written me up invariably described it – this was also my interview uniform), an Arctic-fox fur with a faint, unusual purple cast, and starburst ear-rings.

The cleaner in the glass-walled sun lounge directly opposite the stage-door stopped what she was doing long enough to clock me; but the fishermen on the end of the pier continued baiting their lines or stood with their eyes firmly fixed on the horizon: I could see their dense, concentrated silhouettes against the pale pool of moonlight on the water.

I'd spent months when I was younger practising my signature. That was my only hobby in adolescence: autograph practice. The arrival of the ball-point gave my technique a great push forward. It was the difference between the old put-put planes and jet travel. Now there was no resistance or drag; the pen flew over the page leaving a trail of loops and flourishes in which I could only just make out the elements of my own name. Even now, thirty-plus years later, I have to consciously scale down the action and remember that all I'm doing is writing a cheque or taking delivery of something from somebody who probably wasn't born at the time I'm talking about.

It was surprising, the things you could be asked to sign in those days. The trays from cigarette packets and the backs of match-boxes obviously. But also rent books, dole books, business cards, blouses, packets of nylon stockings, paper bags from Skardon's Fish Buffet, still warm and smelling of vinegar; even – occasionally – bare skin.

A young scaffolder or warp-dresser from the mills once asked me to sign an autograph on his upper arm which he said he was

7

going to have 'needled up' into a tattoo. It was a cold night, I think in Leeds or Bradford, but he stripped down to his singlet in the street while a small crowd cheered him on.

He made a fist and held his arm out straight, then turned his head away while I signed the tough cushion of muscle, as if he was a small boy being given a school innoculation.

He reappeared a year or two later and hauled his sleeve up to show me the blue-green inks of the finished job. 'The man police would like to question has a marked Yorkshire accent and a tattooed autograph of Alma Cogan on his left tricep . . .' That was my first thought.

But then he pulled the back of his shirt out of his trousers to reveal a gallery of even more distinguishing features: four eagles in varying postures, a garland of roses, a peacock, a geisha girl, a selection of hearts, anchors, satyrs, the winged cap of Mercury, a cigar-smoking skull in a top hat, and the legends DEATH BEFORE MARRIAGE and UP THE CITY.

But it's a thought to conjure with all the same: somebody going to their grave with your now flabby signature still inscribed 1/32 of an inch into their person.

There was nothing this noteworthy on the night in question: just a ripe ponging crush of hot-eared young men who looked like their fathers and full-blown, over-talced young women who looked like their mothers, and their earnest, fumbling attempts at familiarity. There was a chorus of shouted goodnights as Stan finally edged me clear and we started walking in the direction of the front, where we could still see the late trams gliding past, lit up like galleons.

A car usually dropped me at the theatre and came back to collect me later. I can't remember if that was the first time I'd travelled the length of the pier under my own steam. What I do remember is the state of disrepair of the footway; the treacherous gaps between some of the boards – easily big enough to break a leg in; the sea churning like cocoa thirty feet below and the incongruous, glinting texture of my shoes in the near-dark.

I also remember the billboarded pictures of myself that I tottered past, clinging to Stan's arm, and my name spelled out in block-letters that had the same drunken haphazardness as the letters that run through seaside rock. Posters were still the products of primitive tech in those days, with red and blue inks that seemed to stand off the paper and create a nimbus effect where the printing misregistered. As a result, the face that stared back at me as I negotiated the North Pier that night is the face I still see when I think back to those times: bright, confused, innocent, blurred, with a dated, hopeful glow around the edges.

The party conference season started when we finished, and a picture of Mr Attlee – an old man in a homburg hat with fatigue and defeat written all over him – had gone up outside the Winter Gardens. We turned right into the narrow streets of the old town where the traditional seaside smells – shellfish, rancid fat, sugared rock – seemed baked into the fabric of the buildings.

We were looking for somewhere called the Helmet – I wasn't aware of the sexual connotation at the time – and found it after several wrong turnings which involved stepping over cooling streams of urine and disturbing courting couples in the recessed doorways of shops that seemed to sell nothing but rusted baked-bean tins and pre-war hats.

'Are you members, darlings?'

It was the second-spot comic, got up like something – something female, that is – from the naughty nineties or the roaring twenties, it was difficult to tell.

'She's not a pretty little lady, is she?' This to me about Stan, who was six-foot-one and still V-shaped from his time in the navy. 'Oh better come in then, cunty.'

The Helmet was what my mother would have called a dive and my mother would have been right. It was at the bottom of two flights of funnel-like, slack-carpeted stairs and consisted of a single room with a small serving bar in one corner and a small raised stage in another, diagonally opposite.

In the minimal lighting, it was possible to see that somebody, almost certainly a previous owner, had carried out murals on a maritime theme. Crabs, starfish, octopuses and other – to me – unidentifiable crustaceans and creepy-crawlies battled for space in patinaed, gilt-framed panels. Flocked wallpaper in two shades of green completed the decorations: with light filtering dimly on to it, it looked appropriately like river-moss.

Stan went to the bar and I parked myself at a table full of faces that I hardly recognised without their tall head plumes and feather-cut wigs and the cheap, raw-edged gorgeousness of theatrical slap. Most of the gorgeousness that night seemed to have been hijacked by a few of the boys from the chorus (and a couple from front-of-house) who had come dragged up in borrowed diamanté sheaths and 'hostess gowns' of ruffled chiffon.

The female members of the chorus, present as themselves, looked like husks. They looked slighter; softer. The softness was emphasised by the cigarettes and brittle painted nails they waved in front of their faces all the time like shields.

Show girls in those days weren't necessarily brassy: it wasn't a condition of the job; and the word itself had yet to become a euphemism for 'tart'. Most of the ones I knew who didn't marry comics married accountants, doctors, commercial travellers and ambitious local government yes-men. They were content to keep house and take their place on the church flower-roster until the children grew up, when they would become, as many of them now are, marriage guidance counsellors, animal welfarists, Earth Firsters, prison visitors and JPs.

Kathie Moody, a former Breams Breezy Babe and seaside hoofer, had graduated in style a few years earlier by marrying Lew Grade. Audrey Smith, a Tiller Girl and can-can dancer, had married Leslie Grade. Then there was old Nora Docker, as if we could forget, who had worked her way up from high-kicking and hostessing at Murray's Club in Soho, to Sir Bernard and the gold-plated Daimler.

10

Even Rita, the Grades' sister, who would soon be constantly on the phone trying to recruit me for her charitable functions and good works, started off on the boards. ('We're all going to feel a little bit taller at the end of the day, would I lie to you Alma?' Rita would launch into her familiar schmooze, well aware that any refusal to put in an appearance amounted to professional suicide. 'It's for a good cause. That road home is going to seem a little bit shorter.')

In the meantime, it was a life of cheap chat-ups and dried-out boarding-house suppers for those who were less well-connected. That night at the Helmet most of the chorus didn't know where they were going to be the same time the following week. This accounted for the cigarette-ends piling up in the saucers and the wreaths of pale smoke that clung to their hair and played around their lively, laughing faces.

' . . . so he said, "I've slept with more people than are in here tonight – and that was on my honeymoon," ' I heard a brunette on my left say. She was shouting to make herself heard above the noise which had already reached a level where talking made you worry about preserving your voice for the next night's performance. Somebody was banging away at a piano; somebody else was murdering a banjo.

'Don't take this the wrong way. But are you ever worried,' the brunette, whose name was Glennis, was addressing me now, 'about being, you know, a five minute's magic?' But before I could answer I was being tapped on the shoulder by Trevor, known throughout the business as Big Rita. (Later in life, when the drink and 'trolling' had begun to take their toll, it would become 'Rita Hayworth's mother'.)

He was gesturing at the table with thick fingers covered in glass rings the colour of table jellies. I thought it was my drink he was after, which was just lemonade mixed with vermouth. But he wanted my cigarette packet: I passed it to him and he slid the silver foil out gently, removed the membrane of tissue paper from the back of it and elaborately blotted his lips. He let the lipstick-stained tissue drift down onto the table and made his way towards the stage.

> 'Electric drill groaning,
> Office telephoning,
> Gracie Fields funning,
> The gangsters gunning,
> Talk of our love,'

Trevor started to sing.

A part of the evening's entertainment, being quietly relished by those of us not directly involved, came from the cross-currents caused by the appearance on the scene of some of the band wives, breaking up various cosy liaisons that had lasted through the summer. A number of the girls who had been displaced were drinking more heavily than usual and hostilely eyeing up the opposition. Margaret, a full-figured but otherwise rather plain girl from Coventry, was one of them.

'I was expecting to be able to come here tonight and let me back hair down,' she complained loudly. 'Then *she* has to put in an appearance. She hasn't got the, excuse me, guts to look me in the eye, if you've noticed. She looks like one of them that'll go fat when she gets older.'

There was a lot more in this vein. Fortunately most of it was swallowed up in the general hubbub which, every so often, gave way to the loud singing of sentimental songs. Then, just as suddenly as the singing had started, it would stop, and everybody would go back to bawling at each other over their glasses.

'Scientists are busy proving the big part personality and looks play in your life. It's all written, you know.' Margaret again. 'They're going to prove that your life is mapped out for you. So why regret what was inevitable? I'm a total fatalist.'

But I had started to experience, and covertly enjoy, the gently rolling sensation you sometimes get when you have spent time surrounded by water; the floor and the table both seemed to be moving. That, combined, I suppose, with the fact that I was now a little lit myself and the noise in the Helmet which had reached the sort of pitch where it was as unobtrusive as silence, dredged to the surface something somebody – an eminent artist, as it happens, his face as red as the wine he was anxiously looking around for more of to put in his glass – had said to me not long before at a London party.

'There are only two things I know that I can look at forever: waves breaking in a long slow rolling turn along a sandy beach with the spray being blown off the top. And – oh yes' – a waiter had finally arrived with a refill; he relieved him of the bottle – 'the movement of a tall poplar's topmost branches and leaves. The poplars I can watch endlessly with the lovely movement they have all the time.'

Everything that happened next seemed to happen at the same languorous tempo; waves breaking on a beach; a tall poplar brushing the sky.

I had been aware of a dancer called Gerard, who I knew was from a small town in the west of Ireland, sitting astride an upright chair on the stage miming to a tape of Doris Day's 'The Deadwood Stage'. He was batting black spiked lashes and had his own blond hair turned back in metallic brackets either side of his face to look like Doris Day's; he was wearing a red-and-white bandanna and something that roughly resembled the buckskin jacket Doris Day wore in *Calamity Jane*. Every time he got to 'whipcrack away, whipcrack away, whipcrack away' he waved around a piece of clothesline and everybody joined in.

Now, though, he was suddenly being jerked backwards off the chair by a man in a dark, American-cut sharkskin suit and what we knew in those days as a Billy Eckstine shirt, who was accompanied by another man who was less flashily dressed. The second man caught Gerard as he fell, then flipped him upright in a single unbroken movement so that he was facing stage-front.

13

This was done with such panache that for an instant you might have been fooled into thinking you were watching a top-line, if somewhat dated, adagio act. If you hadn't been paying attention you might have thought that this was cod-violence; knockabout; pantomime aggro.

But already, of course, you know different. What we were about to witness was an act of violence of the sort that, up to that night, I'd believed no human capable. From that point on, though, it was the sort of vile craziness I would suspect everybody of having the potential for.

Very soon, I could tell – we could all tell; you could already smell it – there was going to be blood. And now – was that a drum-roll I heard? – here it came: a thick rope of blood which twisted lazily through the air, followed by a fine spray which settled on the shoulders of those nearest the stage like sparks from an anvil, like snow. There was a thick slick of it on the leading player's sharkskin jacket that looked like blood on the flank of a tormented bull. Except that it was the bull in this case which was handing out the punishment.

Both men had inserted their fingers into the boy's carefully painted mouth and had looked at first as if they were going to force open his teeth like a vice until he resembled the turkey-necked, screaming grotesques in my friend Francis Bacon's painting, *Three Studies for Figures at the Base of a Crucifixion*.

But these were learner performers. They needed cruder results than that. They weren't prepared to trust the patience of their audience. The brass-ringed fingers hooked into his mouth and tore open the flesh of his cheeks like the wrapping round a promising-looking parcel; they ripped upwards towards his eyes and outwards towards his ears; they simply peeled his face like an orange.

Nobody was ever able to give an explanation for the attack, but it seems reasonable to suppose that there could only be two motives: sexual or financial. If I opt for the former it is because of

14

a comment made to me some years later by somebody who had also witnessed what happened at first-hand. 'There is nothing more vicious than a villainous poof,' he said, and he spoke as one who was in a position to know.

The 'American invasion' of entertainers was at its height in 1954 – Lena Horne, Johnny Ray, Nat King Cole, Frankie Laine, Eddie Fisher and Guy Mitchell had all been over to play the Palladium. Nobody excited as much public interest, though, as Doris Day.

Four months after the events described here, I met her at a reception held in her honour in the River Room at the Savoy. With its kind, modulated lighting, circulating flunkies and stiff linen napiery it was a world away from the sleaze of the Helmet. Inevitably, though, when we were introduced I found myself scrutinising the star guest's ivory porcelain mask for signs of mutilation and invisible mending. (The boy Gerard survived, hideously disfigured.)

The main focus of interest, for obvious reasons, was her mouth. 'No successful singer has an ugly mouth' was something that had been drummed into me by a woman with a perpetually glistening crimson gash who I had gone to for voice lessons when I was younger. And I found myself following the ellipses and painted puckerings of Doris Day's (surprisingly full) lips with such concentration that afterwards I would be able to recall barely a word of our bright, brief cocktail conversation.

It seemed inconceivable then and for many years afterwards that anything could eclipse that as my most vivid memory of the occasion. Events conspired, however, to place even the Gerard episode in a perspective that suggested how far the world had rolled in a direction that no one at the time could have predicted.

My escort at the Savoy that day was a friend called Sammy who had started out in the Delfont office and was now working as a song plugger in Denmark Street. It was a job he did well; Sammy was what he described as a 'people person'. He had extra-finely-tuned antennae. He had a nose for an opportunity; an unerring instinct for the profit-pulse. And at the Day reception he quickly ingratiated himself with a small boy who was sitting alone and bored at the edge of the action.

It didn't take a genius to see that the boy was American – his skin was honeyed, compared to the dishwater grey of English children; and he was wearing a Brooks Brothers shirt and saddle-oxfords. Sammy still maintains he didn't work out until afterwards that his new chum Terry had to be the son of Doris Day and her first husband, the trombonist Al Jorden, who committed suicide.

But he was, and for the rest of their stay Sammy did 'Deedee', as she almost instantly became, and her husband, Marty Melcher, the favour of keeping Terry occupied. Unlike his mother's husband, Terry Melcher wasn't a shlump; he was a nice boy who was remarkably well adjusted for somebody who had grown up on the Hollywood celebrity circuit.

I went with him and Sammy to watch a baseball game at a U.S. army base in Oxfordshire and a couple of nights later to see the speedway at the White City. Both times, Terry fell asleep in the car afterwards, and slept with his head in my lap – I can feel his hair now; smell the soapy, boyish smell – all the way back to the hotel. My instinct all the time was to comfort him for the terrible thing I thought I had seen happen to his mother.

Unlike Sammy, who wasted little time in acting on Marty Melcher's invitation to give him a call if he was ever on their side of the Big Ditch, I made no attempt to follow through or build on the DD connection.

I followed Terry Melcher's career at a distance – the records he made in the early sixties as 'Bruce and Terry', with Bruce Johnson of the Beach Boys (I was pleased – if mistaken – to be able to vote one of them a hit during a stint on *Juke Box Jury*); his

16

successful production work for the Byrds and others who had helped turn his mother and myself into show-business dinosaurs.

It was odd, then, that I should react to news of his narrow escape from involvement in the Manson murders with such a sense of alarm and personal foreboding.

It emerged that Terry Melcher had been the previous occupant of the house at 10050 Cielo Drive in Hollywood where Sharon Tate and a number of others were ritually butchered by the Manson 'Family' in August 1969. Terry had apparently auditioned Manson for a recording contract and turned him down; it was Terry who the 'Family' intended to slaughter that night, rather than Sharon Tate, Jay Sebring and the others.

Terry, I read, had hired round-the-clock bodyguards for himself and his mother; he had suffered a breakdown, gone into the bottle, and had to be given tranquillisers before testifying at the trial.

This was all understandable. What was less easy to fathom were my own feelings of profound unease bordering on panic as a result of events taking place ten thousand miles away, halfway round the other side of the world. It was like a door had opened and the draught had blown out my pilot-light. I was on mood elevators to get me up, Oblivon to bring me down, as well as stuff I took without knowing where it was supposed to take me.

It seemed to me at the time that we were embarked on an unstoppable downward spiral of dementia. That, anyway, is how I rationalised it to the doctors I consulted. And there's a chance I might even have slightly believed it in 1969.

What I very much believed – I couldn't *not* believe it, faced with the evidence of depleted date-books and what I saw every time I more than glanced in a mirror – was that I was thirty-seven and over the hill; yesterday's papers.

When I made the decision to fade away with as little self-pity and as much dignity as possible, I made it quickly, two days into a

17

six-day engagement at an armpit of a club on a newly-pedestrianised shopping street in the Manchester suburbs.

What was the alternative? To hang around until I became the kind of game old dame, the kind of gutsy old *shtarker* who nurses her nervous breakdown on third-division chat shows and whose every public appearance turns into a psychodrama.

In 1969 I was so far from being on the crest of a vogue that I no longer registered as even a blip on the drug-fuddled, booze-addled, youth-annexed national consciousness.

I decided to return to a commonplace existence, and cut the pretence. (What am I saying, 'return'? All my life I had lived in the anticipation, and then the realisation, of being one of those recognised names. The commonplace was virgin territory as far as I was concerned.)

From now on, I told myself, climbing in behind a bombed-looking teenage minicab driver outside The Recovery Room noshery/nitery in Wythenshawe, I was going to wind down from ambition. From now on I was going to live in real time.

Two

The tide is almost out and I am standing at the window watching a man in waders making his way across the river-bed towards a boat called *The Terri-Marie*. *The Terri-Marie* (the man's wife? his daughter? his wife *and* daughter? one of the eighties crop of lost-in-the-mix girl singers? none of these?) is lying at an angle in a gully gouged deep in the mud. There are coils of rope, pieces of equipment I don't have the names for and old paint cans on the weathered and possibly slippery deck (it is close to the end of the year; the year is 1986; it rained loudly in the night).

A bird is pecking at an orange-red berry on the old stone wall directly below where I am standing. Clear water from the surrounding hills runs swiftly along the gullies. Seagulls circle overhead yowling like cats. Other seabirds perch on roofs and on the showily customised cabins of cabin-cruisers, depositing fresh coats of lime. Smoke rises from the pastel-washed bungalows littering the hillside opposite. Something which I now recognise as an aerial root flickers at the top of the window, at the edge of my vision, like a hair in the frame.

These are the touches of local colour attaching to my present life.

But my previous life – the life I gave the kiss-off to what seems a lifetime ago, outside The Recovery Room, Wythenshawe, Manchester; the life I surrendered as reluctantly as somebody getting up from a fire to step out into the cold and bring coal – still tugs at me, often when I least expect it. It is tugging at me at this

19

moment, for example, in the form of music that I'm being force-fed down the telephone.

'I have —— —— for you. Please hold,' the voice (I imagined glasses on a plastic-linked chain, tusky Streisand-length nails) had said. The next thing I heard was the click of technology engaging, a half-second of tape-slip, then over-loud muzak which it took me less than a bar to identify as the Bert Kaempfert version of 'Bye Bye Blues'.

Virtually the only way I could shift records by the mid-sixties was at personal appearances in those big stores which retained the same older department heads who were in charge in the days when I could be depended on to pull the crowds in for them.

I suppose they went along with the charade out of sympathy and nostalgia and, in a few cases, out of the delight that most of us have taken at one time or another in seeing somebody heading for a fall. This particular form of *schadenfreude* showed itself in a manic eagerness to prise people away from whatever purchase they were considering and force them to witness the spectacle of a career in unpretty decline.

Only two records ever seemed to provide the background to these desultory, progressively unedifying side-shows: 'A Walk in the Black Forest' by Horst Jankowski, and Bert Kaempfert's 'Bye Bye Blues'. The push was on then to sell stereo equipment and the paraphernalia of home music-centres; and the Kaempfert especially was perfect for demonstrating the bass-to-treble range and fidelity of reproduction of the new audio technology.

In point of fact, I never found it a faithful reproduction at all. It bore the same relationship to music as the heavy wax fruit I associate with my childhood – was there a home that didn't have its heaped bowl of untouchable, vaguely sinister wax pears and bananas? – bore to the real thing.

The glissando strings, thunking bass and muted trumpets of the Kaempfert orchestra, all existing in their own channels, all separated out in the hyper-real way that they never could be in

20

reality, seemed to point up the dreaminess and sad separateness of the shoppers as they drifted from homely cabinet model to perspex-and-iridium Bang & Olufsen, from spotlit display to spotlit display.

I still find watching people going about their everyday business to a soundtrack that I can hear but they can't – because I'm sitting in a car or coach, for example, or standing at a window the way I am now – inexplicably touching, and once or twice – stopping to let an austerely beautiful but unselfconscious (which was the point) mulatto schoolgirl cross at a pedestrian crossing in New Street in Birmingham, while the Ronettes' 'Be My Baby' played on the radio and drops of rain shuddered diagonally upwards across the windscreen – physically wrenching.

'Bye Bye Blues' has segued (not seamlessly; again there was a couple of inches of tape-slip) into the Carpenters' 'Close To You', a song that smooches along at the same clippety-clop, subliminal blood-pulse tempo. And the man in waders is still making his way towards *The Terri-Marie* in time with the beat, stepping over, occasionally ducking under, the mooring ropes of other boats as he goes.

The psychology behind telephone muzak, of course, is so elementary as to be barely worth stating. It's supposed to divert your attention from the fact that your time is being wasted and you're being putzed about.

There was no muzak in the factories I visited for shows like *Workers' Playtime* for a long time; then suddenly it was there as an airy rinse in all of them, all the time, 'psychologically programmed', round every corner you turned. The only refuge were the boardrooms where we were given lunch after the broadcasts and presented with examples of the factories' output – spectacle frames, nylon lingerie, brush-and-pan sets, glass tumblers, continental sausages – as a token of their appreciation.

Personally I find all kinds of wallpaper music about as relaxing as the yammerings of the happy snappers who used to turn up to take my picture in those days. 'You know me. This isn't going to hurt. I'm not going to try anything violent or unflattering. I'm just going to make you look beautiful . . Super . . . Hold it there . . . And again . . . One more . . . Relax. Marvellous. Don't look so . . . Did I ever tell you I knew Doris Day before she was a virgin? . . . Better. I'm not one of them that's going to poke the camera up your skirt or down your throat . . . Think happy. Wet the lips. Think top-ten . . . A little less *grin*, sweetheart . . . Better. Skirt up just a little. We're getting it . . . This new record's top-five. Cert.' And so on.

The result was pictures I could only bear to squint at at the time and haven't been able to make myself look at for almost thirty years.

There has been a single cursory 'Sorry to keep you' in the three or four minutes that I have been holding for ——— ———. Almost involuntarily, I hang up on Karen Carpenter in mid-trill, bored with the arrogance of the nothings and nobodies who think a job in publishing or journalism, of either the print or broadcast varieties, is a licence to jerk the strings and watch you jump.

The telephone down here hardly rang at all for years. On days when I was feeling particularly laid-by and out of things, I'd pick it up whenever I was passing, just for the purring reassurance of the tone.

The phone still doesn't ring very often. But when it does these days the likelihood is that it's one of the people who seem to have got together and, with striking unanimity, decided that Alma Cogan is once more somehow *viable*.

No longer merely a washed-up relic of the past, apparently; a piece of pop marginalia of interest only to the unyoung, the untrendy, the unmoneyed and the terminally whacko. But – and I have it here in black-and-white – 'an iconic performer', 'a leisure icon', redolent of happier, less complex times. She is an 'emblematic' figure 'reflecting the historical moment'; 'irrefutably part of the fifties Zeitgeist'. Not to mention the fact that she

22

had a colourful reputation in the past for keeping rough as well as more salubrious company, and turns up increasingly in the biographies of dead contemporaries.

I should feel flattered. Instead, it makes me feel like one of those villages that were flooded to make reservoirs at the end of the war and that then miraculously reappeared during the long, parched summer of 1976. They became popular tourist attractions, drawing picnickers like flies, and provided an excuse for a great deal of misty-eyed, inter-generational reminiscing: there was the dairy and over there the Big House; there was the steeple that seemed to reach miles into the sky. All of course only identifiable now as mossy scabs and stunted earthworks.

There's a national characteristic you must have noticed: if there's one thing people in this country like better than pulling somebody down, it's putting them back again. They beat you about the head then pass you a bandage. It's so British.

I can't pretend I wouldn't have welcomed the gesture at certain moments in the past, when I was finding the applauseless life an inconsolably hard one to live.

To be famous, it was once put to me, is to be alone but without being lonely: like Achilles in his tent; like Lindbergh in the *Spirit of St Louis*, flying over the Atlantic, while the world waits for him to land.

An alternative definition, of course, is the inability to be alone or be yourself without an audience; to be unable to exist without constant, positive feedback.

'Do you know who you are!' a man cried out in excitement once, rushing up to me in the street. 'And you're standing *here*! I can't believe it! You're here.'

'Well I have to be somewhere,' I said, and he seemed to find that a satisfactory answer: it seemed to confirm for him that I wasn't merely made up of light and Ben-Day dots, equal parts cathode ray and newsprint; that somewhere behind and beyond all that I was in fact flesh and bones.

23

It's a long way from that day to the point I am at now where – to risk sounding like one of the new Armani mystics, the 'designer Buddhists' you currently read so much about in the papers – I have adopted a tranquil, uneventful life of passive acceptance. I live in pleasant, unembittered obscurity and feel at ease for the first time in my own skin. Cleansed of fame and its unquenchable cravings.

There is a word for what I have come to regard now as my first life. Nabokov used it once: '*A stranger caught in a snapshot of myself.*' 'Alma Cogan', a fantasy of beehive hair and bouffant skirts, ostrich plumes, Leichner colours and tarmacadam lashes, is something I no longer feel able to associate with me. It feels as far away as the doodlebug and the Victrola.

So how is it that the letters and calls from the the-way-it-was, way-we-were, return-with-us-now, kiss-and-tell franchisers and packagers are able to get under my skin and breech my defences so effectively? Why do they hit my system like the first drink of the day (a *big* gin-and-tonic at 6.30 on the nose, in the present regimen)?

If this was a different medium I could use computer graphics to show you: there'd be cartoon crowds, cinemas, taxi-cabs, power stations, chefs' hats, VDUs and supermarket trolleys all spilling out of envelopes and pouring from the earpieces of telephones to indicate city energy; city chaos; the invigorating unfakeable urban clang and clamour to which I confess to being helplessly addicted. Caught off-guard, it can sometimes tear me up with longing.

The usual form, I've been discovering, is a letter carrying a vogueish logo – Art Deco, constructivist, cleverly mismatched hieroglyphs – followed by a call from a person whose position usually advertises itself through one of the 'fast-track' Telecom technologies.

There's the long hold accompanied by muzak, as demonstrated; the cordless model – good for mobility and giving an acoustic impression (not necessarily accurate) of the executive dimensions of the room the call is coming from. Lastly, there is the increasingly popular car-phone.

Calls from car-phones always sound as if they're being made at eighty miles an hour on the motorway or from halfway up a cliff-face, which I suppose is part of their appeal. Every time I pick up the receiver and hear the now-familiar wh-o-o-oosh, I have to know where the caller is *as we speak*.

The replies – heading up Park Lane towards Marble Arch; crossing the Hammersmith flyover going to Chiswick – are always evocative enough to haul me out of my immediate surroundings for the duration of the call: I'm not in the world of tide-tables and seagull droppings, but in a place where the 'in-car environment' of thrashing newspapers and swirling ash perfectly replicates the outdoor environment of sweet diesel and graffiti and blinding grit. O city lust!

I have not met Cat from the Nostalgia Book Club, or Shale or Linzi from *Not Forgotten* magazine; Brick from Charm records, Gully from Star books, Devora from Penguin, or Roxy, Tawatha, Gun, Dyck, Kaff, Swoosie, Chicken or Jalet from Bonham's, Christie's (there is apparently unprecedented demand these days for pop-related knick-knacks and memorabilia), the BBC and Channel 4. But the names themselves, neither entirely natural nor entirely invented, not quite kosher and at the same time not really smile-when-they're-low showbiz, seem to sound a warning.

Read them and you find yourself looking for the tell-tale white wart of Tipp-ex. Roll them round your tongue and you get an idea of what having a split-palate must be like. Say them aloud and the result is queerly cracked; disconcertingly off-centre. They are names that suggest the kind of ambiguities and complexities I have become unused to, hunkered in my bunker, buried in my 'healthy grave' (the Rev. Sydney Smith) down here in the country.

The man on *The Terri-Marie* by this time is doing something which, in boating language, is probably called 'slopping out the bilge'. He's standing on the deck of *The Terri-Marie* throwing water overboard from a plastic bucket.

And now the phone is going again. It's going to be ——— ———, oozing apologies and the usual charming horse manure. I know without meeting him that, if I ever did meet him and offered a straightforward 'How do you do?', he would shift his glass from one hand to the other, tilt his head to what he considers its most pleasing angle (expertly-cut slabs of hair realigning themselves impressively in the light) and say: 'I do fan*tas*tic!'

I'm tempted. Of course I'm tempted. My idea of happiness is the Happy Hour: a bare-brick bar with the office-bound straggling in wall-eyed after a trying day; the Nat Cole and Swingles tapes being swapped for Elvis' 'Suspicious Minds' and the volume simultaneously going up; cold beaded bottles and expensive nibbling bits going on to some no-questions business tab.

I could say 'yes' to a bit of that. I could say 'yes' to quite a lot of it, if I'm honest. But I have to bear in mind the almost inevitable consequences and something I recently wrote into my book.

'A normal, human-like existence is what the majority of the human race aspires to – the aim must be to operate on the same physical and psychological plane as the majority of people – like every natural process, human life gravitates toward moderation.' Gone over in acid-yellow over-marker, meaning 'v.imp.'

In other words, it wouldn't be hard to get talked back into rejoining the conga-line of the professional attention-grabbers and pathologically unignored. Devora says she's convinced she could get a book 'into the sellers'; Brick writes that he's already got the main promotional chat shows 'locked up'.

All things considered, and everything being equal, though – 'Per ardua ad astrakhan' is a phrase which suddenly presents itself here – I think I'll stick.

There's some potatoes that need pulling; there's a dog in the kitchen whining for his feed. So here I go. I'm walking away from this broop-broop. Watch me now.

Three

'Beginnings.' 'Solace.'

If you could wish to have two words spring out of the dark at you, you couldn't wish better than these. If it happened to be the darkness enfolding the countryside where you were about to begin a new life – so much the better.

'Beginnings' – pokerwork lettering on a piece of varnished blond timber – was illuminated in the headlamps of the taxi when we pulled over to let a car squeeze past us at the top of the narrow lane. The car was travelling uphill, away from the village of Cleve, which was our destination, and it slid like a bolt along the high hedges whose sides were grooved smooth from a thousand tight negotiations like this.

We had one more pull-over to make in the dark on the steep gradient. Then 'Solace', the name of an old tub, was suspended in the lights as we carefully negotiated the last corner at the bottom of the hill: the letters were sharp-edged and oddly permanent-looking against the boat's flaking boards, which were mainly that mysterious secondary colour, apart from their paint, which very old boats have.

I had another look at the piece of paper containing the directions which I had been reading aloud to the driver, and realised then that the lighted windows that we'd seen before bearing left round the end of the estuary were the windows of the cottage to which we had been blindly descending.

The driver seemed to realise this without me having to tell

him. 'Nearly got you home, young lady,' he said (a sure sign that the years were starting to take their toll – the years *and* the efforts of my liver to process the brave intake of the night before: the truth was I was still quarter-cut). And then, 'And you, mister' to the dog, who was spiralling up in excitement at the back of the man's head, in between scuttling from door to door.

I had been pathetically reassured to see a rank of what I regarded as 'London' taxis waiting with their engines turning over at the station. Then I had been just as pathetically disconcerted to find myself cheated of the familiar, unreproducible, to me dependably balm-like and curative sounds and smells of the classic black FX4, 'the special FX'.

The back of the cab, I soon saw, had been turned into a replica of the shoebox rooms in the sodium-coloured towers and terraces which made a corridor out of the city for the first three or four miles.

There was what had once been a brightly coloured, now uniformly greasy piece of carpet remnant covering the floor; a stretch-cover so pocked with cigarette burns it resembled nylon netting lay over the passenger seat. Two dish-type lavatory deodorisers were stuck to the back window and a black metal grille had replaced the sliding glass confessional of the London cabs.

The grille was necessary, the driver told me, on account of the number of Navy fares he picked up after they had been lagering hard on The Steyne (rhymes with stain). 'Usually it's just verbal they give you, but sometimes it gets more heavy. You get stacked by women even – smashing you over the head with bags full of deodorant.

'I had one of them do a nasty on me in the back there last night. I only smelled it when I pulled over for a smoke. Sitting at the edge of a wood down by Wollaton here, breathing in the clean air, listening to the owls – "the loud-hooting owl/That loves the turbulent and frosty night/And hallooes to the moon". (*Was this supposed to ring bells?*) Then I suddenly get hit with a whiff of that. I tell you. Nice people.'

The shift from city-and-suburban to country-creepy (hedgerows high as houses shoring up a vast unvariegated blackness; skidding and skeetering movements picked up in the sweep of the car lights) happened abruptly. So abruptly that electric advertising signs from the main road were momentarily imprinted as after-images on the pitch dark, and the sense of strangeness and panic nearly overwhelmed me.

My banishment happened (can this really be right?) six, seven years ago, in the late-seventies/early-eighties. I spent most of the seventies living on or just above the cake line (a crack borrowed from the original cast album of *Pal Joey* which has proved endlessly useful for deflecting cat-house queries about my circumstances).

I've never been ashamed to admit when I've been broke. As my *bobbeh* and *zaideh* used to say, What's to worry? You've heard of people so poor they thought knives and forks were jewellery? So poor they . . . Those old chestnuts. Well that was my parents' parents. Both sets. But regardless of how broke I've been, I have rarely denied myself certain basic luxuries: good gargle, good music, fresh flowers, taxis.

Few evenings were ever able to live up to the taxi-ride through the London dusk which began them. The contrast between the blank, dim, gently vibrating interior and the lights and stark specificity outside (plus of course the couple of stiffeners I'd tucked away before leaving home) never failed to produce that perfect balance between excitement and boredom, anticipation and relaxation that is the condition in which I'm sure most people would live all their lives, if they had the choice.

I always was a great go-outer. My appetite for the social whirl even surprised me sometimes. In the ten or so years before I decided to cut out and head for rural entombment, socialising – partying, lip-flapping, throwing it back – was all I seemed to do. If I wasn't preparing for a drinks, a first-night, a private view, a record launch, a supper, I was picking myself up from the night before. (The formula: sleep, ice-cream, plenty thick brown tea.)

What can I tell you? I enjoyed it. Although I had been there and back myself and was aware of the shallowness, the fatuity, the whatever you want to call it, the truth was that I got a kick out of mingling with faces from the shiny sheets and fresh out of the evening paper.

I liked chewing the fat with the hacks and the stars of the day; adored getting slewed; lived for the moment when the weals and eructations on the hand of the wine waiter, the powder congealed in the crowsfeet and clogging the pores of the waitress offering stuffed dates, quails' eggs, chicken satay, tempura caused feelings of almost overwhelming tenderness to well in me. (Always the signal then to slow up.)

Slipping into a room where the buzz was on and gorillas were mock-menacingly twirling worry-beads at the door (I knew most of them by name) to me was like being lifted out of a rough sea by helicopter. The noise, the smoke, the fracturedness, the social treachery and superficiality . . . all the things that so many people of my acquaintance would cross continents to avoid, were what drew me and started my juices flowing.

(The thing I would cross continents to avoid, even now, are the faces of those friends and contemporaries which I remember – it does seem only yesterday – as being emulsified, as being *rich* with optimism and confidence, and are now, to greater or lesser degrees, opaque with disappointment and the baggy accommodations we have all had to make with reality.

(I'm not talking here only about money: some of the richest are also the most disappointed. Or even about disappointed ambition. Probably the most chilling look is the look of ambition

31

realised – the hollow haunted look of disgust with achievement. You know: Pa-dum-da-da-dum-dee-dum . . . Is that all there is to the circus? That one.)

Most afternoons now, in these weeks close to the end of the year, I come back from my walks with the smell of wood-smoke and garden bonfires rising off me in waves with the cold. This was the smell of my pillow on all those woozy mornings after the nights before. By washing my hair less often than it should be washed – not difficult, given the state of the plumbing (and the condition of my follicles) – it can be the smell of my pillow here in turniptown.

On my infrequent trips to London I can still pull on a coat or a jacket in the reasonable certainty of stabbing my finger on the toothpicks and cocktail stirrers that have collected in the pockets.

My clothes and the bags I carried in those days are littered with match-books for enterprises that went under almost as soon as they were launched and invitations to bashes which nobody in their right mind could ever have hoped would pay their way. Also with cards giving the addresses in 'toney' raised copperplate of men whose names would add up to a bizarre network if anybody – the police, say, or a reporter or freelance snoop – ever went to the trouble of tracking them down.

(I have no idea why this thought should suddenly occur to me now; but the picture of my life which would emerge from such an exercise – sparked off by . . . what? my disappearance? my death? – would be so distorted and grotesque that I have made a mental note to have a major clear-out the next time I go back.)

My determination to be always next to the action was a standing joke among my friends, none of them exactly wall-flowers themselves.

One example. One afternoon sometime in the fifties when I was up there, riding high, my agent asked me what I was doing for the weekend.

'After Sammy's finished his show on Saturday,' I said (Sammy

Davis was in town filming with Peter Lawford and playing the Pigalle), 'I'm flying to the Italian Riviera with him, Betty Bacall, Sarah Churchill and Cary Grant. We're staying with the Rex Harrisons in wherever it is they live overlooking the sea.'

This reply – I honestly couldn't see why at the time – broke him up. His face turned the unbecoming kippered maroon of the leather inlaid into the top of his desk; he laughed until tears streamed from his eyes. 'I kvel when I think of you, Alma,' he said. 'Do you know what *kvel* is? It's a yiddish word meaning I like flip. You really go with the big time, don't you? You'd never go out with a couple of bums.'

'Harry,' I said solemnly, 'I'm sorry, but I find going out with people who are rich, famous and successful simply divine.'

It all goes back to my mother (who else?). In essence, mine is the classic pushy-mother story, so I won't detain you too long with it here.

I have no wish to stick it to my mother (who is still implacably with us, by the way, minus some of her marbles; the lights are on, as they say, but there's nobody home). But it's become pretty obvious since I got out from under her that she set out to use me absolutely cold-bloodedly to achieve all the things she was never in a position to achieve herself.

Family legend has it that she could have been another Callas if she had had the chance. The chance was denied her by her own mother whose violent reaction to the suggestion that Fay be sent to the Conservatoire – this was before the family were forced to flee with their handcarts from Romania – was to become the bane of my life. 'I'd rather see her dead at my feet!' my mother would declaim, imitating *her* mother speaking in another culture (another *language*), in an altogether other time. (Cue tragic pose by the chimney-breast; cue revivifying hit of apricot-brandy from the sideboard drawer.)

A striking facial resemblance between my mother and Fanny Brice as played by herself in *The Great Ziegfeld* – they shared the same ethnic features: proud forehead, bulbous nose, rolling Cantoresque eyes – encouraged her in her belief that the parade had passed her by.

She went to see that film (dir. Robert Z. Leonard, Prod. Hunt Stromberg, MGM, 1936; b&w) in the spirit that other people made pilgrimages to Lourdes: repeatedly, religiously, with a vacuum flask in her voluminous mock-croc handbag and me and my father in tow. There was never any doubt in her mind that it was the transformation of herself from rags to riches, from cheap burlesk to queen of the Great White Way, that she was witnessing on the screen. The comedown afterwards, as she rode our family bone-shaker the few hundred yards home, was pitiful to behold.

Inevitably, as it seems now, my mother met my father at a tea dance at the Café de Paris in Leicester Square. He was a familiar figure outside the stage-doors of the London music-halls and the legitimate theatres of the West End and as incurably star-struck – he wore it in his eyes – as her.

The Kogins had disembarked in England from Russia, thinking it was America, and stayed. My father's father, whom I never met, was a tailor. My father, whose name was Mitya, or Mityusha, or Mityenka, or Mityushenka – less euphoniously 'Mark' – sold women's dresses from a shop in a genteel seaside resort on the south coast. In time he would build the one shop up into a small chain.

I must have seen the sea every day when I was a child but have retained no memory of it at all. My childhood was miraculously, certainly quite unnaturally, protected from the elements. I was, after all, conceived as an all-singing, all-dancing showtime spectacular and, like the exotic bloodstock that suggests, raised in what virtually amounted to laboratory conditions.

By the age of two I was being coached in voice and tap by Madame Rogers and her daughter, a stringy girl, splay-footed as well as tone-deaf, known to us as Mamzelle Leonora. There was something about the Studio – two rooms above a Burton's the tailor, sharing a landing with a dangerously dingy billiard hall from which damp sawdust trailed, as out of a butcher's or a burst teddy bear – that smacked of the gutter glamour to which I have always found myself ineluctably drawn. My parents, needless to say, saw it as merely glamorous.

Back home after every lesson I had to stand on one of the broad lino margins around the living-room and give a demonstration of what I'd learned, the metal taps cracking out into the room like gunfire.

'Don't stop 'til I tell you,' my father would cry. 'I want my shilling's worth.' My mother, meanwhile, perched on the edge of the sofa scrubbing on a ukelele, Formby-style. (She can still, at a pinch, and even out where she's orbiting, play accordion, trumpet, clarinet, trombone and harmonium, God help us.)

By the time I was ten I could walk into a cinema and tell you which studio – Warners or Metro or Fox or Gaumont-British – had made what was showing just by looking at the print. MGM's lion; Paramount's snow-topped mountain; RKO's radio beacon, and Columbia's diaphanous Miss Liberty were the dominant images in my childhood, the last two especially so because I wasn't altogether sure what they were meant to represent.

Monday nights and Thursday nights – the night programmes changed at the Troxy – were when we went to the cinema together as a family. We usually made up the head of the queue at what my father still quaintly called the Electric Palace (it was only years later, many years after his death, that I noticed these words done in plaster, amid baroque twirls, high above the contemporary facade).

The balcony at the Troxy was thrillingly raked and canti-levered and we would dash to claim seats in one of the two curved corner sections which swung out over the stalls like Waltzer cars. This was part of what, in the late-thirties, was the owners' much-vaunted Odeon-modern look. My mother was super-taken with a colour scheme she insisted was 'carnation and mango', and with the way the gilded sconces and scrolls that went with a past that pre-dated even their past had been blocked and negated and streamlined out.

A game I liked to play – only with myself, who of course was too young to know the Troxy as Mark and Fay had known it – was to seek out evidence of what the Troxy had been like in the days of the silents, when the decorative theme was apparently south-coast Samarkand; in the days, that is to say, immediately before my arrival on the scene.

I would gaze about me and quietly note a palm cornice here, the tip of a barley-sugar column there, a swan-neck gas bracket concealed behind a sweeping parabolic plaster screen. Stupid, I know, but it was almost as though Mark and Fay – Poppa and Momma, Tateh and Mameh – had been trying to keep something from me and I'd found them out.

I was a strange little girl. But not as strange as the little girl who, singing, dancing, acting and dimpling, would tower over us, spit curls bouncing, hammy knees hamming, toxic in her winsome-ness.

Baby Take a Bow, Our Little Girl, Bright Eyes, Little Miss Broadway, Curly Top . . . There was no end to them. Shirley Temple films came thick and fast. And we sat through everything One-Take-Temple, America's Sweetheart, ever made.

There was always a special tension between the three of us when we went to see a Shirley Temple picture. I could sense meaningful glances being exchanged over my head each time the precocious one launched into another number. Many encouraging smiles were flashed at me in the flickering half-light and there was a marked amount of cosying down in seats and metaphorical clucking.

I felt them willing me to like her and want to follow her down the thorny path she had beaten. I was given a Shirley doll for my third or fourth Christmas with moving and sleeping eyes and jointed arms and legs and her name branded into her head under the human hair wig.

But I pointedly ignored what I have no doubt is now a much-coveted collectible, and instead lavished all my affection on the plastic likeness of the ice-skater-turned-movie-queen, Sonja Henie.

Too late in my own career – the Teds were on the rampage; Elvis was being denounced as morally insane – somebody put an Alma doll on the market. The manufacturer took the bath on it that I predicted. But if you keep your eyes peeled, you can still sometimes spot me sitting on the top of a TV set in place of the lava-lamp or the Spanish lady that film-makers invariably dig out when they want a shorthand way of establishing a certain kind of birdbrained, latently violent, Darren-and-Sharon fish-finger ambiance.

In the event, it was the other regular weekly fixture in our life as a family which was to prove most effective in realising Mark and Fay's ambitions. On Wednesdays, halfday closing in town, we would join many of our neighbours and friends from the business community at the tea dances which were held in the Famous Name Danse Salon on the front.

I don't think I need to go into a great deal of detail about this. The Famous Name is the kind of place that is familiar from a thousand period reconstructions. Suffice it to say that it was peach-mirrored and below pavement level and suffused with the smell of naphthalene fur protection from the ladies' Persian- and beaver-lamb coats and chinchillette hug-me-tights. They carried their own and their husbands' shoes for dancing in homemade bags with draw-string tops.

In the films, there was never any suggestion that fur, which was constantly being tossed and draped and trailed across night-club floors, could ever be in any danger of infestation or rotting. Or that the stars were ever anything less than the flawless beings they appeared. I was too young then to appreciate the important part played by lighting, camera angles, and the scalpel.

I just knew that the scrutiny demanded by the movies terrified me. I was a little Jewish girl: dark-skinned, lank-haired, short-sighted, horribly fat; no amount of reassurance that my big nose would 'photograph cute' was enough to convince me. The cinema demanded perfection, and I didn't have it.

I remember the day I decided I could make a singer, though.

I was wearing a touch of something from my mother which smelled strongly of cantaloupes and oranges ('You want a man to like it, go after the food groups' was her position on perfume, which she still calls scent) and gliding around the floor in the arms of my father at the Famous.

I danced with Mark and Fay by turn, and had tea and cakes with semi-transparent icing while they took their turns with each other. I came up to chest-height on my mother, whom I seem to recall having heavy, pendulous breasts even as a young woman. The part of her where my hand rested had a stiff, packaged feel and was gently corrugated from her boned girdle.

I came to just above waist-height on my father who, as usual, was wearing a suit of a heavy winter fabric which lightly inflamed my cheek. The band had only one shantooz or canary, a lilting lovely and curvaceous cutie whose general standards of presentation and personal grooming were as formidable as anything I encountered at the Troxy.

In her dress of rhinestone lights, standing in a pool of light, never making eye-contact, singing always above the heads of the dancers to the middle-distance, she was a mirage – bleached, evanescent, shimmering. It was as though she was both standing in the light and at the same time helping to create it.

It was an effect she was able to sustain (and I was able to learn from) by never appearing in the public parts of the hall. She seemed to dematerialise when she was out of the spotlight. I had never seen her arrive or leave, and had never spotted her anywhere in town while shopping with my mother.

June Satin (not her real name – that has gone, unfortunately) was as other-worldly, as *unearthly* as anything coming out of the Hollywood dream factories. Her farts even probably smelled of violets, to revive a saying I was rather fond of (but never allowed to utter) in those days.

On the day the scales fell from my eyes, she was wearing a dress of yellow (blue?) tussore with blue (yellow?) ornaments and bright lemon-coloured gloves extending to the creamy upper part of her arm.

The bandstand wasn't very far from the ground and I had skirted it several times in the stiff embrace of both my father and my mother before I noticed something that seemed impossible in my eyes: June Satin had a mend in her stocking!

Her immaculate toes were as usual framed in the brilliant straps of her slippers. But there, in addition to the dark hint of nail polish that was always visible, on the cusp of her big toe, at the summit of the pretty stairway of her perfect foot squatted what looked like a medulla, a *tarantula* of last-minute mending. Hallelujah! Succour for the week! Hope for the suffering! Was blind but now I see!

June Satin's toe-hole was a chink through which the light suddenly seemed to come flooding; it exploded off the mirrored ball turning slowly under the ceiling (people were walking above us), lighting up a world of the possible. Suddenly now the shoes of the band personnel, for instance, weren't uniformly glassy, but horizontally striped with the dust in the creases. There was a button hanging by a thread from the sleeve of the double-bassist's jacket. The band desks, monogrammed and slickly finished from a distance, proved to be scuffed and jerry-built on closer inspection. (And offered a microcosm of the showbusiness life, as I was to learn with experience. You should have seen some of the things those boys kept back there – pictures of their wives and

39

kids, pornographic pictures, chewing-gum, packets of biscuits, rags to hawk and spit in.)

So hats off to Junie. Hers was an invaluable lesson in the crucial part attention to detail plays in sustaining an illusion. I became a fanatic about footwear as a result of that small moment of awakening, and a perfectionist with a prickly and enduringly 'difficult' reputation.

The strongest memory I have of my mother is of her in turban and apron in a steam-filled kitchen, boiling dyes in order that a pair of shoes might exactly match the colour of my latest over-the-top stage creation.

This was our regular drama: her sweating and stirring, mixing and matching; me shaking my head dismissively and sending her back to come up with something better. A heartless image, I agree, loaded with pathos.

So let me quickly set beside it another – of me, the biggest-drawing entertainer in the country and a mature woman, through television and radio a virtually inescapable presence, living in trepidation (I was a baroque, moygashel- and shantung-hung definition of the word) in case anything should happen to prevent me putting in my nightly call to the widow Cogan.

Wherever I happened to be, whatever I happened to be doing, a call, preferably on the stroke of eleven, is what she expected. Failure to deliver resulted in extraordinary scenes and recriminations.

Anguished calls to the police and the papers, for example, reporting my disappearance (they knew to humour her). Locks changed on the flat we lived in together after my father's death in London (although she always saw it as *me* living with *her*). Records smashed (*my* records – records, that is, with my voice on them – for preference). Clothes that turned out to be slyly mutilated the next time I went to wear them . . .

Oh she was something, my mother.

This peculiar ménage, of just myself and Fay and no sign of a male presence, was something which, understandably I suppose, people used to find intriguing, even in an era when nice girls didn't.

The conversation would always proceed along predictable lines whenever the 'human interest' scribblers (gossip-mongers) came calling: uneasy opening pleasantries, then a trade-off of industry gossip, leading to the interview proper – biographical background (no matter how many times they'd read it); current hopes/ambitions/corny quips/crackerbarrel philosophising – 'I have always prided myself that my fans are not the unruly type. I feel the attention of the fans is flattering to me as an artist.' The usual bushwah, in other words.

It was only when notebooks were being pocketed and the smell of alcohol was finally starting to defeat the smell of the tobacco that had been used to disguise it (lavender-scented cachous, I seem to remember, were a favourite ploy of the ladies) that they would broach the subject with which of course they had always known they were going to be leading: discland's most eligible bachelor girl and the man question.

'Miss Cogan' – a casual crossing of the legs; a rush of blood to the ears (those boiled lugs); perspiration flooding the pancake between nose and upper lip – 'your love life seems to fascinate a lot of people. They find it strange that a good-looking girl', etc.

'Not so strange. I just haven't met the right one. How can I think of marriage until . . .' You can easily fill in the rest.

The unlikely truth is that, although I grew up surrounded by men who were far from shy about showing off their bodies – the boys in the chorus were tirelessly exhibitionistic, rarely bothering to close the doors of their dressing-rooms and padding around more or less a hundred-per-cent peeled – I was alarmingly vague about the male anatomy.

41

I had no idea what went on in the downstairs department. Really went on, I mean. I had a vague idea that something was put somewhere, but where and how was a giant mystery.

('Meat injection', an expression I had overheard once or twice, was pretty graphic. But I remained ignorant as to the exact mechanics, not to mention the motivation. I didn't even find out what 'B.U.R.M.A.' or 'E.G.Y.P.T.' meant on envelopes until long after the war was over. When I was told they stood for 'Be Upstairs Ready My Angel' and 'Eager to Grab Your Pretty Tits' – and, worse, that 'N.O.R.W.I.C.H.' was code for 'Knickers Off Ready When I Come Home' – I blushed crimson.)

All this may seem strange – it may even seem barely credible – of somebody who by the mid-fifties would be able to count Diana Dors and an actress I later learned was known in Hollywood as the British Open, among her friends. But what you have to remember is that we're still talking about the years of buttoned-upness and relative austerity before the lid blew off in the sixties.

I didn't know I was living in 'the vice capital of Europe' in 1952, which is the year we moved to London in the interest of furthering my career (I was twenty). I hadn't yet been introduced to the basement drinking clubs that had sprung up almost outside our front door in Kensington – Frisco's, run by Frisco himself ('Ah's the biggest buck nigger in town'); the Little House; Ruby Lloyd's Maisonette. (I still didn't drink.)

One club I had been introduced to – The Court Club in Mayfair – I visited several times without realising that the constant traffic through the curtained door at the side of the bar meant it was virtually a brothel.

I see now I was green as goose-shit. I knew Diana Dors's husband, Dennis Hamilton. I had been to his parties and he had occasionally been to mine. But I was as shocked as anybody by the revelations about his 'fish book' – his directory of available knock-offs – and the two-way mirror installed in the bedroom at

'Bel-Air', his big house in Maidenhead, and then at his London perch in Bryanston Mews. I suspected nothing.

I had known Paul Raymond since he was Paul Quinn, touring the number-threes (which were too good for him) with a mind-reading act he'd bought from a couple of palm-readers on Clacton Pier; I'd even known him before that, when he was Geoff Carlson, a part-time drummer and full-time hawker of nail varnish and hairnets at the funfairs.

I was in a party that he took to Ciro's the night he was fined £5,000 at the London Sessions for keeping a disorderly house at his Revuebar. (The mood was celebratory; in court there had apparently been talk of 'lust' and 'filth' and 'disgustingness' and he had been prepared for the worst.)

After dinner we moved on to the Bal Tabarin, Raymond's club in Hanover Square, where we were joined late by a dark-haired girl with a distinctive gypsy look: high-piled black hair, dark-rimmed eyes, a fortune in loose change worn on chains around her waist and neck. He introduced Liana as the Revuebar's 'big vedette'.

Liana, it turned out, was a snake-charming spesh act: she performed with three boa-constrictors and a python while shedding her clothes and, despite her name and the exotica, talked in a homely North-country accent (Huddersfield-Barnsley, would have been my guess).

'I have a self-imposed rule of not stripping off completely,' I remember Liana announcing at one point. 'Nothing full-frontal or risqué. Straight T and A only. I have always worked on that principle – I look on it as my insurance in life. Who knows – you might one day be prime minister!'

'She's doing her f-f-f-fire act when we do the turn-around,' Raymond said, covering the girl's hand with his own, which was noticeably hairless and weighted with gold sovereigns. 'Sets fire to a carpet then boogie-woo-woo-woogies on it. Eats fire. Going to c-c-cost us a wedge in insurance. S-s-some versatile girl, this one. Sticks a broom up her arse and sweeps the stage for an encore, eh babes? Finish your e-education, she would. You should pop round.'

The point I'm trying to make is that, not knowing what we were supposed to be looking for, Fay and I regularly failed to see what was staring us in the face. You could have told us shit was sugar in those days and we would have believed you. We took it all at face value.

Toot, for instance. Cocaine. Happy dust. I wouldn't have recognised it if it had jumped up and played 'Ole Man River' on the spoons. Or 'jazz woodbines', as joints used to be called when they were just making the crossover from the jazzers to the pop boys, and the pop boys' blissed-out chalky faces were just starting to mingle with the showbiz 'Mantan' at our parties.

When I came across some musicians soaking gauze from inhalers for the hit of benzedrine it gave them and they told me it was a new kind of tea they were trying, what did I know? I believed them.

Self-analysis, navel-gazing of any description, had never been my strong suit. But it's pretty obvious to me now that I started bringing names from the shows home out of a sense of guilt, as a way of keeping my mother happy, in the first instance.

My mother, though, was never happy being merely a passive recipient. From the beginning she organised sing-songs, forfeits, ham-and-egg cook-ins (we were never that orthodox), charades.

Unfazed by having some of the biggest entertainment names in the world in front of her – and a not-untypical gathering might include Noel Coward, Sophie Tucker, Danny La Rue, Michael Caine, Peter Sellers, Rudolph Nureyev, various Beatles – she'd call for her banjo and knock out some of the oldtime numbers: 'When It's Nighttime in Italy It's Wednesday Over Here', 'If I had My Life to Live Over, I'd Live Over a Delicatessen' (which John Lennon always particularly requested, although I suspect it's not

44

the kind of information to set Jez, Hicky, Caro and the other media monkeys' pulses racing.

(It certainly didn't seem to do a great deal for the girl employed by Lennon's chief American biographer when she tracked me down here – I found her peering through the wisteria into the window one morning when I came back from doing the shopping. 'Oh *brilliant*,' she said through a watery smile, sneaking a quick glance at the train times she had inked onto her inner-wrist.)

Without us ever doing anything to consciously promote it, Fay and I found we'd got a reputation for being the most happening after-hours spot in London.

Where we lived was in no way grand – nothing like as grand as most of the people who came there were used to. On the other hand, it wasn't totally predictable.

Having (or at least affecting) a rather advanced contemporary taste in decoration, my mother had avoided the showbiz staples of English Vicarage, Hollywood Medieval, Cockney Moroccan and that style that by now is almost generic – flocked lamps, cascade chandeliers, 'Regency' telephones, deep blush velour – known in the trade as Chapel-of-Rest Cheesy or Jewy Louis.

She'd covered the walls and floors neutrally in buffs and drabs and installed a few good pieces of modernist, low-to-the-ground Italian furniture. Apart from lamps and some vases and ashtrays, there was little in the way of what she dismissed as *tchatchkas*.

'Never collect inanimate objects, or in the end they will possess you, and you will lose your freedom,' she'd say, parroting verbatim the latest gem picked up from the women's magazines or the radio. 'Only invest in jewellery, so that if everything else gets taken you still have something left to sell.'

('Was hectored in the usual scarifying fashion by that stout little woman who is always at Alma Cogan's – by and large charming – parties in Kensington claiming to be her mother,' Noel Coward noted in his diary of March 5, 1963.

('What a truly odd phenomenon. Whoever it was said we can't choose our parents must surely have had Mrs C. – could there ever have been a Mr C? – in mind. Somebody ought to drop the word that professionals really must be allowed to show off to their hearts' content, without too much competition from amateurs. Rather gratifying, though, to have the Paul Beatle at my feet for much of the evening. The drummer, however – Ringo? – remains butchily surly.')

There would be no point giving a roll-call of all the people who packed themselves into our small rooms like rice in a bowl between, say, 1956 and 1964, when for a time London really did feel as if it was the centre of something. It wouldn't be a case of dropping names so much as spilling them like marbles.

Let me just say that, in that period, virtually everybody who was anybody in the world of entertainment, plus painters, book writers, politicians, academics, sportsmen (and more than a smattering of gentleman villains and others 'from the flip-side of the social disc' – Donald Zec in the *Mirror*), came and went.

'You know, this place has become a kind of Lincoln Tunnel,' I remember a visiting American drawling on one occasion. 'I know by coming here I'll meet all passing traffic.'

When the time came and I was no longer the hotcha-potatcha I once had been (and it was always coming), I had plenty of favours to call in. Not that I ever had to do much calling, to be truthful.

There wasn't a party in London – and few outside – that I couldn't be guest-listed for, if I said the word. I was constantly on the receiving end of offers of tickets, holidays, expensive dinners, clothes. A number of people whose names you would recognise, but who want to remain anonymous, continue to slip the occasional life-saver into my account. This cottage, the childhood home of a friend of a friend, is just one example of supporters rallying round.

It had become obvious to other people that I was going to have to get out of London long before it became obvious to me. But when it happened, it happened with more of a whimper than a bang. There were no histrionics; no chewing the scenery. I didn't disgrace myself in public. The police weren't involved. It was simply that, after years of steadily upping the intake, the drink started to have a depressive effect. There were some small signs of memory loss. I was rarely up and about before mid-afternoon. Then I sneaked into the papers again.

The celebrity snappers hadn't wasted any film on me for a long time; in fact, they made a point of gloomily turning away whenever I de-cabbed. Then one day, because I happened to be standing shank-to-shank at a reception with somebody high on the current wanted list, I turned up in the 'candids' section of a Sunday supplement.

'Sugar in the morning, sherbets in the evening . . .' the caption read. 'Oh dear. Who let Aunt Bertha in?' The picture, basted in the usual citric, achromatic light, was of a piece of meat with a grease-mottled, lipstick-smeared glass in its hand.

The chipolatas clamped around a chipolata turned out to be my fingers. The meaty midgets head-butting each other were my knees. The red tones had been brought up in the printing so that all available flesh (too much – very much too much) looked flayed; it was mottled, purple-on-purple, like hung game. As for my face. I won't begin to describe my face.

The calls started coming in straight away – geared-down Sunday-morning voices trying to gear up to a sense of weekday commiseration, outrage, concern. 'Think of yourself as a great glass bell, yeh? Filled with junk, yeh?' monotoned one born-again chanter or meditator, newly put in touch with her breathing planes and alpha waves. 'Clear the junk out, y'know, and then polish the bell so it can reflect what you really think and feel.' Peppy advice. Fax'n'info. Bits of jolly-up. On and on.

'Let me tell you something Scott Fitzgerald once wrote. "I was drunk for many years", he wrote in his notebook, "and then I died." '

47

'Of course you know what your trouble is. You're life-lagged.'

But they could have saved their breath, well-meaning as it (mostly) seemed to be. That picture was all the prompting anybody could need. I was out of there already. I was already gone. Faded, as my friend Sammy would say, in bolivion.

I had hoped to get to the village during daylight. But I'd ended up taking a later, and then a still later, train. So now it was dark.

The cottage, when we eventually arrived there, was on the edge of the village, just off to one side of a lane, standing on a small quay on its own.

Lights were burning in one of the rooms and there was smoke rising from the chimney – the work, I knew, of a Mr Brotherhood, who lived nearby and took care of the place when it was empty.

The panting of the taxi sounded loud and queerly familiar in such an unfamiliar place. When I had paid him, the driver drove to the end of the quay, where his lights swept along an outbuilding and then settled for a couple of seconds on a boat slip where the quay dwindled informally away to seaweed and stones. He did a tight turn, tooted and sailed past me with a wave.

I watched while he went over the stone bridge we had crossed coming in the opposite direction, and marvelled that half an hour could have him back in the land of bar-fights, Kebab-U-Likes, and puke-ups in the back seat.

It was June and there were certain accents on the air which of course I had no way of naming (plants, flowers, all manner of maritime and rural things). There were boats moored to the quay, and standing out of the water on the edge of the quay, balanced between trestles. Viewed at such close quarters they appeared as strange as Venusians; they loomed above me, and I felt a compulsion to step forward and touch one, put my hand against its rippling flank, as if it was a thing in a zoo. Smaller

48

boats were moored out in the river. Their metal masts made a clean clinking sound in the dark as hawsers (I guessed they were called) and other bits of metal beat against them.

The background to all of this, though, the incidental music about to be *prioritised* now, was the sound of water. It reminded me of something. And what it mostly reminded me of was itself: water lapping in even waves against the hulls of boats with odd kitschy names and breaking on the bits of shingle beach.

But as I stood and listened and it grew louder – it was now the only sound there was – it reminded me insistently of something in addition to – an approximation of – itself. But what? I couldn't remember. And then I remembered. It was the sound of a thousand working men drinking a thousand pints in the loud swilling sheds where I ended my professional career.

Drinking on that scale and in those circumstances can set up a sustained note, a kind of drone, which could – frequently did – throw me off-pitch. I hear the crack of coarse fingers against a microphone and the plaintive – self-pity can be a voluptuous pleasure; I can get a lump in my throat for myself – 'Give the poor cow a chance!'

I found the key where I'd been told to expect it, under a spongy log to the right of the front door. The door opened into a small flagged space with a scrubbed bench and a plain shelf above it holding a decoy pigeon, a child's torch and a single (adult) glove. There was a row of painted nails – the paint smooth from where it had accreted over the generations, drip-on-drip – for hanging coats. A kitchen – stone-flagged also – was off to the left. The sitting-room was up three stone stairs to the right, with another room up another short set of stairs at the far side of it.

I was struck immediately by the sense of solidness and permanence, the simple volumes and surfaces, the absence of pretence. All the walls were thick, rendered in irregular plaster

49

with primitive storage spaces, repositories of family pictures, common family detritus, chiselled out of them.

The walls by the doorways had been worn smooth over the years, and there was efflorescence running along under the ceilings. I noted multiple examples of discoloration and variegation, like ancient maps or age blotches on skin.

All this I absorbed in an instant. In the next instant, having arrived at the heart of the house, I experienced what I can only call a grace state.

When I think of the moment now I think of it as consisting entirely of three kinds of mixed but incompatible light: the light from the fire that Mr Brotherhood had set, liquefying the ceiling and walls; a swimmingpool light coming from sun on the river, delirious, mutable, rinsed blue; a buttery summer evening light falling on the backs of sheep being herded down the lane running close to the rear of the house.

And what about the figure? Where am I?

Paint me black. A full-length standing figure in silhouette – dense, matt. Eyes and features blank with nothing to indicate that what I'm thinking is this: I have arrived. I will be happy here. And then when the time comes I will leave with reluctance but without regret, to go back into the world.

Four

There was a magic act popular in my time. It involved, as many of these acts did, a volunteer from the audience coming up on to the stage.

For this particular trick, the volunteer was shown a number of books and invited to pick a single title (the books were 'presented' by the magician's assistant, balancing on the balls of her feet and wearing a scooped-out sparkling leotard, in the time-honoured fashion).

Having made his selection, the volunteer would be asked to tell the audience how many pages there were in the volume he was now holding.

He would then be asked to nominate a number ('Pick a page! Any page!') between one and the number he had just mentioned. This done, he would next be asked to pick another number corresponding to a line of text on that page and to read the line aloud slowly to the audience.

As he read, the magician would chalk the words on the board, writing rapidly, dotting the 'i's noisily and using other bits of stage business to bring up the dramatic tension.

I would sense the hush and hear the urgency of the scrape of chalk on board as I sat waiting to go on. And when I did, I would invariably reach out and turn up the volume on the Tannoy in my dressing-room in order to catch what the odd words, wrenched from their context, were this time around.

The act would be brought to a conclusion by the conjuror

removing a cigarette from a silver case, showing it to the audience with a flourish, bringing a light to it, and exhaling a long puff of smoke up into the spotlight to prove it was real.

Then, taking care to ensure that it flashed a semaphor in the light as he produced it, he would take a razor-blade and carefully slice through the cigarette paper from top to bottom. Finally (drawing back his cuffs conspicuously to show that the hanky-panky didn't happen at this stage), he would tamp the loose tobacco into the cupped palm of his assistant and pass what was left to the volunteer from the audience.

'Would you please read what is written on the piece of paper you are now holding in your hand, puh-le-e-e-e-ze!' And what was written, of course, was what was spelled out on the board which the assistant was now parading across the stage like one of those girls in savagely-cut satin hot-pants who go around with the round-cards at championship boxing matches. Cue walk-off music. Cue applause.

These meaningless snatches of sentences, recited importantly several times in the course of a few minutes, in a disembodied, almost an incantatory way, could be oddly potent. With the repetition, some sort of meaning seemed to coalesce around them.

Many times I would be halfway through the first song of my set and I wouldn't have heard a word that I'd sung; my mind would still be snagged on some random string of words which, more often than you would think possible, seemed to have a haunting-ness or mysterious resonance.

I can now remember only two of them.

The lights grow brighter as the earth lurches away is one.

'You've dyed your hair since then,' remarked Jordan, is the other.

Why I should have remembered these two and wiped the rest, is impossible to know. But the fact is that they stay lodged, stubborn as meat between the teeth, when many things of much more obvious relevance or significance have been casually flushed away. It has encouraged me to nail my flag to the mast of randomness and chance.

It is something I think about often in the evenings when I find myself idly leafing through a book here in Kiln Cottage, waiting for something to leap out and grab me.

When it does, I might include it in the notebook I keep for the purpose. It was 99% virgin when I came here, as her record company used to boast of Joni Mitchell in the sixties. But now the covers are ringed from cups and glasses, and some of the pages are stuck to each other with make-up, spilled coffee and dog-slobber.

There is no television in the cottage, but it is well stocked with books. There are full bookshelves either side of the open fireplace in the sitting-room. Books line the upstairs corridor. There are even books wedged under one of the legs of the bed in which I sleep, compensating for the way the floor dips away to the window overlooking the quay – E. Keble Chatterton's *The Yachtman's Pilot of 1933*; and, on top of this, a dog-eared copy of Arnold Bennett's *The Old Wives' Tale*, with a cover painting of a woman by Toulouse-Lautrec – only her hair and a hand rather tensely gripping the back of the garden bench on which she is sitting are visible.

If I was ever serious about making good the gaps – the outbacks and Saharas – in my knowledge, the last few years have been the perfect opportunity. The trouble is, I lack the application. I have always been a dipper and a browser; have always enjoyed what in today's terminology I believe is called 'grazing', rather than the full tombstone read.

Books, like churches and classical music, have always made me feel turned in on myself and involuntarily gloomy. It gives me no pleasure at all to say it, but there's hardly a book that I've started at the beginning and read all the way through.

The only exceptions are the American pulps, the paperback shockers which circulated on the long train journeys we were always undertaking between engagements in the fifties. They completed my education.

Like violets, and small saucers of prawns and whelks, they were sold by men with trays around the pubs in Soho and the equivalent areas of the bigger towns, and this contributed to the sense of illicitness I always felt about them. 'Any health mags, love stories?'

I always picked them up from where they were lying in a studiedly casual way and read them with a growing feeling of guilt and a packed hotness behind the eyes.

They will always be connected in my mind with stalled Sunday-afternoon rail journeys between, typically, Middlesbrough and Nottingham; with northern industrial light working its way across worn carriage-cloth; and with the unfamiliar, not unpleasant, sensations they started up in me.

Sin Circus. Shame Slave – She knew the little tricks that fan lust in men and women. *One Hell of a Dame* – The naked story of lusty-bodied Sheila whose uncontrollable desire put her name in lights. *Resort Girl. Diamond Doll. She Had To Be Loved. Gay Scene* – Every time a man had her it was rape. But with other women it was love. Gutters of lust ran wild in this *Sex Town*.

Along with the American magazines you found on sale at some station bookstalls – *Zipp, Abandon, Caress, Hollywood Frolics* – these were titles which struck me then as a kind of concentrate of eroticism. (And recalling them now, I have to say, still gives me a certain frisson.)

As the fifties drew on and the profession started attracting a higher percentage of what Fay called 'strollops' and professional good-time girls, I was dimly aware of scenes from the covers of *Shame Slave* and *Sex Town* – spectacular cleavages (the breasts very boldly shaped and divided) and Bri-Nylon Baby-Dolls; rippling torsos and luxuriant chest wigs – playing themselves out in the digs around the country where we stayed.

Despite the standard rule about no 'take-in', these places were

54

alive with sexual activity: Atomic Armfuls . . . Bikini Bomb-shells . . . sexsational sex romps and hi-jinks . . . dolls on dope . . . daisychain dollies . . . The News of the Screws got it more right more often than probably it even realised.

When I returned to London at the end of my first hike around the provinces, I recall my mother taking me firmly by the shoulders (she had to propel herself on to her toes) to give me the third-degree. 'That's it,' she wailed after an interval. 'I knew it. It's happened. You've changed. You look hard already.'

I was always promising myself that I was going to read something more nourishing. I appeared to have plenty of time at my disposal. The problem was that it was effectively dead time – too long to do nothing in, but too short to do anything in particular.

Every day was geared towards the evening's performance. I was obsessive about protecting my voice. I was always detecting coughs and infections. For years I endured breakfast-time (that is, lunch-time) witticisms about what I was hiding behind the foulard scarves with which my throat was lagged. Most nights, as I think I've mentioned, I was sick until my ribs ached before I had to go out and be the vivacious little miss with the bubbling personality. Books never had any place in this programme.

The countryside represented one of the holes in my knowledge of which I was most conscious.

'Country' to me was the sleepy boring bit between the incident-filled narrative of the cities; the nothingness spreading out beyond town boundaries, where the trolley-wires terminated and real life dwindled to an incandescent dot, and then quickly faded to nada, like television at the close of transmission.

I only knew the flowers everybody knew. I didn't associate flowers with the seasons. Roses were something that arrived wrapped in cellophane, with a small white pill in an envelope to prolong their life. It remained the case even when I became a variety advertised in the bulb and seed catalogues myself.

In the days when it was as much a part of the celebrity ritual as being hi-jacked for *This Is Your Life* and being greased up by that old phoney Roy Plomley on *Desert Island Discs*, I had a rose named after me: a pale tangerine-coloured tea- or damask- or old-rose that turned slightly less anaemic-looking when (perhaps it was well-named after all) it became bloated and blown.

The naming ceremony took place at the annual flower show at Chelsea and was performed by the Queen Mother. She was wearing one of her Monet-print floaty outfits with a major hat and a flesh-coloured elastic bandage under her stocking on one leg.

We passed a happy few minutes talking about digging in manure and bonemeal and how to deal with root rot, and 'the incredibly beautiful Madame Alfred Carrière, and her cousin, Mrs Herbert Stevens', who I gathered just in time were both roses like myself. The whole conversation could have been in Gujarati for all I understood.

These details feel real: I can also remember (I think I can) the satin scalloped lining of the tent, the sickening thick aroma of the exhibits and the music of a pipe-band.

But the occasion is one of hundreds in my life which I am more and more convinced I can only have read about or seen on television and which must have actually happened to somebody else.

Some of my most dream-like recollections involve the royal family (and are therefore made more dream-like by the awareness that they are the country's favourite fantasy-figures). The most dream-like of all – it plays itself back in SloMo shot through medium gauze – involves the present Queen.

I performed at Windsor Castle several Christmases running. There was a show in a private chapel, converted for the occasion, followed by high-tea and a party for the staff and the family. My first visit is the visit I remember most vividly.

Edmundo Ros, the Latin specialist, provided the music for

56

dancing that year (it was almost certainly 1956 or '57). And the evening wound to a close with everybody snaking around the state-room in which the dance was held doing a ragged, high-spirited conga.

But for reasons of etiquette or protocol (I didn't know the reason) the Queen found herself excluded. She was still a young woman then, as of course I was, slim and pretty. And I happened to look up at one point and see her standing alone under a Flemish tapestry of Actaeon being torn apart by dogs, smiling happily and clapping in time with the music.

On an impulse, I dropped out of the conga-line and approached her. I might have curtsied first – a quick dip – but the next thing I remember is placing my hands on her waist and steering her on to the floor to join the dancers. She was wearing a suit which was double-layered – coffee lace over blue – and I remember thinking even at the time that it felt like net curtains against windows to touch.

I was aware, in the short time that I maintained this taboo contact, of my whole system going into overload in an effort to accumulate all the information it could – the look, the feel, the smell (I was almost certain I recognised 'Miss Dior'); all the data ordinary subjects are unable to access – and running a flash-check on it against what I knew of these properties in other women, including myself.

I wanted to know, I now realise, what the hungry stage-door touchers and gropers were always wanting to know about me: if, and in what way, I differed from ordinary mortals. Whether the close eye-balling, the constant exposure, the incessant reproduc-tion of the image had added to, stolen from or in any way affected the composition of the in-the-round, blood-and-guts person.

Was I in any essential way different from them? Was Elizabeth II, great-great-granddaughter of Queen Victoria, direct descen-dent of Dick the Shit and Henry VIII (true? – history is almost

57

as much of a black hole as nature studies), was she in any tangible way different from me?

I look at myself sometimes when I'm out walking in the country, at the waxed jackets and bush hats, the warm-up trousers and sights-of-Roma headscarf, the army surplus mittens and vinyl trainers and other items borrowed from Kiln Cottage, and wonder whether it's possible to read in my present appearance anything about what I once was.

Do I look like a woman who witnessed a violent disfigurement, was the subject of *This Is Your Life* and conga-d with the Queen in the same brief span of her life? Or do I look like all the other women out walking their dogs along the edge of the cliffs on the coast path – thick-thighed, unhurried (nothing to hurry home for), of indeterminate age and sex until they come within polite 'afternoon'-ing distance?

In all these years, only one of them – mail-order trail boots, duvet jacket, lovat tweed headgear, a classic example of the breed – has given me any reason to believe that she might be anything other than she seemed. 'They try to mount her and she doesn't like it,' she said when she saw my miniature Pinscher worrying the business end of her Sheltie. 'Not unless they buy her a drink first.' Said with the kind of pale smile that contains an entire history.

At the beginning, I held out against being the shapeless rag-bag I am when I go out these days. I wore obviously unsuitable things on purpose, as a way of billboarding the fact that I didn't want to join the club. Being slapped around by the weather a few times quickly brought me to my senses.

Now when I think of my clothes I tend to think of them in the terms in which, in his published diary, Alan Bennett says his mother thought of hers:

My other shoes
My warm boots
That fuzzy blue coat I have
My coat with round buttons

I made a note of that at around the same time I made the following note, which seemed a perfect encapsulation of the person I was trying to get away from.

> She is the kind who feels a protective tenderness toward her own beginnings. It is part of her strategy in a world of displacement to make every effort to restore and preserve, keep things together for their value as remembering objects, a way of fastening herself to a life. (Unattributed)

There was a time when I couldn't let anything go. I used to have three or four sizes in everything because I never knew what I was going to fit into; I had to rent rooms in the flat of the woman downstairs to store the overflow in.

Now I enjoy living in this temporary way: unanchored; unburdened, often not even able to call the clothes I stand up in my own.

Some days the cliff path is buzzed by military planes from the base along the coast. They scream in over the fields, follow the line of the cliffs for a couple of miles, then wheel away over the Channel, leaving behind a low rumble followed by silence, and the dog pressed against my leg, cowering, and the wind thrumming and the sheep unconcernedly cropping round tough plants with pink and mauve and yellow flowers which are called campion, ragged robin, thrift, sedum and veronica, but which is which I don't know.

From above, and at speed, and thrown at a panoramic angle, it all must appear pleasingly unified and inevitable – the picture elements, although discrete, psychologically understood as composing one continuous picture.

Everything in Kiln Cottage – books and furniture, cutlery, crockery, all the household bits and pieces – was from the people who had been there before.

This was Mr and Mrs E, Staff's parents.

Staff was a London showbusiness lawyer whom I felt I liked, although I knew him only vaguely. He belonged to that group of people, and it was a large one, whom I had only ever met when either one or both of us was three sheets to the wind; half-seas over, at some party or other.

Staff was born at Kiln Cottage. He grew up here and his parents lived here until their deaths.

Through the clusters of pictures in the downstairs rooms it's possible to trace his development from toothy schoolboy to public schoolboy to his Moroccan-sandal and tie-dye phase. The pictures stop some years short of his present bi-continental, sherbing-and-jogging, prinked and polka-dotted urbanity.

Mr and Mrs E had three children, whose faces are now all as familiar to me as my own from their pictures. Susie ('Sookie'), the younger daughter, obviously had theatrical ambitions at one point. There's a grainy *Spotlight*-style portrait of her wearing the copper ring, Juliette Greco hair and exaggerated cow lashes which were de rigueur in certain circles when she was young. She is gazing heavenwards out of the left of the picture in response to the lensman's no doubt husky request for 'misty eyes'. *Make magic with that face*.

Ruth, the elder daughter, is the breeder. Pictures of Ruth's compliant, button-nosed children hang in velvet frames in several of the rooms. If I think of the children as being – how shall

I put this? – dead, of having retreated from, rather than moved forward into their lives, that is partly the effect of the Polaroids, which have become sun-bleached (the light here most of the time is hallucinogenically bright), giving the young flesh a green, loose-on-the-bone, sickeningly disinterred look.

But it is also partly the fault of the faded burgundy velvet which surrounds these snaps and the grime-stiffened pieces of ribbon to which they are attached.

In the days when I was still noticing them – still noticing everything that I now accept as just everyday domestic clutter, mere atmospheric fill – I was tempted several times to remove the pictures or turn them face to the wall. What stopped me is the thing that has always stopped me making any kind of even minor change in the years I've been dug-in here.

It pleases me that, with the exception of a couple of personal eccentricities which we will no doubt take a turn around later, there is hardly any more evidence of my existence in the cottage today than on the day I arrived.

The names and numbers in the book that lies by the telephone are in Mrs E's hand. It is Mrs E's recipes that are written on plain four-by-five cards in the tin box in the kitchen. I sit in Mr and Mrs E's chairs, sleep in their bed and eat my meals from their plates with their knives and forks. My clothes hang next to the few items of clothing of theirs that their children, for whatever reason, have decided not to let go.

I lie in their bath at nights listening to the riotous knocking and screaming in the pipes which, on the rare occasions they were away from it, must have formed a part of their memory of the house. Lying in bed in the dark, you can still hear mouse claws clicking in the rafters and the reassuring noises of the house settling around itself.

They have laid claim to it in so powerful, apparently permanent, a way that, although in many respects it was blindingly obvious, it came as a shock the first time I realised

61

that other people had lived in Kiln Cottage before Mr and Mrs E.

'Know what this is?' Bob Brotherhood asked when he broke off from pottering in the garden and came in for a cup of tea one day. He was sitting in his favourite 'elbow chair' with his cap flattened across his knee. His country colour as usual was alarmingly high. He was rotating the tiny leather clog off the bureau in his chipped and worn old fingers.

(My thoughts immediately flew to the clog-shaped hole it would have left in the collected dust, and the bad report he'd put in to Mrs Brotherhood when he got home. He has an unusual attachment to the cottage and misses nothing to do with its well-being and maintenance.)

'Found it in the wall, I did, when I was helping knock through here, time I was a boy. Put there years sin', so they say, to ward off evil spirits.'

The cottage was originally three workers' cottages. The original tenants were apparently jobbing gardeners and journeymen carpenters, masons and tailors, washer-women and domestic servant girls, all topped-and-tailed, incestuously shoe-horned in together.

The conversion to a single dwelling accounts for the surprising changes of level you now find between rooms; going upstairs, in some instances, can leave you standing no further from the ground than where you've started.

The cottage is wedge-shaped and built sideways into the foot of a hill that starts off as a sheep field so perpendicular the sheep look like fridge magnets stuck to it. As the hill descends, it becomes a combination of ploughed red earth and grazing pasture, and ends up at the quay and the river.

Kiln Cottage is named after the lime kiln which now makes a picturesque ruin at the foot of the garden. The cottage stands alone between the quay and the lane which takes traffic down and round into the village. This is so narrow it's possible to look into cars and see what brand of cigarette the driver is smoking while washing dishes at the sink. Or, alternatively, watch the flies gorging themselves in the mucus draining from cows' nostrils when they're lumbering past. (You can see how easily I have adapted to not having a television.)

'The foetor there must've been them days,' Mr Brotherhood said, absently polishing the child's clog on his cap now. 'Days before the invention of sanitary science. Open drains. I remember when the families what lived here had earth-closets. Wasn't so long past neither. Slop-pails in the kitchen that smelled to beat the band. Smelt it when you were passin', you could. But those days evbody roun' these ways was the same.'

'More tea?'

'Often occurs to me to wonder who that little girl might have been,' he said, peering into the shoe now as if something on the inside could give him his answer.

'Would you like your tea heated?'

'Just half a cup,' he said, setting the mug down between his boots, which was the cue for the dog to make a dive for it from the other side of the room. (All my dogs have been tea drinkers.) 'I'll have to let some out first.'

There is a set of photograph albums stored in one of the cupboards. I didn't look at them for a long time. But when I did, less out of any sense of genuine curiosity than as a way of filling an empty hour (there are some things you don't want to know, and will put off knowing), a number of things became apparent.

Staff's parents had moved into Kiln Cottage as young marrieds, when this place obviously represented what I recently saw described as 'one of those Shangri-la-type concepts'. (Their well-bred young English faces – the eyes shy yet determined; the skin drawn tight across the bones – weren't blurred with the inevitable loneliness apparent in the later pictures.)

They had also changed the cottage over time to suit their

needs. A second bathroom, for example, had been added off the kitchen. ('This sink leaks' a notice posted here used to say when I arrived; still there but illegible, like all the other notices around the cottage – 'The kettle sometimes switches itself on, so after use please switch off at socket'; 'DANGER: the water from this tap can be VERY hot', etcetera – it adds to the sense of layers; it forms the newest layer of secret surface information.)

There had been several other modifications. The original thatched roof had been replaced with slate at some stage. An asparagus patch which was fertilised with seaweed and lay between the cottage and the kiln, had been turned into a tufted sloping lawn with a clear view over the water.

Most disconcertingly, what I still think of as the front of the house – the part of it which opens on to a small plot of garden and then the quay – used to be the back. As some of the earliest pictures in the albums make clear, the large cupboard on the lane-side of the living-room is built into a hole where the old front door used to be.

These discoveries about what had seemed such a rock-solid, unchanged and unchanging set of circumstances left me feeling oddly skewed for a while. I felt the way I felt when I learned (more recently than I care to own up to) that all matter is perpetually in a state of vibration.

I was still at the stage then when I believed that, simply by quitting London, I had entered a world in which all contradiction and complication had been swept away. In their literal matter-of-factness, the names of the cottages I passed every day walking through Cleve seemed to confirm that this was the case.

Rose Cottage (roses round the rustic gate, roses round the door). Plum Tree Cottage. White Cottage. Blue Shutters. Round House. Greystones. Court View Cottage (overlooking the municipal tennis courts). Smithy Cottage (opposite the old smithy). East Wood. West View. Churchunder. Steps End. End of the Strand. Slipway Cottage. The Slope.

They were the very embodiment of the life of certainties and 'real values' that all town-dwellers are supposed to aspire to as some kind of earthly nirvana. And for a long time, as I say, I bought it.

As the in-comer from a world I had no doubt they all regarded as ugly and tawdry and meretricious, violent and distasteful (I could hear them mouthing off at choir practice in the village hall, over whist, at the Young Wives' Thursday Afternoon Club and the W.I., righteous eyes blazing, lips pursed in distaste), I kept myself scarce.

It took me a long time to get my eye in; to find out who the madmen are.

'You can tell by their gardens which class they're from,' I overheard one woman saying to another shortly after I arrived. Well I couldn't. Not at first. (And, if I'm honest, still really can't. Not the way I can tell at fifty paces genuine Rolex or Chanel from the Hong Kong bootleg. Short of match-practice as I am, I could still walk into most clubs and tell you what the bar take is to a penny.)

Cleve is really two villages, Cleve and Coombe, one on each side of a steep valley. The oldest parts of the two villages are down on the waterside, where a rough causeway connects them at low-tide.

The causeway is made of cement which must have been of some special fast-setting kind to resist being washed away by the current. In fact, impressions of water-movement are visible at certain points along its length – smooth, swirled areas fixed into the surface, which remind me of those time-stop shots of dandelions releasing their clocks, and the technically enhanced pictures of the motorcade in Dallas that purport to show a section of President Kennedy's scalp being blown away.

Near the water is where you find the traditional whitewashed cottages, black-tarred at their bases, which in the early days I fondly imagined housing unruly families of honest-to-God shit-kickers and decent, atmospherically stinking fisher-folk.

The name-plates attached to the cottages – hand-decorated and -fired tiles, and loftily inscribed lozenges of local slate (both styles no doubt the work of rat-race drop-outs and hairy back-to-the-earthers) – should have alerted me to the fact that these were all now either holiday homes or the homes of young commuter professionals and comfortably-off retirees.

A few hoorays come tooling in late on Friday afternoons in the spring and summer months and immediately set to it arranging themselves in outdoor tableaux straight out of the creamier advertising pages of *The Tatler*.

Almost all the locals are tucked away in the council houses tastefully screened from the main road by a stand of spruce and elm, and shop at the Co-Op, which has a rather forbidding notice displayed on the counter – 'Unlike boots and shoes, the words please and thank you never wear out. Use them as often as you like' – but gives stamps.

There's only one shop on the Cleve side – a post office-cum-general store with a psoriatic old dog dumped in the doorway and only swampy lettuce and purpling scrag-end identifiable in the Neapolitan gloom inside. 'We can *get* it for you' is what you get if you ask for anything outside the basic range.

A fish van (prop. a recycled public relations executive, dried-out but still noticeably stress-clenched) comes round once a week. For everything else, you have to cross over to Coombe. This means the tide decides when you shop.

There is another way to Coombe, on dry land. But this means climbing a hill steep enough to bring the blood taste up into your throat; you also risk being flattened by on-coming traffic. It is this traffic whose headlamps and tail-lights I can look out and see at nights, the only things moving in the dark.

From halfway up the hill, Kiln Cottage on the other side of the valley looks like a picture-postcard or sampler of itself, 'quaint' in a way it never feels from the inside.

Taking this route, you have to walk through a sixties development of houses tricked out with Andalusian arches, ships' bells and carriage lamps, and jacked up on stilts facing the river as if straining to catch a glimpse of the passing show.

These houses have names like 'Thousand Fathoms' and 'High Standing', and deep dark picture-windows where you sense the curtains twitching even when they're not. ('Rattle the corner of the curtain to show them you're still there,' was the advice an old pro gave me on the art of taking bows when I was just starting out.)

Going to Coombe by the river route is more scenic. Not only that, there's the added excitement of miscalculating tide times and being left stranded on the wrong bank.

At low-tide, the river turns into a kind of concourse or pedestrian precinct, dotted with shoppers and awash with nonbiodegradable junk. It's a short walk across the rocks and seaweed, through the Mmmmmm-Matteson's bacon wrappers and washed-up tumble-driers and spaghetti-hoops cans to the crossing-point, and the dog gets a chance to unload a couple of doo-doo's on the way.

I've been caught on several occasions by the tide and had to whip off my shoes and roll up my trousers to beat the water pouring over the causeway, with the dog splashing along behind.

Queueing is still as much a way of life in these parts as it is in Moscow or Gdansk. Shopping is regarded as a branch of the performing arts, with scripts that are polished and well-worked rather than improvised.

'If I were obliged to eat no meat for the rest of my life, on the whole it would be a relief and no hardship . . .'

'I always think the flavour of asparagus is the very flavour of late spring . . .'

'Very young, slender runner beans are almost as good as asparagus . . .'

'Until I got a steamer I was always depressed about rhubarb . . .'

'The joys of having one's own new potatoes are worth any amount of sweat . . .'

'A free-range egg is simply a different species from the stale, fishy-tasting battery variety . . .'

'The best part of the flower becomes honey, and when I eat honey I like to believe that flower becomes part of me . . .'

The most important platform – Coombe's Olivier or Drury Lane – is the shop run by a fleshy, middle-aged Jesus-freak. The most conspicuous thing in the village is the tall cross erected on the roof of Loaves and Fishes. Its surface is a skein of thousands of faceted foil pieces which lighten or darken with the sky, and shimmer brightly at night like an elementary demonstration of all matter being in a state of perpetual agitation.

The owner of Loaves and Fishes prides herself on being nutritionally, as well as spiritually, right-on: although it's the only place for miles around where you can buy a zinc bucket, cast-iron doorknocker or nylon washing-line, she sees herself as being primarily in the health-food game.

Inevitably, her customers take this as a challenge to come in and ask for things that they know she hasn't got: rapeseed oil, balsamic vinegar, falafel, Star polenta, Greek-style yoghurt, nitrite-free crisps.

She reaps her revenge by employing no help and taking several minutes to weigh out a paper-twist of yeast or blanched almonds or peppercorns; by slopping around on big bare gristly plates-of-meat, and larding receipts with religious texts which she programmes daily on the computerised till: 'Jesus is wonderful. He is doing wonders in my life'; 'Know Jesus, no problem. No Jesus, know problem'; 'All I care for is JESUS and the power of HIS resurrection'.

There then follows an address for the International Miracle Centre, in one of the poorer postal districts of London.

Housewifely zeal extends to every corner of village life. A trend I've noticed in recent years among the afternoon walkers on the cliff path, for example, is voluntary doggie-doo retrieval. Out comes the carrier bag, down goes the tissue, and another part of the national heritage is saved from desecration.

It's thanks to the various environmental, heritage and ramblers' agencies that the turf along the many miles of the coast path is kept in the sort of condition that, if it was in a house (certainly if it was in my mother's house), it would have a plastic runner thrown over it for protection.

The timber of the gates and stiles along the route is architectonically sunk, oiled, tongued and mitred. The benches have evidently never known a lovelorn Bev or Gary: they haven't been gouged at or signed with graffiti. The sheep and rabbit pellets seem a last authenticating touch of the set-dresser.

It nagged at me for some time that I wasn't having the proper response to the untamed beauty, the uncouth majesty, and so on, of the scenery. That I wasn't experiencing those lashed-to-the-mast, big feelings that waves crashing on rocks, Turner skies, the sea's rhythmic thrusts and sighs, were supposed to inspire. The dispiriting underwhelmingness of the experience kept reminding me of the old cockney one-liner: 'You're fuckin' me, aren't you? I can hear you.'

I worried that I didn't have a feel for nature.

Only slowly did it come home to me that this was largely because the nature I was surrounded by had been patiently house-trained and suburbanised; toned down like Chinese and Indian and other ethnic flavours to suit the English palate.

This was impressed on me during my second winter. It took that long for the strength to come into my legs. And one day, in a fit of uncharacteristic enterprise, I decided to give them a test-drive by investigating a small bay that I knew lay beyond the perpendicular hill at the back of the house.

It was cold but bright when I set out. After a few hours, though, the weather went into full-dress gothic – thunderbolts, boiling black clouds, curtains of dense rain. I was clinging to a rock at the time, my feet skidding because of the cladding of red mud they'd collected, and my arms shaking from the effort of hanging on.

The tide was coming in fast in spitting white rollers and the dog kept almost knocking me off the narrow ledges I was timidly inching along to safety. At last I was standing in a small cove where a rusting ladder was set into the cliff. At the top of the ladder was more sharp rock, then crumbling earth – I had to snatch at grass clumps and outcroppings a couple of times to stop myself hurtling towards the abyss.

By now, you'll gather, I was being visited by deep thoughts about those great elemental forces; I was getting it all in spectacular Sensuround and Vistavision – my nails were bleeding, my fingerends were shredded, I was soaked to the skin. I shuffled left and crawled what seemed hundreds of yards on allfours until I came to a piece of sailing rope leading to who-knew-where.

I hauled myself up – the dog was peering down at me, his knuckle tail whirling with excitement – and, through a hole in a hedge, found I was eyeball-to-eyeball with a fishing gnome, complete with ornamental pond and cloche-covered runner-beans, and a wrought-iron sign on a gibbet saying 'The Retreat'.

I was in the caravan park that is still the target of perennial local complaints about 'caravandalism'. The vans were a uniform pea-green colour with threadbare fifties curtains at the windows and wizened TV aerials on the roofs. They squatted in their decorative plots like favoured pets, too old and settled in their ways to be going anywhere other than here.

That was my last piece of freelance activity. Since then I have been happy to fall in with the local rhythms and observe the established codes and practices.

I stay tuned to gale warnings at nights so I can hold my own on the weather. I keep abreast of the latest health scares – listeria, BSE, glass in babyfood, carcinogenic trace-elements in coffee – in case I'm called on for a comment while kicking my heels (and biting my tongue), waiting to be served. I wrap the empties in newspaper when I throw them out, so as not to embarrass or alarm.

I take my walk at the same time every day and see the same soaps, chat shows, quizzes, and somnambulistic sporting occasions – the electric green of field and pitch and billiard table lending a pleasant aquarium air to the stolid, moteless rooms – through the windows I pass on the way.

Now and again the talking hairdo on the screen doing continuity or selling double-glazing or miming the meaning of 'Easter' or 'sandwich' to an animated machine operative from Chorley (whose prize of a weekend in Jersey or bench-top dishwasher hangs in the balance), is one I once shared a bill with at the Chiswick Empire or the Tivoli, Hull.

People can say all they want about the so-called totalitarianism of the totally pleasant personality. It has all contributed to the sense of physical well-being and security I have known in my time here.

Steer clear of the rivalries, feuds, tensions, and petty vendettas, as I have managed to do, and the atmosphere is dull and soporific, admittedly, but also unthreatening, undemanding and benign.

I quickly acquired the habit of leaving the doors unlocked when I went out. (Although, for a time, I went through a routine of checking the many hiding-places in the cottage, humming a happy tune, when I got back.) I only lock up at nights in the winter.

At least that was true until some months ago, when something happened that I am taking as the sign (for which I have sensed myself becoming increasingly receptive; my radar for a long time

71

has been silently sweeping the sky), that my time out of time may be reaching the end of its natural span.

Something you hear said occasionally is: 'the only thing wrong with Cleve is having to look at Coombe.' What they mean is the toothpaste-coloured bungalows looming out of the dark ilex trees, with their breeze-block barbecue pits and canopied outdoor loungers.

Cleve, by contrast, is mostly weathered natural stone – biscuit brown, sky grey – and lichen-covered tiles. One of the few post-war houses on this side is the first house beyond the slipway at the end of the quay; I pass under its picture-window and plastic tear-drop chandelier walking along the river bottom on my way to the shops.

The people who live there used to be regular weekenders but, since the summer, have become permanents. She is stocky, long-suffering, capable; he is the sort of man who tucks the short end of his tie into his shirt and wears crackling diamond-patterned socks with a track-suit and trainers (this is guesswork – I've never been close enough to find out).

Even at a distance, though, he seems to bristle with repressed fury and self-hate. It comes off him like static. He kicks out at the debris trapped in the seaweed, slams car doors, changes colour like a traffic-light, and glowers. His neck is in a neck-brace, probably as a result of this pent-up rage. Sometimes the light catches the perspiration standing on the satiny neoprene rim of it in a way that makes it look as if it is beginning to melt.

There is a sign on the heavy gate on the road side of their house, aimed at scaring off burglars. It features a picture of a Dobermann and the slogan: 'Go Ahead. Make His Day.' But there is no dog. He is a dog-hater. (There's a lot of them about.)

The river at low-tide is a popular place for exercising dogs, for obvious reasons. They can swim and chase sticks and do what they have to do, then the tide comes and handily sluices it away.

The couple in the house near the slipway have always kept a

72

particularly unsightly sign in their kitchen window, where no dog-walker can miss it: a line-drawing of a dog squatting to take a dump with a broad red diagonal through it. (They seem to have a *fetich* about laminated signs and badges: the rear window of their car is spattered with stick-ons from stately homes and safari parks, in addition to one advertising another pointless untruth – 'Child aboard – keep your distance'.)

Recently, though, a home-made effort went up, close to where they park their car on the far end of the quay by the slipway: 'Please do NOT allow your dog to defecate in front of this house. Or please TAKE THE FAECES HOME WITH YOU'.

The contrast between the drawing-room language – 'defecate', 'faeces', the reiterated 'please' – and the crazy underlining and piece of old board on which the words were chalked, seemed evidence of a personality coming apart at the seams.

My last walk of the day is one of the parts of the day that I most look forward to. Taking the flashlight and walking along the river last thing has become one of my unshakeable rituals.

On the darkest nights, when there is no moon (it's a connection I've only made since I've been here), it reminds me of being backstage in the time before I was due on, just out of sight of the audience, which I always found a companionable place to be.

It's where every day was headed. The relief to have arrived, plus the condition of total black-out – the only light was the light bleeding from the stage – was conducive to a kind of careless intimacy that I knew nowhere else in my life.

If somebody had to do a quick change, they came off and did it where they stood. Chorines were constantly flinging off one piece of flim-flam and throwing on another. Behind the flats were steaming heaps of towels, tights, athletic supports, brassières, dressing-gowns.

It was a refuge that was always available. A settled environment. Somewhere to retreat to out of the light.

A thing I learned early on was never to play a theatre blind. You had to know where the exits, pillars, balconies, bars and, most of all, where the lavatories were located if you wanted to avoid being thrown by stray blobs of darkness moving in the dark during your turn, like elements of the dark reordering themselves.

When you go out on stage, go out smiling, look at your audience, start at the top balcony, captivate your audience, look at them and smile, then take your eyes down to the bottom balcony, look from one side to the other, and go into your number.

If it's a night when the tide is out far enough for me to walk most of the way to where the causeway links the villages, I can see the scales of the illuminated silver cross throwing scrims of light into the street below it, giving the steep street the appearance of a stream negotiating stones and other small obstacles on the way to emptying itself in the river.

A blurry blue light comes from windows on both banks in rooms where people are watching television in the dark. If this had been earlier in my life, the probability is that I could have told you, almost to the minute, what they were watching.

I carried television and radio times in my head without even thinking. Gazing into windows as we came into strange towns, I could take the elongated shadows playing across curtains and ceilings and instinctively convert them into familiar faces and settings.

The dark has never held the usual terrors for me. On the contrary, I'm happy when night comes. I welcome it.

Recently, though, I have felt their eyes on me. Felt sure I was being watched. I've seen shadows moving behind their bedroom window in the dark.

74

A few weeks ago, playing the beam a few feet ahead of me as usual as I went, I lit up a series of symbols drawn on the quay in fresh white chalk.

There was a diamond, a circle and a triangle, all geometrically precise and aligned, and in the centre of each was a turd.

Directly above the circle was a chalked square and the words – there was nothing hurried in the writing; the opposite, in fact – 'Next pile of filth?'

I checked the cupboard under the stairs (one pair of naval binoculars, six jigsaw puzzles, several suitcases, one horsehair shoe-brush, the coin-box for the phone), the pantry and the cave-like dressing-room off the bedroom where I sleep, when I came in, feeling what I would describe as both thrill and dread.

Many nights now I lie awake far into the night, straining to catch some wrong note in the creaking of the rafters, an off-chord in the cooling of the pipes or something unresolved in the noises the fire makes as it prepares to fall in on itself.

Five

There are, I would guess, several hundred pictures of me in existence somewhere, frozen into my glamourpuss-with-pooch pose.

Along with bathing-belle-with-beach-ball and pulchritudinous-package-with-provocatively-jacked-up-Continental-shelf, it was a formula snap of the day. (And, on the day, it was a formula for which I was genuinely grateful: it was something to hide behind; a reflex that was useful if you were taken unawares. When in doubt, pout.)

The dog would invariably be decked out in the slinky, boudoir-coloured leads and junk gem-encrusted collars that were gifts from the fans and therefore compulsory in public. (Freshly boiled bricks of lights, sheep lungs and cow udder were also deposited at the stage door daily in certain towns in the north. They came wrapped in newspapers, occasionally with damp, smudgy pictures of me uppermost, and always with hearty messages – 'Have a grand week!' 'Shall be in every night!' – inscribed along the margins.)

For fifties lensmen, the alignment of a small dog and a female bosom seemed to add up to the kind of dumb-bunny cheesecake with overtones of the forbidden that was their stock in trade. A champagne bottle (full or empty), a champagne glass (ditto), a large motorcar (a turquoise-blue Armstrong Siddeley in my case, then in later days an MGA roadster, neither of which I learned to drive) and scarlet sting-look lips ('Hot it up, darling!') were also regarded as indispensable for the same reason.

I suspect it's these pictures that ———— —— and his cronies have in mind when they rhubarb on about iconicity and retro imagery and the 'solid, uncomplicated, talismanic Englishness' (that is, counterfeit Americanness) of the immediate post-war years that I'm supposed to represent.

(I would lay dollars to donuts on him having one or two choice examples pinned to the bulletin board in his office this minute, along with xeroxes of 'outrageous' front pages from the *Sun*, storyboards, jacket laminates, wads of computer print-out and festive-looking flow charts showing projects in development/in production/on hold.)

What they're really saying – which is okay – is that I was a cliché.

Now, as I've explained, I have become that other cliché with a dog in it: the old dog with the old dog trotting off on her daily constitutional.

Almost from the day I started travelling, I travelled with a dog as a companion. I can measure my life out now in miniature Pinschers.

There is nothing intrinsically *Come Dancing* or frou-frou about the breed. The miniature is a perfectly scaled-down version of the full-size Dobermann. Head wedge-shaped. Coat smooth, short, hard, thick and close lying. Tail docked at the first or second joint and appearing to be a continuation of the spine without material drop. Colour black, brown or blue. Markings red rust in colour, sharply defined, appearing above each eye, on the muzzle, throat and forechest, on all legs and feet and below tail. Eyes showing intelligence and firmness of character. Temperament bold and alert. Form compact and tough. Gait light and elastic.

I was given my first Pinscher by the founding members at an early fan-club gathering, and have stayed loyal to the breed ever since. As soon as one starts to show signs of being about to check out, I am in touch with Mrs Wood, the breeder, to enquire about a replacement.

In theory, Dawn Wood and I should meet about once every twelve years. In practice, because of accidents and various health complications resulting in animals going belly-up before their time, the intervals between our meetings have sometimes been shorter.

They have never been so short, though, that we have failed to register the physical changes that have overtaken us both in the interim. We were in our early twenties when we first met; now we're coming up to sixty and conscious of the fact that, if not the next dog, then the one after, will in all probability represent the last transaction.

This gives our encounters a poignancy of which I think neither of us is unaware. I notice the spread of melanin blotches across her hands, the painful torsion of the veins behind her knees, the fact that the loose flesh of her upper arms now reminds me of the skirting around a hovercraft, and that her hair is a more emphatic colour than it was (she looks younger when she lets some grey show through).

She takes on board the fact that the three-string necklace of creases round my throat has been etched deeper and that the thread-veins on my cheeks have grown more entangled; she sees that the fine skin around my eyes is growing tired and that the whites of the eyes are not a good colour, but of course both of us say nothing.

We rarely go very deeply into the latest cause of death: there isn't much to say if it's because of the heart packing up or one of the cancers (colon, bowel), which has generally been the case.

There was one occasion when I did go weepy on her, after a dog had died prematurely and in a particularly unpleasant way. And there was a period some years ago when there were problems in the family with a teenage daughter and she unburdened herself to me.

I held her hand under the buttony gaze of the Pinscher portraits on the walls. She said she felt she could talk to me more easily now I no longer cropped up on the television all that often. I detected a note of reproach in this (it's a wild world) as well as some satisfaction that things were beginning to even out.

After that we became more reserved and formal. Our encounters have always followed an established pattern. Once the standard pleasantries have been disposed of (our eyes gliding over the latest ravages, our voices resolutely up), we are drawn by the smell of simmering bones and bagged biscuit meal to the kitchen, and from there to the outhouse beyond the kitchen where the puppies are whelped.

What would you call a smell so evocative that it has come to seem somehow fused with your existence, an indelible part of your life? One for which you can develop an irrational yearning and that you often find yourself trying (uselessly) to imagine? A smell for which you feel a kind of nostalgia even while you're in its presence? Proustian? (Only if you were really pushed.) Primal?

You can smell the smell before the door to the outbuilding in Mrs Wood's garden is unlatched – it out-smells the tarred weatherboard of the walls, the tubbed midget-pines making a path to it, and the leaf-rot which oozes underfoot in autumn.

The ingredients are simple, if unreproducible: milk from, for example, Smoky Ghost Sovereign Lady (that is, the mother – pet-name 'Tara'); paraffin from the heaters; urine and creamy crap soaked into the shredded newsprint covering the timber floor; the tang of surgical spirit; the oiliness of glycerine; the nubby rubber of hot water bottles.

At three weeks, the puppies are still sexless and blind and squirm in a heap together like something under a laboratory microscope. They are as undifferentiated as oranges or melons. Choosing between them involves the same level of choice as a waltz along the produce aisles at the supermarket.

Or it would if Mrs Wood, with an unerring instinct for what I'm after, hadn't already chosen for me. After very few minutes she'll rummage with one hand among the gummed eyes and

79

satiny pelts and leg buds and, having found what she's seeking (a businesslike inspection under the tail for confirmation), set it in my palm like a sack of chocolate dollars, the pay-off in some secret and ancient ceremony in which we are participating. 'Your new Psyche . . . Look out for each other.' Always these words.

Just as I have stuck to male dogs for no other reason than that is what the first one was, so I have gone on using the name which the dog that started all this was given by the fans.

'Psyche' was the dog in the 1950s radio comedy, A Life of Bliss. He was played by the birdcall specialist, Percy Edwards, a portly, classic countryman figure, in twills and knitted waistcoat, whom I saw frequently during broadcasts from the Paris Cinema in Lower Regent Street, anxiously waiting to come in with his high-pitched whines and welcoming yelps and the other reaction noises they relied on to bring Psyche alive for the listening audience.

Although there was very little commercial exploitation of the character, on the strength of his radio life as a dog, Percy rose to second-billing on the number-two tours (the Palace Attercliffe, Her Majesty's Barrow, the Hippodrome Aldershot) where his impersonations of burning buildings, trains in tunnels and gale-force winds also went down very well.

Choosing a new Psyche is part one of the process. Taking possession is part two. In the glory days this was very simple: Mrs Wood would drive up from her home in Surrey and deliver the dog to the flat, where my mother would have prepared by burying the carpets and all the upholstery under copies of the *Mirror* and the *Daily Sketch*.

This service stopped some years ago, however. It's an indication of how the balance of our relationship has shifted that I now have to meet Mrs Wood at the services close to the Leatherhead exit of the A3, which is literally halfway.

The first time we rendezvoused there, this was a Gingham Kitchen, with everything gingham-patterned – tablecloths, staff uniforms, beakers and plates (the chequered close-weave sealed between layers of moulded plastic, which reminded me of some shoes I once had with tropical fish suspended in the chunky perspex of the heel). The friend who drove me there had a 'lobsteak' which poisoned his insides and put him out of action for five days, while we were waiting.

By our second (and latest) link-up, the same place had become a Happy Eater. Everything was the same – the breathy noise of the power-brakes on the heavy goods vehicles, the whacked-out trees, the trampled lawns, the slashing rain in the tungsten downlighters. Only the signage and corporate coding were different.

Mrs Wood got out of her car and placed the travelling-case with the puppy in it on an outdoor table with fibreglass figures of the Mad Hatter, the White Rabbit and other *Wonderland* characters seated around it, as the fat tomato logo winked and litter hurled itself vertically into the sky and the commuter traffic on the overhead ramps threw refracted technicolour splashes showering down onto the traffic on the lower levels.

Psyche flicked his hot tongue in and out of my nostrils all the way into London, a habit which he has never lost.

Writers on the pops have always talked about the 'Hey Doris' effect of reaching out to their readers. I am a fund of doggy 'Hey Doris' facts and trivia.

The tenor Luigi Ravelli, for instance, would cancel a performance if his dog Niagra growled during the warm-up vocalising.

Maria Callas gave all her poodles the same name: Toy. (I discovered this long after I'd adopted the habit.) 'Only my dogs will not betray me,' Callas is reported to have once said.

Freud thought a lot more about his chow, Jo-fi, given to him by Marie Bonaparte, than he ever did about Frau F., and he spent a lot more time with it into the bargain. Freud declared that an owner's feeling for his dog is the same as a parent's for his children, with one difference – 'there is no ambivalence, no element of hostility'. Shrink sessions were up when the chow rose from beside the couch and walked in a circle.

Brigitte Bardot shares Colette's belief that 'our perfect companions never have fewer than four feet'. 'I have given my youth and beauty to men,' Bardot announced when she sold her wedding dress and jewellery collection at Drouot recently. 'Now I will give my age and wisdom to animals.'

My friend, the pop impresario Larry Parnes, has dedicated a lounge to the memory of his Rottweilers, Prince and Duke, in the showbiz twilight home where my mother is presently eking out her days. The dogs' cremated remains are displayed in a vase in a scalloped alcove, dramatically back-lit and surrounded by photographs and a personalised epitaph.

A fox-terrier called Pincher at Hawkesbury station on the Coventry and Nuneaton Railway was famous for ringing the station bell at the approach of stopping trains. One day after performing this act he ran from the signal box on to the line and was cut in two.

Montgomery of Alamein once said he had heard of a man being able to bear severe persecution, even torture, and then breaking down completely when his dog was taken.

Dennis Nilsen, the murderer of Muswell Hill who made goulash of his victims, did all his weirdnesses in front of a dog called Bleep.

When she was told her pet dog, Puppet, had died while she (and it) were in police custody, Myra Hindley said: 'They're just a lot of bloody murderers.'

(A couple of nights ago after giving Psyche his run I stopped in at The Creel to pick up the bottle I had forgotten to stock up on earlier in the day. There was no one about. The dining-room was empty; the bar was full of the smell of cellarwork.

(As I slipped behind the counter to help myself, as I sometimes do, I saw that the television was showing aerial shots of what

82

looked like a moonscape populated with indistinct hooded and black anoraked figures, moving across the difficult terrain in the inching, semaphoric way of the organised search.

(The bandit was doing its pieces, giving out spacey chirrups and generally cawing for business, so the voice-over was obscured. But there was something about the blistered and regular grid of the hussocks, the dispersal of the figures and the sombreness implied by the poor picture-quality – these were snatch-shots obviously – that was immediately and queerly familiar.

(The next image that flicked up on the screen told me what it was. Here, her time-warp, black-and-white features brightened by the Christmas lights in The Creel and animated by the blobs of light from the bandit pulsing on the dusty curvature of the screen, was the cruel-nosed, meaty-mouthed iconographic (yes!) mug-shot of the dog-lover, child-killer Hindley.

(It seemed – and I know now that this is the case – that they are back on the Moors, searching for the graves of other children tortured, sexually abused and then murdered by Hindley and her partner Brady and buried on the wastes of Saddleworth Moor more than twenty years ago.)

As he lies under my hand I can tour the scars that Psyche has collected in the six or so years we've been together. It's a familiar bodyscape of tendon, polyp, knuckle and gristle.

The corrugation on this knee is the result of a cartilage operation. He got the raised worm on his belly from impaling himself on a fence. The twin rivets under the hair of his right ear are where a Boston terrier's teeth went through. The recent wound on his forechest is from barbed wire. The tissue around his upper mouth is tough and permanently engorged from the afternoon on the cliffs when an adder bit him.

The pads are always the first to go: from Velveeta, they quickly turn into rasping, industrial-strength vinyl. From there it is a short step to them being permanently marked-up, damaged goods.

It's a process I saw happening around me in theatres for many years among all the fluffy little struggling dolls of showbusiness. They arrived bright and unblemished and in no time were consorting with characters in mercurochrome suits and concealing bites, bruises, welts, scalds, and disfigurements whose circumstances you couldn't let yourself imagine (cigarette burns on the lower-back, blue fist-prints on the thighs), under the layers of peach-coloured Pan-Cake makeup.

'I don't care if you've been fucking all night,' one well-loathed producer would stand in the door of the dressing-room and harangue the girls, 'when the show starts, I want you to get out there and *show them teeth*.'

Psyche 2 died at the age of two, murdered, although I could never prove it, by a schizo stagehand who saw it as a way of getting at me. I should have been alerted when he started bringing him back from walks with claws missing; he eventually broke his neck, blaming it on a fall down some stairs while he was carrying him to the dressing-room area.

Psyche is out like a light; dead to the world. His eyes are turned up in his head, his scrotum (still some small signs of dermatital infection there) is twitching, and his feet are kicking against my leg in a choppy approximation of running.

A plane has just flown low over the cottage. It was loud enough to agitate the river into a sizzling, quilted pattern. The dog's usual reaction is to dart for cover when this happens. Half an hour ago, though, I slipped him a mickey – just enough Mythium or Lythium, Oblivon or Halcion to keep him under until we've made it back to London.

Very soon it will be time to lift him into the zippered carrier I use to smuggle him onboard the coach. Roy, my regular driver from the village (motto: 'Church bells not decibels' – it's printed on the mesh of his trucker's cap, plastered across his bumper) will assist me in this and then, experience has taught me, work the phrases 'dogsbody', 'dog tired', and so on, into the conversation as many times as possible in the half hour it takes to travel from here to the coach station in town.

The arrangement I've got at Kiln Cottage is unconventional, but it seems to work. Whenever Staff or his sisters want to come back on reacquaintance visits (which is never for very long and not very often – there are too many other options open to them) I upsticks and go. These visits tend to coincide with the school holidays and the influx of happy campers and Sunday sailors into the area, so I have few complaints.

Temperamentally it suits me to be going against the flow. Even since before I was awake this morning I have been hurtling along the one-horse highways and high-hedged lanes that will carry me away from Cleve, the window wound down to give me a full hit of the phenols, benzines, hydrocarbons and other toxants and pollutants that hang in the air over the trunk road at the top of the valley like vodka in tonic and give the same sort of violent kick-start to the system.

Sometimes in the mornings when I was pulling down £500 for playing a week in Grimsby or Stockton or Wakefield, I would throw on a headscarf and a coat belonging to the owner of the digs where we were staying and slip out past the all-night poker school in the kitchen and the bleary club hostesses who were the previous night's take-in and climb aboard the buses taking the cleaners, mill-girls and factory hands to work. I'd sit in the fugged sleepy atmosphere, ingest the smell of newsprint and tobacco, and bask in the anonymity.

(Under normal circumstances I refused to be seen without full make-up, even first thing in the morning. If I'd ordered a meal in my room in a hotel, I would hide in the bathroom until it was served to avoid being seen by the staff.)

On the return run, we'd load up with the shop-girls for the

85

Victorian department stores whose windows were still full of berserk-looking, putty-coloured models in stingy post-austerity fashions. From the upper deck you looked out at the wallpapers of rooms that had been half-demolished and had fireplaces and doors suspended halfway up them, or down on to the exotic plant-life that had swarmed over the bomb sites.

I used to feel sometimes, although I'm pleased I was never called on to prove it, that I would be able to say which city I was in in those days simply by the noise coming from the football ground.

The roars of the Nottingham Forest crowd, for instance, rose on thermals and became diffused as they crossed the Trent, while the cries of triumph when County got one in rolled straight into town like fog.

The wave of noise of Newcastle supporters used to break against the walls of the Palace theatre in an explosion which seemed to release the earthy sweet smell of yeast from the Blue Star brewery which it carried before it.

Bradford's Valley Parade location resulted in the crowd sound from there being particularly big and bottomy and mysterious – the hollow-cosmos effect of the first Mitch Miller mike-in-a-lavatory-pan echo-chambers – 'putting a halo around the voice' is how he described it – which was later beefed up and operatically OTT-ed into the Spector sound.

With their composition floors and bare brick walls, dressing-rooms tended to amplify anything – people arguing, a toilet flushing, football crowds. The crowds functioned as a sort of locating mechanism. Constantly on the move, as I was at that time, they gave me a bearing.

Perhaps the best way to explain it is in terms of the way some actors used the heat generated by the studio lights of the early talkies to get themselves into the correct camera positions.

'Any film-stage properly lit becomes a veritable crisscross of unseen light beams of different focus and intensity. These soon became my secret tools for correct positioning,' one of the old-time movie queens relates in her memoirs. 'Realising that my facial skin was sensitive to subtle differences in emission of heat from various combinations of light beams, I came to correlate and memorise the patterns of heat and action established during rehearsal and used this knowledge to maintain correct changes of position during filming. What I recalled was a rehearsed pattern of heat. My knack involved sensing the difference between a patch of skin on my forehead and a cooler area on my cheek. Combining this fact with my memory of where I had been in rehearsals, I could even sense if my head was held in the right position.'

When a goal was scored while I was in the empty theatre gearing up for a show on match days, it could sometimes sound as though generations of applause had freed itself from the plasterwork and was rumbling eerily around the auditorium. At other times it was as if the building itself was exercising ancient lungs and ventilating.

I am sentimental about the old neighbourhoods associated with football grounds and variety theatres. Where they still survive in any recognisable form, it's there that you're likely to find isolated pockets of the working poor and all the textbook examples of multiple deprivation. But it is also where you will find the characteristic sparks of individual eccentricity and urban energy, advertising themselves in back-street businesses with names as impromptu and hussled together as the clapped-out premises to which they're tacked: Kumincyde, Bed-E-Buys, Connectuphere (cellular car phones, pagers), Sheeba Video, Vidz 4U.

Street-corner hairdressers have always provided a direct line into private fantasy and wish fulfilment. ('Alma's' were very popular when my name was prominent on the showcards that hung in the windows among the ads for 'Drene' and 'Knight's Castile' and still painted big on the gable-ends.)

Shobiz Hair, Hair you!, Curl Up and Dye, Eboné Stylez, Maggie's Thatchery, Scissors Palace, Shear Class, Toffs and Tarts are some I have spotted when the bus has lurched off the motorway en route to or from London and gone barrelling along close-crowded streets that are a riot of information overkill.

It is this diversity and animal vulgarity that I miss in the de-industrialised dreamlike dead-zones that the railways stations have become.

They are places where you can buy life assurance, compact discs and twenty varieties of croissant at midnight and hop aboard a train almost as an afterthought, secure in the knowledge that there will not only be more of the same, but identical climate-modulated concourses and graphic accents, foreign-exchange franchises and spandex activewear concessions, disposed in an approximately identical layout, at the other end.

What happened to 'the immense and distant sound of time' hanging under Brunel's great roofs, shrouding his cast-iron columns and arches? *Men came and went, they passed and vanished, And all were moving through the moments of their lives to death, All made tickings in the sound of time.*

All this – a no doubt naive belief in what I like to think of as the romance of real life; an aversion to the security-scanned timeless present, to Sock Shop living – adds up to reason one why I ride the buses.

Reason two is financial.

Reason three is here in the person of our hostess today – Sue, as she will announce herself after a hacking cough into the mike and an attack of the giggles – 'Hello, my name is Sue. Your driver today is Nige. Your video today is *The Mannequin*, a present-day fable of our time set in downtown Philadelphia. I will be coming round soon to take your orders for refreshments' – once we are up and running.

An air of reverie surrounds Sue, which I would put down to a hangover. She has the beginnings of the hard look which comes with a hard life and age – I'd place her at about forty-six, half a generation younger than myself.

She has dark hair which she is in the process of growing out: the growth-stages are marked in shallow waves which she keeps fingering and straightening in an attempt to cover the tattoo of fresh love-bites – plum purple, no signs yet of yellowing – all in a row in the soft trench at the base of her neck. She keeps repositioning her neat, lipstick-stained company cravat for the same reason.

Although, as her passengers, we regard her with the affectless, disinterested gaze with which we regard each other, my guess is that I am not alone at this moment in imagining up the steamy scenario surrounding Sue's overnight turn-around activities.

A few lager and blacks down the Steyne at the The Blackie Boy, The Happy Struggler, The Spanish Patriot; a few Baileys and Parfait Amours at Berlins, Boobs, the Studz Bar (topless d-j, spacey globular lighting, Bonnie Tyler, Whitney Houston, Barry White in stomach-lurching quad); some fuel food – Taiwanese, Chinese, Greek, curry sauce optional; and so to the main business of the evening (a bit of split-crotch boogaloo? tarry Nepalese temple fingers? gummy African bhang? French ticklers?) In other words, the old Joan Collins never-too-old-to-rock'n'roll and the whole nine yards.

Nige doesn't figure in any of this. At least not in my version. Nige is the quiet studious type in navy V-neck and sun-sensitive glasses who, two inches into his second pint, can be relied on to divulge an unusual interest or hobby, an unsuspected inner life – a passion for English spatter-ware of the late eighteenth century, say, or a competition-keen knowledge of the life and works of Rider Haggard or the Brontë clan or John Buchan. Just the type who can be depended on, in other words, to get you up the motorway in one piece and keep the bus a Valium-free zone.

But if not Sue-and-Nige, then Sue-and-who? I tried to spot Sue's partner of last night among the hostess-and-driver teams milling around on the apron at the bus station before we pulled away. Early favourite was an in-shape, light-complected Negro with a morning paper poking out of his pocket at a pardon-my-pistol angle, but I decided that this was probably just sexual stereotyping.

The atmosphere – scuzzy sex and booming hangovers and complex interpersonal dynamics – brought back memories, as it always does (as I look forward to it doing), of all those mornings when the tour bus was loading up to head off for another town in that period in the mid-to-late fifties, roughly between *Blackboard Jungle* and Little Richard finding God and dumping his jewels in the Tallahassee, when the world seemed to be being made new and new energy was flowing into all departments of everyday life.

In 1957, the business was still coming off that big beautiful sound of Patti Page and Perry Como and Kay Starr. That was fading away and the new sound was taking over. But it wasn't an overnight affair.

When I spent the early part of the year touring the Moss Empire circuit with Britain's first homegrown teen scream sensation, the remainder of the bill was made up of a clown who doubled on drums, a magician, a pair of trick roller-skaters, Borrah Minevitch's Harmonica Rascals, and a man who made shadow-pictures with his hands.

Audrey of the Skating Avalons became the first casualty when she was 'struck by a projectile' (a commemorative Coronation compact scrawled with the words 'We love Tommy') while simultaneously revolving at speed on a high platform and spinning from a harness round her husband's neck by her teeth.

Pea-shooter armies were out in force (their actual ammunition was pellets of stinging pearl barley), and it became a custom as we proceeded around the country for the front rows of the stalls to stand with their backs to the performance, with older members of the audience yelling at them to sit down, until they got what they had come to see.

By the autumn of '57 I was the token female on a package that played more dance-halls and cinemas than theatres, and for one night only, and from which all the old-stagers, with the exception of a comedian-compère, had been expunged.

The band balladeers who I'd come up with had tended towards conventional notions of beefcake: cleft chins, square jaws, crinkly hair, boxy shoulders and trousers with zero crotch-definition. The boys of the chorus, on the other hand, inevitably tended towards the swish end of the spectrum: they were always a little light in the loafers.

The new breed of male on the pop packages that were being hastily slung together was hybridised from these two types, with the addition of a heavy US overlay ('western' shirts with lace-up fronts, nodding Tony Curtis quiffs, tight high-water pants that stopped several inches up the ankle).

A smattering of the Rons, Lens, Terrys and Harrys who had reinvented themselves as Jet or Rock or Deke or Ricky were familiar to me from La Caverne, The Condor and other clubs around the London scene: pretty-boy hustlers and actor/drifters who made up the shifting entourage of the leading managers and promoters and were in the pop racket as a career move, getting while the getting was good. They needed no lessons in how their hair should be puffed and tinctured or in how to pack their jeans.

Most of the fledgling idols and stage-struck musos, however, were pubescent lathe-turners, panel-beaters, spot-welders, abattoir attendants, hot-dog vendors and pub pot-boys, getting their first taste of showbiz.

'I'm young, dumb and full of cum,' the bassist or rhythm-guitarist for the Congars or the Krew-Kats or the Cameos announced as he climbed on board the bus on his first morning and, over the next few weeks, proceeded to prove it.

The buses reeked of sex. The bench seats at the back of the bus at the end of every tour used to be scabbed and caked with it. The windows and chromium appointments were bloomed with it.

The walls and ceiling seemed to be smeared with it. They were all cock-happy. It was like a contagion.

Because the cost of where they stayed at nights came out of their own pockets (and because it tied in with their new idea of themselves as rebel rockers), many of them chose to doss in the coach, parked in some municipal car-park or round the back of the hall.

At every stop there were the same eager mouths, arcade eyes and hungry hands swarming round the bodywork in a recognisable formation. Most mornings saw cheap-speed blondes frantically ratting their hair, applying spit-and-mascara and stuffing their knickers in their handbags before staggering off to work at the Market Café, C&A or the Co-Op. (Where they sluiced their sticky dumpling thighs, flaked the glueyness out of their intimate seams and gullies? Or opted perhaps to go through the day with the funk of bus sex clinging to them; to wear it on their fingers as a kind of trophy or memento and share it around with their workmates and customers? I was certainly curious and tempted sometimes to ask them.)

The newly-minted Shels and Troys, meanwhile, washed their underwear in the handbasins at transport cafés between gigs, then hung them to dry with their shirts and socks along the luggage-rack inside the bus in ludicrous parodies of what they had seen their mothers do on boxy verandas or in soot-streaked council-house gardens.

'I got nipples on my titties big as the end of yo' thumb/I got somethin tween my legs can make a dead man come . . .' In the beginning, they used to sing this sort of stuff because they knew it made me uncomfortable. I used to go up front and talk to the driver when it was dirty-joke time. But then I learned to face it up.

The realisation that I was the only one present who knew a crotchet from a hatchet (if only just), who could tell a C-chord from a head of lettuce, heralded a switch in attitudes. I started to join in on the Lucille Bogen and Big Mama Thornton numbers. I began to get attuned to an atmosphere which was a combination launderama, approved school, pleasure charabanc and knocking-shop.

There was the usual delinquent mooning and synchronised pissing and hurling half-pound bags of flour at passing traffic. Some of them acquired shotguns and would get the driver to stop at the edge of fields to let them shoot at bottles (and sometimes birds, though I didn't want to know about that).

Dean Vance's (of the Venturas) history – absentee mother, drunken father; a smoker by nine, a drinker at ten, first conviction at eleven years and nine months for wounding with intent; at fourteen charged with assault causing actual bodily harm; at fifteen with housebreaking and larceny – was extreme but not untypical.

I got it in bits at night as I painted black eye-liner and navy-blue mascara on his eyes and smoothed nacreous Max Factor factor-5 over his violent viridian face pustules and chest acne. He tended to dwell on the idea that his mother had been murdered, and there was nothing anybody could do about this preoccupation because nobody knew where she had gone when she suddenly disappeared from home with the off-licence takings. He spent much of his time on the bus working on a song about it – the Everly Brothers out of Leadbelly – which, to the best of my knowledge, never got finished.

Obviously this was a lot different to life on the road with Betty Kayes and her Pekinese, The Balcomes, Fun on a Revolving Ladder, Kay and Kimberley, Balancers Plastique, Winnie Atwell, Pat Hatton and Peggy, Tommy Wallis and Beryl and all the other mum-and-dad acts who I knew were still out there, still *tummling* away.

I knew because I encountered them most nights when I put in at digs which, with their stuffed fox-terriers and formal 'best' parlours and moans about kid singers wearing mops of hair thick enough to hide a crate of kippers, were the pre-war world preserved.

All the talk, widespread at the time, about 'modernisation' and 'affluence' and 'the crust of conventional life cracking from top to bottom' went straight over their heads. They saw what was happening in the wider world as a parallel of what was happening in the business, which is to say: a fad, a freak of fashion, a flash in the pan.

(Many of the performers rehearsing for the 1956 Royal Performance wept openly when Van Parnell walked into the stalls of the Palladium late in the afternoon and announced that that night's show had had to be cancelled owing to the grave international situation. At the time, though, nobody gave it any great significance.)

The Archie Rices were staying with what they knew, which was all they knew, and, as a consequence, were losing it. Unlike myself, I need hardly add, who was plugged into the new mood of youthful vitality and powie fifties optimism.

For me this found its most concrete form in the first solid-body 'planks' and 'axes'; the Fender Stratocasters and Telecasters, Epiphone Coronets and Wilshires, the Gibson Les Pauls. With their futuristic shapes and colour-ways and textures – lemon yellow with gun-metal fleck; graphite with graphite mica – they seemed excitingly in step (what did I know?) with the new concrete environments of ring-roads, tower-blocks, transportels, expressways, sky-lounges, skylons and sputnik-style sportatoria.

My problem was that, although I was thinking 1959, image-wise I was marooned back in 1954. I was locked into a persona that no amount of remoulding and remodelling and cosmetic rehab seemed able to break me free of.

My original style had been an outgrowth, a cartooning I suppose you would now have to say, of the New Look that came in a couple of years after the end of the war: hand-span waists, immense spreading skirts, bell dresses with warehousefuls of sequins, bugle-beads, tinsel, crackle-nylon and a lot of padding, pleating, stiffening, corseting and boning going on.

I was a work of conscious and total artifice. I wore long nails because I had stubby little hands. I wore high-heel shoes because I was short. I wore my hair big because my hair wouldn't do everything I wanted it to. I thought that part of whatever appeal I had lay in the fact that I looked totally artificial but was totally real.

This look reached its apotheosis on the occasion that I had to be physically swung into position like a Portaloo or section of partition-wall when the outfit I was wearing – a real 'Hey Doris' number consisting of a floor-length ostrich-feather cape over a dress of jet beads and chainmail – proved too monumental to make it onto the set any other way. I had reached a degree of *thingness* from which the time had obviously come to beat a retreat.

By the package tour era, I had slimmed my outline down almost to street proportions. I'd also updated the press-button-A ballads and cutesie-poo ditties from my usual programme to a style that seemed more in keeping with the younger trend.

They were developments that had my manager, among others, climbing the wall. 'You're still a terrific piece of merchandise,' he'd remind me every time he came on the line. 'The less you change, the longer it lasts. You know what I'm saying? You *know* what I'm saying. *Leave it alone.*'

But unfortunately my ear had been turned. Instead of a clear horizontal simplicity in the music, I was now hearing the potential for notes to be chopped up, jammed together, halved, augmented, twisted, stretched and dropped. Instead of a regular chugga-chugga pulse, I was learning new ways to bend, tease and subvert the regularity of the beat. Which was the beginning of my *tsuris*, as I should have known: the more I tried to break out and move from the old style to the next style, to introduce a more modern idiom, the more it went over like the proverbial turd in the punchbowl. To the point where I had to admit defeat and backtrack to the well-worn and familiar, the tried and tested. (More hits followed.)

I believed at the time of the package shows that my heightened awareness – I have to call it that – could be attributed solely to the new range of musical experiences I was being exposed to, the race music coming in on record from America, in particular.

But that alone couldn't account for the soaring energy levels, the unusual alertness and receptivity, the unprecedented appetite for performing. Or for the dilated pupils, the popping nerves and the sense sometimes of being put in another dimension.

For that, I now know (though I didn't then) I had the 'nigger minstrels', the black-and-white slimming capsules the boys on the bus were feeding me on a daily basis, to thank. The reason I was feeling so up for such a lot of the time – and so swimmy and strung-out for the remainder of it – was because I was staying permanently dosed on ups.

Now – today, I mean: November 20th, 1986, which happens to be a Thursday – I can experience the same speed-freak sensations merely by being back on the road, riding in a Rapide double-deck Shuttlelounge or Scenicruiser, with Sue or Sammy or Donna in the kitchen corner nursing a hangover and wrestling with the clingfilm and the sandwich-fillings she has raced round doing the last-minute buying for in a post-euphoric haze.

Having a doped dog in the bag planted between my feet whose unpredictable smells and movements could suddenly result in him being discovered gives that added extra urban top-spin to the experience. I've been feeling out there ever since I got on. I've been feeling acid-blazed.

An hour ago it was sunny. The sun lit up the individual fibres of the pseudoplush on the seat-backs so that they seemed to be sensitive to every breath and vibration and swayed in the frazzled air in here like the fronds or stamens of anemones.

The wig worn by the black woman sitting in the seat in front was similarly ablaze with nylon filaments and fat perspiration-points, each one of which appeared to hold a perfect image of the shimmering, sun-bleached infinitised interior. The shaved pubic strips of velcro which anchor the head-rest slips bristled with a similar harsh black sheen.

It isn't so apparent now that it has clouded over – the sky has a lowered, snowy look. But a while ago, every synthetic surface seemed to be animated with a jazzy streptococcal patina: the window stanchions, the window sills, the tissue head-rests, the seat-surrounds, the drop-trays – all could be seen to be evenly, but variably, textured, like different skin-types examined minutely in a purpose-adapted light.

When she came round with the first in-coach refreshment service, about forty miles in, I saw that Sue herself was glittering with these semi-subliminal patterns or patinas, which were over-printed on the polyesters of her otherwise solid-coloured company-issue skirt, shirt and jacket.

The woman directly across the aisle has been weeping intermittently ever since she got on. She hasn't looked up from the door-stop novel in her lap (a Virginia Andrews) for over an hour. She has been eating crisps and occasionally wiping her fingertips clean on the fibrous pages of the book.

A small Asian girl several rows in front is screaming in what at first was a nerve-jangling way, but has now become like a mantra. The elderly man with her, whom I take to be her grandfather, keeps repeating the same phrase – 'How do you do, little lady? . . . How do you do, little lady?' – in a desperate counterpoint.

I can see the title of a magazine article that somebody's reading: 'Ever so Crafty Main Meal Super Soups'. I can also see a complicated elastic-band device keeping a pair of glasses on a man's face, and the headline 'Nick Nick Jim Punched At Disco'.

(How do I know that this is a reference to the young Cockney comedian, Jim Davidson, when most of the time I have no access to a television, take no daily paper, and rarely listen to the radio?

(The answer, I suppose, is that I know in the same way that I knew immediately without thinking what Sue meant when I asked for a packet of peanuts from her tray and she said, 'Wet or dry?'

(It's in the air like the weather, and you can either duck it or let it wash all over you, coating you with that distinctive late-in-the-century patina.)

Moving along. The videos are located at the front and centre of the vehicle. So far they have shown the motorway playing itself out in a melancholy way, as a wavering scribble on a screen, the trace-line of a dicky heart.

Now *The Mannequin* – 'a present-day fable of our time set in downtown Philadelphia', you will remember – is being teed-up with trailers for *Police Academy 4* , *Lethal Weapon, Who's That Girl?* – 'films that will fill your home with *quality* entertainment' – and other offerings from Warner Home Video.

I recognise the voice doing the talking-up – a disc-jockey from my own time, apparently still going strong.

I look out the window and see the computer-generated logos and graphics spinning and cavorting as a reflection on the bland agribusiness landscape through which we're travelling.

Reality digitised and broken down into megabits or bongo-bytes, then replayed as a kind of endless fidgeting or fluttering on the periphery of experience, at the edge of vision. Motes dancing on the air. That's what I see. That's what I seem to be constantly seeing.

We slow to a crawl for no obvious reason. We are apparently climbing a steep gradient, although no incline is visible. Then we pick up speed again and glide past a racecourse with deserted grandstands and hand-painted numerals slotted into a big churchy frame giving the date of the next meeting.

The past, in the shape of a shingled farm building, a farm dog skirting the edge of a field on its half-haunches, a plot of country graveyard bordered by slabby barbered yews, will occasionally be glimpsed in profile for a few seconds before the road presents itself full-face and sets you back on course across the surface.

'Minute in the mouth, month on the hips,' I hear a child a couple of rows back chastising its mother.

'It's one of the places where you can get really *good* camel's hair.' This from a character in *The Mannequin*, a frail but feisty old lady, evidently the owner of the department store where the action – a bit of love-interest, a lot of knock-about – takes place.

I find myself wishing it was time for Sue to come round again taking orders. (There are no catering committees involved, no portion control practised here. It's a system that allows the personality some play. Sue's chicken roll with Paxo stuffing and honeyglaze ham with pease-pudding now both sound particularly good.)

I know that at this point, though, Sue will have got her head down, squeezed in among the cases of no-brand cherryade and cola, the caterers' jars of beetroot and brown sauce that occupy the back seat and mark out her territory.

Her bit is the bit next to the toilet cabin. 'If you sprinkle when you tinkle,' a rather startling little notice in there says, 'please be sweet and wipe the seat.'

Turbo-Intercooling. Chilled Distribution, the rolling logotypes say in the winter dusk.

Imagesetting. Interprint. Computrans. Superdrug. Control International. Corporate Synergy.

Then: Get In Lane. Filter Right.

We slide past convoys of wagons on the left, their house-sized loads mysteriously belted and tarped. There are no heads visible, only ghostly forearms and slicked denim thighs and the unexpectedly homely cabin bits and pieces brought along to fend off the loneliness of the road. (Already some Christmas lights are in evidence – strings of coloured lights looped round windscreens to give a festive/sad, lyrical/tawdry Santa's grotto feel.)

We have slowed to a crawl again, due to some obstruction or

accident. We sidle alongside a lorry carrying an alp of giant concrete pipes. There is a dog curled up asleep in the seat next to the driver and a newspaper flattened against the steering-wheel.

SHAMEFUL, CYNICAL AND CRUEL it says in letters as black as death across the front page. And, over the constantly-retrieved, flatly-lit picture of Myra Hindley: 'Police step up macabre search for young bodies in the snow as Moors murderess Hindley confesses after 20 years'.

The picture (blurring slightly with the movement of the engine) fills almost the whole of the page. Is it possible to discern evil, as many have supposed, in the cavernous upturned eyes, the pasty planes, the heavy bones, the holed hedge of bleached blonde fringe, the fondant of deep shadow, like a choke-collar, under Hindley's chin? Is this the look – frontal, insolent, the unintimidated direct address to the camera – of *ein richtiger Teufelsbraten*, a true devil's dish?

The features are individually too familiar by now to be read as an integrated, blood-warmed face. As usual, Hindley looks like a composite, an identikit, a media emanation, a hypothetical who never existed in the flesh.

But we are moving again. Or the wagon is. I have to look across at the dark field, the stripped trees, the traffic on the distant feed-road to get a bearing.

The cabin dog staggers to its feet, makes one and a half circles, then folds itself back into the hollow made by its body. Between my feet, in his bag and still, I hope, sedated (there are two hours at least to go), Psyche performs the same bit of business in perfect unison – as if one was the object and the other the shadow cast by it (remember all those Fred and Ginger routines?); one the voice and the other the echo.

I'm confused about how to react, whether to feel beguiled or repelled (why did I almost say 'warned'?) by this sudden, oddly haunting piece of synchronicity.

As he inches ahead, I see that there's a fresh and feminine-looking continental quilt bunched up behind the driver's head and a bunk-space it must feel good crawling into at the end of a hard driving day.

Six

Four days back in London and no contact so far with my mother nor any attempt to make any. So I have forced myself to make the effort to stir my stumps and take the trek (and it is a trek) today.

It's like the war again in the Tube. During the war the identification boards on stations all over the country were painted out to fox the enemy; the trade papers for the week billed you only as appearing 'somewhere in East Anglia'.

Stations all along the line are being given a facelift. Station names are obscured by scaffolding and ladders and the clouds of demolition dust that gust out of service tunnels and ventilation ducts, adding to the curious world-in-flux, sand-bagged atmosphere.

The result is a lot of craning and straining at every stop from people like me who are not familiar with the route, and tired looks from the desk-jockeys and Tube rats who know its every lurch and door-slam better than they probably thought they were going to know anything in their lives.

The work in progress means an unbroken blankness that brings the blackened walls pressing in and accentuates the snugness of fit between the bore of the tunnels and the poreless silver skin of the trains.

The ads have been cancelled with blackboard paper: its surface seems stretched and buckled with the vitality of what lies concealed underneath. Occasionally it is possible to see beyond the screens that have been erected on the platforms to sections of the rind-like saloon-bar and lavatorial tiling which is in the process of being overlaid with wafer-thin mosaic and ceramic tiles in more up-to-the-minute, razzle-dazzle designs.

Also advertising panels where posters from as far back as the thirties have been roughly ragged-out and lie exposed in archaeological clarity/complexity, like layers of the city's skin.

An awareness of the present being a membrane grown over the past (and of the future constantly threatening to occlude the present, in an imperceptible lapping movement towards the centre from the edges) has been with me since I was a child planted between my parents at the Troxy.

One of the things about growing older is that you start to develop a kind of X-ray vision by which any building can suddenly appear as depthless and liquid as a slide image thrown on to whatever you remember standing in the same space at an earlier time.

I feel certain that it is to avoid these woozy sensations and achieve a less slippery fix on things that people in their declining years (Cleve of course is full of them) move away from the areas they have known all their lives and re-root themselves somewhere where the past is less likely to rear up and go boo! and there is a sense (a sense at least) of immutability and permanence. To stay is to risk the psychic dizziness that in the end can drag you under.

The pace of change has been so fast in the decade or so I've been on hold that certain districts of London for me are like a chimera.

The supermarket which I use almost on a daily basis when I'm in London was, in an earlier incarnation, a theatre I played many times. I was a regular on a popular variety programme, *Chelsea At Nine*, which Granada Television put out live from there on Monday evenings in the mid-50s.

It is inevitable now that as I hesitate in the space between the delicatessen counter and the chiller cabinets, which, by my reckoning, is just about where the pass-door from the stalls was located, I sometimes seem jostled by ghosts and golems and uneasy souls – many of them not released yet from their earthly vessels.

Because of its fashionable location rather than its history (though I do wonder how big a part that plays) it's a place that attracts a reliable sprinkling of famous, or nearly famous, or formerly famous, faces. (The papers have run items on it.)

The striking thing in almost every instance is how fleeting the resemblance is between the popularly circulated public image, the official template, and the patsy with the wire basket.

Stripped of that elusive X ingredient essential to the projection of the well-presented, value-added self, they (*we* – I can't leave myself out of this) appear not only deflated but somehow dully denatured.

The low-wattage of the has-beens is understandable and mostly involuntary and can be put down to age, obscurity and the extended season of disappointment and failure.

The former footballer, the disgraced children's television presenter, the *Army Game* actor, the *Z Cars* star, the playwright who has been famously blocked for twenty years, the precociously successful novelist who has since lost the thread, the clapped-out dress designer, the one-time prince of the voice-over, an actress of whom it was once said she couldn't ad lib a burp after a Hungarian meal . . .

When we see each other we take avoiding action or, if it's too late, exchange brief nods of recognition and turn hurriedly into another aisle, although this doesn't always work.

Some time ago I found myself in the check-out queue next to one of the beefcake balladeers from the old days, a passable Vaughn Monroe copyist, who was clearly in the grip of some personal sadness – grandson a junkie, had up himself for shoplifting or persistent importuning; I honestly didn't know.

He had a Walkman headset clamped over his ears. It was tuned to one of those all-talk, a-problem-aired-is-a-problem-shared stations specialising in opinions by the mile and round-the-clock confidences, confessions and hair-curling personal disclosures.

He never listened to music, he said. Music brought back sad memories. His skin had the texture of days-old orange peel; it was crystalline with whiteheads. The headset went on whispering into his chest as he spoke.

Listening to the news and phone-ins was like listening to a never-ending serial – things were happening to other people, and they were mostly bad. 'It takes you out of yourself and instead of brooding over your own problems you're listening to and living in other people's messes. And it keeps you company. Music puts me in a melancholy mood. I start thinking about the past. It makes me want to go and get loaded.'

Since then I have seen him palming cherry tomatoes from the salad bar and chewing contemplatively on them as he dragged his big feet around, zombie-fashion.

But it's the others, the ones whose careers still have some heat under them, who are currently making some noise in the world, who seem if anything *more* ghostly, more spectral – shadow creatures bewilderingly adrift from the lustrous, confident, open-featured people (the people with something to sell, always some aspect of their own uniqueness) showcased in the newspapers and the colour supplements and radiating from the television screen.

It is difficult to believe, for instance, that the small, pinched, rather furtive woman who always takes an unusual interest in what people are putting in their baskets can be the celebrated writer familiar from the magazines that I get third- and fourth-hand from a neighbour in the country.

The truth is I had thrown the relevant issue – A Home In the Life or A Day of My Own or This Hectic Life or My Favourite Tipple – away with the rubbish (I'm the last one in the chain) before it dawned on me where I had seen that burnished old bird, posing in a shaft of light in her Chelsea salon, before.

(She had her bathroom painted half a dozen times before she achieved the exact shade of cerulean blue. She has an aversion to cats and is devoted to Jean Muir's classic simplicity.)

In the shiny pages she is palpable, coherent, identifiable, *complete*. In the supermarket in her frazzledness and ordinary dishevelment, indistinct and all but invisible. And she is not alone in her invisibility.

The actress who lives with the American novelist; the model-turned-actress who is combining a successful career with bringing up a Downs baby; the Lloyd-Webber lyricist with the eighty-foot kitchen and industrial hob, the newsreader who has just run his first half-marathon, the singer with the on-stage rasta hair extension, the controversial architect, the quiet Stone, 'the girl with the laugh in her voice' – all are equally phantasmagorical, intimately familar yet worryingly unplaceable to the tricked, the tired, the glutted eye.

It seems odd to me now that I ever had to invent strategies for going unrecognised. Today I walk past old friends and acquaintances in the street and I might as well be Myrtle the Turtle. They don't see me.

The me that they remember looking like ten pounds of shit in a five-pound bag (as one of them has unsentimentally described my seventies appearance) is now bantam weight, standard-looking, almost stringy. Most of the excess poundage has been eroded and chivvied away over the years as a result of all that walking and cliff-top buffeting.

Sitting shoulder-to-shoulder with the sleepy commuters as we hum forward through the underground tunnels of north London, I see my fifty-four-year-old face staring back at me from the depths of a dirt-dappled window, looking all of that, yes; a touch reptilian and leathery, certainly; but with nothing uplifted, tucked-upped, sliced off or surgically repositioned.

In middle-age I've developed a sort of deracinated, nutty gypo look that I play up whenever I venture out in public with vaguely ethnic bits and pieces – cambric shirts, tortoiseshell combs, metal-threaded prayer shawls. My hair is longer – what my mother (oh Jesus, my mother) calls bedroom-length. It's been wrecked by the sun and salt, but that gives it a careless, tendrilly appearance that I can live with for the present.

My hands, as it happens, are the part of me that has altered most. From being porky soft and mottled, they have turned spartan and squared off, like the hands of market traders and old landladies that I admired – women who thought nothing of going into a chicken up to the elbow to haul out the giblets or into a stopped lavatory to the shoulder; who unflinchingly saw to the corpses of family and neighbours and rose well before anybody else in the house to lay fires on chilly, misty mornings.

(Fire-lighting is one of the skills I have acquired: it gives me unreasonable pleasure to be on my knees among the clinker with coal-dust under my nails, taking the sulphur of struck matches in through the mouth and exhaling it through the nose.)

Having said all of the above, however, I have to confess that Ronnie, among others last night, recognised me as soon as I stepped out of the lift into Seigi's.

'Hey what the hey. *E*lma!' Ronnie said, seeming to take my coat, relieve a tray of a fistful of glasses and steer me towards the table where he was sitting, in a single movement. 'Look what the wind's blew in. Crazy-looking threads!'

> You got a smile so bright,
> You know you could've been a candle.
> I'm holding you so tight,
> You know you could've been a handle.
>
> The way you stole my heart,
> You know you could've been a cool crook.
> And baby you're so smart,
> You know you could've been a school book.

I remembered this – the way you were aware of the music as a distant pulse before you'd finished paying off the taxi; how it entered you through the soles of your feet as you stood waiting for the lift to come; how it steadily increased in volume as you rose through the building, past stone corridors and darkened offices with doors of rippled glass; and how finally the noise embraced you, along with the smoke and the human hubbub and the heat; how it played you like a flounder and then slowly wound you in.

A plant glowed emerald green in the foyer. Bottles shone behind the bar; waitresses went back and forth in the sketchy light wearing waist-high tutus. But the dominant feature of the room was, as it has always been, the nightscape like a painted backdrop or diorama – the night city achieved effortlessly in a few broad strokes: splashes of white to suggest lighted windows or reflected light or a swathe of light glancing off rainsoaked bricks high up in the night; torch bulbs for the hard bright stars.

It would have seemed old-fashioned as decoration if it hadn't been real: too cornily concrete in a world tuned into the associative, the abstract. If you went up to the window you could vaporise part of the city with your breath on the great cold pane.

'ElmaTonyaTonyaElma,' Ronnie said. Tonya was a peach-blonde no longer in the summer of her years. She was wearing shiny black ciré stretch-pants and a panther limned across her angora sweater with sequin-peaked ears and red ruby eyes.

'Elma and me go way back, like . . .' – Ronnie flubbeled his lips with his fingers, obscuring how many – '. . . years.' He tapped the untipped end of a cigarette quickly on his thumbnail and sucked in a long blue flame. Tonya indicated that she was already lit. 'Ohyeah. Yewshaw. Like for life. Am I right El?'

But even with one eye closed against the smoke Tonya was giving me a look I recognised. I knew that was coming next. 'Weren't you . . .'

The champagne flutes were generous and thistle-shaped,

108

made of an industrially-etched crystal sharp enough, if gripped hard enough, to cut your hand.

'Yes.'

Club lighting is an under-acknowledged art – the pin spot, the subtone wash, the optimum angle. I knew she wouldn't have rumbled me without it.

Tonya herself had chosen her place intelligently, half in and half out of the creamy glow reflecting from the table and just to one side of an uplighter concealed in the plant trough running along the back of the banquette.

She was pushing a few scraps from the complimentary buffet unenthusiastically around her plate with a fork that looked enormous in relation to her beaky white knuckles. 'You're not much fun, are you?' Ronnie bawled at her over the music. 'Look at it. A wall of wet paint.'

Tonya brought a napkin to the corner of her mouth, taking exaggerated care not to smudge the velvety brown line that defined her lips. 'It's a cordon bleu cook sitting here,' she said. 'Trained.' Then to me: 'Not that I want to eat well all the time. I can eat, let's say, baked potatoes every day, but now and again I like to put a spoonful of caviar on top, you know?'

Pernicketiness about food is a trait that has been shared by all of Ronnie's girls, which suggests they must get it from Ronnie: it is what he expects; part of the high-living etiquette. Whenever you saw a plate of steak going back to the kitchen at the Stork Club or the Empress or Churchill's, you always knew that Ronnie was in with one of his *tsatskes*.

He reached over, grabbed something wrapped in flaky pastry from Tonya's plate and jammed it in his mouth. His teeth gleamed momentarily in a face that is lavender-orange from going under a sun lamp every day as well as from the tanning cosmetics Ronnie wears all the time. He had his initials set in rolled gold on his middle finger and a monocle on a gold chain twisted loosely round his wrist.

His hair – the little hair he has left these days: red-grey field stubble on top, blue-grey wings either side – was razor styled. His shoes were ostrich, showily pocked where the quills had been pulled, and the knot in his tie was shiny and very small. (It was later, when we were out on the duster-sized floor, that I saw that the white-on-white stripes in his shirt said 'Yves Saint-Laurent Yves Saint-Laurent' like that, which told me it had to be bunce from the barrows, a bit of Korean buy-in.)

Ronnie, if you hadn't already guessed, is a character with a colourful criminal back-story. (And, from what I could gather last night, a colourful near-criminal present. When he isn't leaning on the crews of shoeshine boys he currently runs in the City or the gangs he sends to erect stands 'for the lardee' at point-to-point meetings, he's employed as a technical adviser on TV cop-operas and docudramas that can harness his specialised knowledge.)

In the sixties he was a bag man for the Who and other bands, taking charge of the 'now money' they demanded from promoters before they went on, and disappearing with it in carrier bags out the back door.

But when I first knew him, Ronnie was a gofer, fixer, set-up man (it didn't pay to enquire deeper than that) for Tony Dalligan, who kept the Kray twins out of Soho and the West End.

That was thirty years ago, when the different London worlds of film people, showbiz, sportsmen, Chelsea layabouts, Indian aristocracy (the Maharajah of Baroda – 'Charlie', the Maharajah of Cooch Behar), politicians, rag-trade, property developers and the East End criminal element were just starting to run together.

The venues could be anywhere from the society photographer, Baron's, bottle parties at his studio in Belgravia, to the coffee stalls in Queensway where everybody congregated to swap notes at the end of a long night.

'Alma, sometimes I wish someone would really hurt you so I

could kill them,' I once recall Tony Dalligan telling me in what was intended to be a romantic interlude.

He was handsome, charming and very pleasant, with that aura of danger about him that Billy Daniels at the time, and many other male stars since, have tried to cultivate.

But what I remember best about him is his abnormal passion for cleanliness. He wouldn't get into his car without first making certain that it had been recently sprayed with a perfumed antiseptic. He kept his own monogrammed bed-linen in places where he slept regularly and paled at the idea of using a towel more than once.

Naturally such fastidiousness made him an instant hit with my mother. 'That Tony,' Fay would purr, 'he's so cavalier. An absolute gent.'

When I was away on tour Tony made a point of including Fay in parties for nights on the town. Even when I was back from the road she usually managed to get herself roped in.

As he would only eat at places which allowed him to examine the kitchens whenever the whim took him, this narrowed the choice down to a regular half-dozen: Harry Meadows' Churchills, Bertie Meadows' The 21, Bruce Brace's Winston's, Harry Green's The Jack of Clubs (under Isow's restaurant in Berwick Street, where I had my name painted in gold on the back of my regular chair), Patsy Morgan's Torch Theatre Club in Knightsbridge, Eric Steiner's The Pair of Shoes.

Being Tony Dalligan's guest was never easy, especially when you knew the performance that lay in store when it was time to settle the bill. 'Wader, can I get the check?' he'd call out across the room in a terrible B-feature accent. But nobody laughed.

Nobody acted like they'd even heard. The stories about the cut-throat and the sword-stick (also about the blow-torches, electric cattle-prods and concrete kimonos that later emerged) were to be believed.

There then followed a period of drawn-out haggling, at the end of which he'd offer to settle things on the toss of a coin: heads, he'd pay twice what was written on the bill; tails, the waiter would cover the cost out of his wages over the next six months.

The opportunities for embarrassment were multiplied, of course, whenever Fay was along. 'Do you want a lousy tip,' she'd ask the waiter, rootling busily in her handbag, 'or a beautiful picture of my daughter?' (The memory of this makes me want to get off the train now, cross to another platform and start going back in the direction I've just travelled.)

Tony's dead – offed many years ago by somebody in the same line. Ronnie's still around to tell the tale, but it's been touch-and-go, from what I've been able to piece together.

'I had a breakdown not so many years ago, I had two, and was very near to death,' he was quoted as saying in a Me and My Health feature in a newspaper that the fish happened to come wrapped up in one day.

'I found my wife dead in a room, my mother had her leg amputated and died, it all piled up and I had a breakdown and a haemorrhage, the house was splattered with blood, all up the walls, over everything. I was taken to hospital a dying man, and I wanted to die. I didn't care. They were all round the bed and that was the end.'

(I often used to get the feeling that the public thought everybody they heard on the wireless or saw on television all lived in a big house together and loved each other; that we were constantly pouring our hearts out and weeping on each others' shoulders. The truth is, personal revelation remains even more of a rarity than in straight civilian circles: we know most of what we know about each other the same way everybody else does, from what we read in the papers.)

One of Ronnie's major pluses as a person is that he hates to dwell on the past. We could, for instance, have jawed about when Seigi's, the very club where we were sitting, was lined floor-to-ceiling in fake fur and traded under the name Wips.

(There was a tank of famous piranha fish just where you come out of the lift which Ronnie plunged his bare arm into more than once and took it as a personal affront when they refused to bite.)

We couldn't see the view of the night-time city from where we were sitting; but we knew it well and felt it like a breath on the neck – the lemon-bleary winter light, the oily sliver of silver river, the broken grid of cranes, the illuminated contractors' signs swaying hypnotically in the wind.

We were content to sit and watch and listen to Tonya discuss Christmas shopping, Andrew and Fergie, the pound-against-the-dollar, religion ('I change religions like I change clothes. But I am now in one of the most confused parts of my life. Philosophically,' I'm almost certain I remember her saying, 'I'm back at the Socratic "A"'), until it was time for the event that was the excuse for us being there to happen.

'Woman' was the title of a book and the name of a perfume being launched by the former wife of a former (dead, in his case) sixties super-swinger. The snappers who had been mooching around looking for 'faces' in the shadows were being corralled together in front of a low platform, and the pros took this as their cue to load up on drinks before the free-bar closed and a pay-bar came into operation.

The introductory speech was made by the owner of Seigi's, whom I had known since he was a child and his father had part of the Freddie Mills Nite Spot. (Fay would frequently get up on the stage to sing 'A Foggy Day in London Town' and 'This Is A Lovely Way to Spend an Evening' with the ex-boxer.)

He was wearing his working uniform – a Japanese-style black silk suit with a big brooch made out of fragments of broken mirror in the lapel. Later he would change into cords and a Barbour, collect the lurcher and the pointer that were tethered to a radiator in the back room and go deer-hunting near his house in Sussex.

'I'm not a lady as you may have gathered' (this didn't get the laugh he had been expecting), 'but I have sniffed the fragrance and I think that it's very, very subtle, it's very, very gentle, it's very, very sophisticated and it's very beautiful. And that is why this particular lady is putting her name to it because she is every one of those things, believe me. Could I invite you to applaud . . .'

Maureen was that odd phenomenon, a para-celebrity – a celebrity by association. Now, too many years down the road, she was still trying, as the survivor of a 'heady, frenzied' era, to make it play for her.

As they closed in for the kill, I saw the photographers exchanging sneaky glances behind the snouts of their Pentaxes and Leicas, which meant they were going to make a monkey of her; she was going to come out with multiple chins, a mean-looking mouth, eyes as wild as a bedlamite's.

They got her to aim perfume at their lenses in a sticky cascade; then squirt perfume in a crossfire under her nose; then to recline on the black velvet display trestle, scattering books and cheap cardboard boxes, and revealing more of herself than was sensible, including a repair ticket on the dim plastic sole of her shoe.

'I've never sold *my* story and I can't really understand how they can do it, being beastly to people,' I heard one of those familiar goo-goo little-girl bedroom voices say behind me. 'I'd have an amazing list, but you can't go round shopping your friends, can you?' Pause, for an inhale or a sip. 'I might easily change my mind, of course, if things went badly wrong and I was offered staggering bread.'

The towers of books had been reduced to dog-eared rubble; dozens of pocket-sized 'flacons' of the fragrance had instantly gone walkies.

I returned to where I had been sitting and had only been there a couple of minutes when under/around the noise I thought I heard somebody say my name.

'Alma Cogan, yeh?'

Starting from the feet we had: suede cowboy boots, pressed jeans, Navajo buckle, turquoise Navajo ring, plain T-shirt, linen jacket, inflamed nostrils, pupils like coal-holes, tumbling long blond androgynous hair. A portable phone jammed into his back pocket had the incidental effect of drawing the denim tighter at the front and showcasing his (bulked out?) thing (many hours in front of the mirror evidenced here). 'Knockout. Well-pleased. Would it be cool to lay my rap on you since you're like here?'

An expensive education lay close to the surface of the lame-brain rockbiz pose. I saw Sundays at home in the country with the parents; I saw a forest of lovingly-angled family pictures, tiny saucers under the castors on the sofa, brass occasional tables from the service days in India, smelly ('whiffy') elderly labs, tepid gin-and-tonics, knicker-blinds, tables with skirts.

He began to tell his story. But before he had got very far I discovered I knew it in outline already from the couple of letters I had received from the desk of 'Jase' (this was his name – a corruption of – what? – Jasper? James? Wholly invented? There were no Jasons thirty years ago in his particular neck of the woods).

Written on the paper of his marketing-production-management company, the letters were peppered with *catalysing a little further evolution of*s and *synergising with the psyche of*s and *emblem of showbiz culture*s and *déjà vu factor*s.

The top-and-bottom of what he was suggesting was to put me together with a client who had recently made a 'boldacious' cross-over from the club dance scene and was now coming off a couple of ginormous hits in the pop chart.

The idea, as he had explained it, was to establish a whole new category of pop duets – 'the epitome of the fifties-eighties pop collision, with shades of sophisticated boystown disco and clear bright-eyed melody'. I would figure in this as 'a kind of art statement'.

'One, with experience, gets this tremendous feeling. We've got power play guaranteed on it already. Every hour, on the hour. It's a potentially enormous entity.'

Jase had just got his feet under the table when he was stopped in full flow by Ronnie, who was a bit fiery by now and wanted to know if he was from the papers.

'I've only got two uses for newspapers,' Ronnie said before I'd had a chance to explain the situation. 'To cover the bottom of my budgie's cage and to train my dog on.' (Having some deal on the boil that would benefit from a bit of friendly image-tweaking in the tabloids – that was different.)

'S'funny,' Ronnie said, plopping a placatory paw on Jase's shoulder, 'I went for a Chinese last night. He hadn't done nothing. I just went for 'im.'

This was a twist on Ronnie's most famous saying from the old days. Asked what had happened to some individual who had been causing trouble (or who Tony Dalligan suspected was *about* to cause trouble), his answer was always, 'He became punched.'

After a few more minutes of banter, Ronnie drifted off into the crowd again and Jase ('Some wild dude') continued as if there hadn't been any interruption.

'What I'm saying is it could add up to a hellacious combination. It's supposed to be secret. Like, deep graveyard. But already there's an incredible industry buzz.' His mouth was so close to my ear now I could feel the consonants popping. 'He's so impressed by how primary you remain in the culture. I can send you clips where he talks about what an avatar you are. He grew up with your records. His mother's always been like a mega-fan. There'd be video product, other cross-media tie-ins . . . And you'd have points. Which could mean we were talking serious numbers.' And so on.

But my fingers were exploring the recesses and under-edges of the seat upholstery to find the cigarette-burn that, like the hardened wad of chewing-gum, is always there.

At the same time my mind was fixed on the view that you get from the upper-deck of the coach at a certain point on the Hammersmith flyover: you look down on the raft-like canopy projecting over the entrance to the Odeon theatre and the red plastic letters that have been thrown down among all the crud that has collected there until the next time they're picked up and hung together on the big white light-box that fills the whole of the facade to spell out the name of a headline attraction.

I also hadn't forgotten a review I had read of the latest career re-launch of a near-contemporary (she's slightly younger, but not much) where she was described as looking like 'a minicab driver in Bacofoil'.

I took the business card to which he had added his direct number and the number of his car-phone and promised Jase to think about his offer and let him know.

I went on somewhere else with Ronnie and Tonya after leaving Seigi's, then somewhere else and (probably) somewhere else again. I woke up this morning with the usual misheard and stray snatches of conversation swooshing around my system with the after-effects of the alcohol.

I was sure I could remember, for instance, somebody (could it have been Tonya?) talking about going to an erotic sculptor to have her 'pussy' sculpted: 'I had it done in dental clay and painted blue and silver and now it's sitting on my mantelpiece at home. I think all men should have them in their offices instead of the usual dreary picture of the little woman.'

The general atmosphere is vivid (there were peppermint-coloured nuclides of neon playing on the surface of my drink; *Lady In Red* was the record playing at the time); but key details, such as the identity of the speaker, couldn't be sworn to.

I have a hazy recollection of Ronnie putting me in a cab and scrunching a large note into a ball as he passed it through the window to the driver.

It was only a couple of hours ago, when I was getting myself organised for the schlep across London to visit my mother, that I found the samples of 'Woman' stinking up my bag. They were probably put there by Ronnie, thinking he was doing me a favour. I decided to leave them and take them to Fay and the other old girls who spend most of their time experimenting with hair and make-up and dressing up like weenyboppers.

The first sign of my mother disappearing off the radar was when she started swanning around in the guise of Alma Taylor, the silent movie star who she named me after. I would come home to find her with her face whited-up, sitting in front of the mirror with candles lit, pulling faces and striking poses she remembered from fifty years ago.

The next step was thinking that people on television could see into the room. 'Pull your skirt down. He's looking at you,' she'd whisper during the news. Or 'Close that drawer. He can see right in there. It hasn't been tidied for months.' She wasn't even an old woman – not *old* old. She was sixty-eight when all this started to happen.

I got her into Dorothy Ward House by calling in a few favours. Strictly speaking, it's a retirement home for variety performers exclusively. But by the late-seventies, it was a purely academic distinction in my mother's case. By that time she was convinced it was herself, rather than me, who had had the career.

'The Old Pro's Paradise', as it used to be referred to (unironically) in the profession, is a bizarre and unnerving place to visit. Very few of its three-dozen inhabitants believe they were anything less than the toast of the town in their day. The difficulty lies in deciding which Hollywood lovely or Broadway legend, which king of comedy or matinée idol they see themselves being this week.

You've heard the old joke: Open the fridge and she'll do twenty minutes when the light goes on? Welcome to Dorothy Ward House.

The escalator at this end was roofed in with corrugated iron and chicken-wire. Sprawled on the steps outside the station were a gang of Stone Age derelicts with violent contusions and scabs on their faces as exotic as Ubangi tribesmen.

The sweet rotted smell of cider lufted from the gardens at the bottom of the hill where they go to relieve themselves. It's still thick in my throat now that I've climbed as far as the Victorian villas with pink and apple-green garden paving and bottle-holders with little clock-faces on them to tell the milkman how many pints to leave and caravans and motor homes standing waxed and raised on bricks in the gravel drives.

How well I feel I know this street (and how much I loathe it). The question that nags at me every time I find myself panting up it is: what are the chances of me coming to know it even better? How strong is the possibility that I may one day have to end up seeking refuge here myself?

It's inevitable that I'm going to sound as though I'm weeping in my beer when I say this, but I own virtually nothing. The flat in London is in my mother's name. In the event of her death – not very far away now – the tenancy is not transferable.

Yet every time I step into Dorothy Ward House (past the mezuzah on the door-frame, under the arch 'Stage Door' sign in the porch) and see the cracked and faded trade ten-by-eights, the old show-bills in their framcs, the collections of china dogs and toy ballerinas set out on the tops of walnut chests in rooms labelled Hippodrome, Empire, Tivoli, Coliseum, Palladium, and so on, I am reminded why I have been happy to see my own souvenirs and career cast-offs dispersed like a wig in the wind.

There are no pictures of me around my mother's flat (and none in Kiln Cottage). There are only pictures of my mother here in my mother's room: Fay being introduced to the Duchess of Kent; Fay making up a card school with Roger Moore, Michael Caine and Stanley Baker; Fay refreshing her lipstick at a bottle-crowded table at the Talk of the Town (Tony Dalligan is just visible in the bottom right-hand corner).

She accepts a kiss on her downy, doughy cheek but obviously

has only the haziest notion of who I am or what I might be doing there.

She is wearing black lace gloves with cut-off fingers, white PVC knee-length boots and a purple dress I haven't seen before. Ash dribbles down her front. By her elbow on the bedside table is a schooner of the Tia Maria that she keeps in the wardrobe (I have another bottle in my bag).

'See that Rolls out there?' she says abruptly and with such conviction I half-turn to look at the window. 'It doesn't mean a light. Truthfully. I thought it was all going to be different when I was a star. Not a bit of it. Don't you think I'd like to go into town to the shops, have a rummage round? But it's impossible, you see. The commotion. I'm a prisoner.'

Her room is at the back of the house, with a view of the garden. All that's out there is a wooden bench and a blackened bush in a circular bed on the lawn. Everything else has been brought inside for the winter.

It is early evening. The low murmur of the TV news comes from other rooms on the corridor. There is a chrome bar along the wall just inside the door and support-handles by the washbasin and the armchair. There's an emergency buzzer by the bed.

'I've been on bills with stars recently,' my mother continues, 'and I've been in the number-one dressing-room where they used to be and they're down the corridor now. Which embarrasses me terribly. I couldn't see my name down there on the bill when I was up there once.'

Silence. I shake out the few items of clothing that are lying around and fold them neatly in a pile. I open the door of the medicine cabinet and quickly shut it again. I prise some white hairs from a brush using the handle of a metal comb and, reluctant for some reason to throw them into the empty, paper-lined bin provided, flush them down the sink.

They wrap themselves around the spokes of the plughole. I

poke at them with the comb as if they were something unpleasant I'd just discovered and let the tap go on running long after they've disappeared.

The sound of water is immediately followed by the sound of a voice coming in our direction and announcing, 'This is your five-minute call, ladies and, gentlemen . . . Five minutes.'

If you didn't know the sound had a human source, however, you wouldn't identify the cheese-grater purgatorial mechanical croak as a voice at all. Connee Emerald played saxophone and sang in an act called the Emerald Sisters and Michael. She was a celebrated West End 'Peter Pan' in the years before the war. Now cancer has eaten her face away and she has a throat box.

Without saying anything, my mother drains the last of her drink, makes some tiny adjustments to her appearance and begins to make her way along with the others to the lounge (the 'Larry Parnes Lounge' – it says this on a chafed brass plate by the door) where the evening's programme of entertainment is about to begin.

A regular part of life at the home are the 'chat shows' in which the residents take part. It is all done along professional lines, with television make-up and a spotlight beamed from the ceiling and a 'conversation area' of three armchairs set in a two-on-one formation directly below the alcove containing the remains of Prince and Duke.

The 'host' is the resident manager of the home, or 'Super', as he prefers, a blot-shaped man with glazed candle jowls and perfect cuticles who talks in the ingratiating, stupefyingly ebullient style that he has perfected from the box.

The unfortunate thing is that the old stagers, who nearly all have a tale to tell, have been pressed into following his example. Which means that originality – of point of view, of experience, of expression – is not only not expected, but not encouraged.

The bland generality, the formulaic utterance, the quip that has been round the block a few times – they are all preferred to the texture of lived experience. The audience has also internalised the rules of the game: they come in with a laugh-track whenever the Super's bared teeth and lifted shoulders suggest that it's appropriate, exactly on-cue.

'It's been some fun days, I tell you,' Bubbly Rogers is saying and winning loud murmurs of approval from the hair-dos in the gloaming. (A hairdresser has been in in the afternoon and many faces, including Bubbly's, are still heat-blotched and par-boiled.)

She was a vocalist with Vic Oliver's orchestra in the thirties. The bow of her lips is exaggerated and pearly pink, and so is her wispy nest of hair. 'I think you can control your destiny,' she says, leaning forward in a confiding manner. 'You and God.' (Applause.) 'No, God and you. Watch out for the billing!' (Laughter.)

'I never go to the cinema any more. You get through the door, and five minutes and they're in bed. I'm not a prude, I just don't like it. I don't like it at all. I don't like bad language in films.' (Loud applause.) 'I don't like it on television, it frightens my dog.' (Loud laughter.)

Norman Long ('A Song, a Smile, a Piano') has slipped into the place next to me on the sofa, making me the filling in a sandwich consisting of himself and my mother. He has done it in the casual-conspicuous way that reminds me why I was never able to deaden the tedium of long afternoons in strange towns by going to the cinema on my own.

I half-expect his sclerotic old hand to come sliding over and start working its way up my skirt. Instead he starts plucking at my sleeve and jerking his head in a way that says he wants me to follow him out of the room. I look at my mother; she is moving her lips, silently mimicking Bubbly Rogers' answers with her, so I do.

The wall-lamps in the corridors are the kind that drip plastic candle grease: many of the shades have toppled sideways and become scorched from the heat.

We pass the doors of the Prince Littler undenominational chapel (there is an artificial Christmas tree on a table, waiting to be dressed) and then bear left in the direction of Norman's room.

After his solo career was over he'd been props-man for Tommy Cooper for many years – the person in charge of the doomed tricks and other famous bits of comic business that made Tommy the institution he was.

He'd been let go for some considerable time when Tommy Cooper collapsed and died on-stage at Her Majesty's Theatre during a live television broadcast in 1984.

The curtains are drawn in Norman's room. The only light comes from a lamp on the bedside table which has a chiffon scarf thrown over the shade. Illuminated in the light above it – he has insisted I take the only chair, while he himself perches on the edge of the bed – are a number of personal mottos, hand-inscribed and framed in cellophane and black tape: 'You've either got it or you've had it' is one; 'Teach a kid to blow a horn, and he'll never blow a safe' is the only other one I can read.

He offers me a whisky; then an apple or a boxed date. He pours a small drink for himself then bends forward from where he's sitting and loads a tape into the video machine.

There are a few frames of a man and woman at a kitchen table but these soon stutter into the opening credit sequence for *Live From Her Majesty's*. The curtains open on a high-kicking chorus, who are followed by the compère who tells a few jokes before introducing a girl singer who lip-synchs.

Norman fast-forwards all this. Only when Tommy Cooper comes on to take his first spot does he allow the the tape to play at normal speed. Cooper comes in on the revolve with his familiar fez on his head and a purple velvet-covered pedestal of tricks in front of him. But when he opens his mouth to speak, Norman hurries the tape on again.

'. . . like a log. Woke up in the fireplace,' Tommy is saying when Norman takes his finger off the button. During the laugh an assistant comes out of the wings and wraps him in a shiny kimono which causes some camera flare. As she exits, Norman freezes the frame.

'Now!' he says, moving the tape on inch-by-inch. 'Don't blink. Here it comes!' On the screen Tommy has begun his backwards fall into the curtain. The next frame shows him with his mouth open gasping for air. By the next – 'There he goes – he's going over!' Norman almost shouts – he is on the ground.

He fast-forwards through the commercial break – the super-laminate images, the galloping colours, the sweat beading on Norman's head – into part two of the show in which a young comedian has been brought on to cover for the confusion backstage.

'But he's still there!' Norman says, moving back a few frames. He leaps from the bed and stabs with his finger at what he says are a pair of feet pointing skywards amid the static and muck of distortion at the bottom of the screen. 'He's still there. They're breathing in his mouth! They're jumping on his chest! He's too heavy to move!'

The deteriorated quality of the tape in this section – it has the milky opaque look of sugar that has been spun and stretched – shows how it has been run and re-run over the heads, freeze-framed and examined pixel-by-pixel, played and re-played in the hope (I assume) of isolating the moment of death.

'Death deserves dignity,' Norman Long says as I stand to go (an apothegm that would probably be hanging on his wall some-where if I cared to look).

He produces a flat tin from the darkest corner of the gloom and opens it to show what is inside. 'Heroin, morphine, ampheta-mine. Add gin or whisky and what does that make? The Brompton cocktail! Set sail for happiness! I'm all prepared.'

The search for bodies on the Moors has been suspended until the weather lifts. It's snowing in the North.

Yet here there is no sign of snow. The night sky isn't its usual depthless city black, but lit up with tea-scum, coffee-scurf clouds of the same pastel spectrum as the inmates' hair.

Seven

The boats have been lifted out of the water; they are lined up on the quay with tailored hoods and sleeves fitted over the cabins and masts and leaves slicked to their pedigree hulls.

Odd, as old Bob Brotherhood has occasionally remarked, watching members of the happy-go-crazy set and cases from Berry Bros going onboard during the season, that there was once a time when they built boats here from the wood up.

'Two hundred years ago,' so it goes, 'a woman making bread had to start with grain, and a man making a boat had to start with a tree. Simple components, d'you see what I'm saying, simply joined.'

The long nights signal a flurry of social activity in the village – the Friendly Wives' Club's 'Twenties evening', the cricket club's 'Derby night', tombola socials, jumble sales, domino suppers, talks, demonstrations – cake decorating, 'Christmas decorations from garden and hedgerow' – inspirational-religioso choir workouts, and panto rehearsals (Englishmen in frocks – the annual drag-fest, but all for a good cause: Horticultural Therapy, unless I'm mistaken, will be the beneficiary this year).

Most afternoons a Viva or Nova with a couple of oldsters on board will putter to a halt across from the cottage and a performance as stylised as the ghost dance or Kabuki will begin.

It starts with the unwrapping of sandwiches, the unshelling of eggs (a tissue over the knee to catch any fly-away pieces), the tremulous pouring of hot drinks.

126

He will fill a pipe while, with the concentration of somebody performing triple bypass surgery, she cores and peels an apple, the skin spiralling agonisingly down into a neat pile in her lap. Her offer of a clean scraped section will be refused with an impatient shake of the head.

After the shipping forecast he will check on the movement of his shares (part of a standard retirement package) before turning to the TV page, where, with a series of ticks and circles, he will plan their viewing for the evening.

By this time she will be sleeping with her mouth ajar and an irregular whistly-wheezy noise coming from deep down in her sternum.

The countryside is littered with these tin semi-tombs at this time of the year – whiskery mouths and jellied turkey wattles and slow-flowing drools and dribbles pointed towards glorious 'views' of wooded peninsulas and boiling sun-flecked seas.

When snooze-time is over and spectacles, hearing aids and upper-palates have been pressed back into service, it is time for more tea and biscuits out of tins bearing ancient images of the corps de ballet from Sleeping Beauty or the old king or the Castle Gardens in Edinburgh viewed from Princes Street.

If you ever needed convincing that All life is sorrowful (the first Buddhist saying) here is your proof.

It is scenes such as this which explain why we all eventually devise ways of putting ourselves in places or states of feeling that bring us back to the inner rhapsody of being alive and reconnect us with the *now* feeling of life.

In my years alone here the formula has been unvarying: a small room, sepulchral lighting, a drink with a kick like a dromedary (a Negroni with Carpano substituted for the Campari, plus a splash of sweet Cinzano, is always guaranteed to hit the button), plus music, including the cheap, thin, popular songs I spent years trying to deny had ever floated on my breath.

I always loved singing. Long before I was alerted to the

ambitions my father and mother were hatching for me in that direction, I sang all the time.

There was a man, a neighbour of ours, who used to have me over to help him do things in his garage, and he'd give me a threepenny piece to sing. I sat there and watched him do things, and I sang. I was four or five.

At the peak of my powers I had a voice that could peel lemons. But time takes a toll on voices, particularly those of women. The vocal cords calcify and, in extreme age, the result is a high cracked sound.

These days the only exercise my voice gets is during the cocktail hour here in the cottage, when I am shut into the small spare-room packed with lumber, that, in my single incursion into what I still regard as borrowed space, I have turned into a makeshift mood module.

One of my regrets is that I haven't spent as many hours in bars in the course of my life as I would if I had been a man. It's a passion that can be dated back to my first visit to New York in 1956, when I was booked for two appearances on Ed Sullivan, plus three weeks of cabaret in the Persian Room at the Plaza.

It's something I had been pushing for for long enough (from the beginning). Fog delayed our departure from London for three days. The flight took thirteen hours, and I arrived tired, under-rehearsed, and nervous.

On opening night I was, to quote one of the early notices, 'tense as nine newly-tuned pianos'. The *downbeat* critic described me as 'another femme singer'. (And, in a city that had femme singers coming out of the paintwork, he had a point. I was 100% ersatz Americana; a warmed-over version of the real thing.)

New York didn't exactly beat a path to my suite at the Plaza, which had what was called a cathedral-ceiling living-room, and a terrace overlooking Central Park from where it was possible to watch a polar bear endlessly prowling backwards and forwards in his rocky compound in the Zoo. (It is an image which remains peculiarly vivid, and yet I can't say for certain it isn't something I read about later and projected my own predicament on to after the fact.) I remember it now as a gleam among the green, like the light off a naked body.

I was mentally preparing to go out and face them on my second night when the phone rang and a voice from downstairs announced that 'I have Mr Davis wishing to visit with you.'

Naturally I knew Sammy Davis by reputation – hip-dressing, wise-cracking, finger-snapping, ring-a-ding-ding-ing member of the showbiz inner-élite. 'More *tchotchkies* than Sophie Tucker,' as somebody had it, 'and twice as sentimental.'

I loved the image. And he was no disappointment in the flesh. He came in through a door to the suite I hadn't realised existed until then, a tiny black man in a retinue of Italianate white bruisers, and stood ten feet away for maximum effect – the skinny-fitting shiny suit, bluest black, with a blue-black shadow stripe; the eggshell shirt with the generous soft high rolled collar; the boots (with lifts) made from the hide of unborn calf; the saucer-sized St Christopher and other medals bucking on his tie; the black moiré pirate patch covering the eye lost in a road accident eighteen months earlier; the processed elcctro-violet Congolene pomaded hair.

To say he looked exotic is to seriously undersell the effect – he looked imagineered, cuboid, like a Picasso painting or an Easter Island sculpture. It was plain that here was somebody who didn't know what it was to take life in small steps.

I, on the other hand (still unversed of course in substance abuse; in chemical coping skills), had never before felt so entirely grounded or earthbound – never so aware of my physical musculoskeletal self.

I felt the dead weight of my plumbing and blubber and heavy organs; saw myself as heaving viscera in a bag of hot skin – and at the same time for what felt like the first time saw my ideal self: a

129

frictionless black man talking jive-talk and living a life whose basic premise was that the normal, the dull and the average – square, white-bread, cutems (I was prepared to put my hand up to all three) – had simply ceased to exist.

He moved to where I was standing and brought both my hands to his lips. 'I hear last night was a real bitch kitty of a performance, doctor. Tonight you'll be even better. We're going to be in forya tonight, and tonight you're going to knock them square on their *tuchis*. If you don't turn 'em on, then they've got no switches.'

(They *were* in; the performance I gave wasn't a noticeable improvement on the night before's. In all my performing career I never learned Sammy's trick of burning off fear and releasing the clean, unimpeded impact of personality which jolts an audience to life.)

But it was what happened next that set the seal on the future pattern of our friendship. I'd been feeling so shredded and put through the wringer since I arrived that the only time I'd been out of the room was to go to work.

So the private lift lined in buttoned white leather that we got into was new, and so was the labyrinthine yet intimate bar buried deep in the Plaza that turned out to be our destination.

We slipped behind a velvet rope into an alcove, Sammy ordered – 'A little taste for the face, a little toddy for the body, *Eduardo*' – and snaky hipped black boys and solid middle-aged men with Cork-American accents danced attendance on us as if we were deities.

I felt a nice exhilaration, sitting in the electric-plotted twilight, drinking from the Steuben glasses. (I was going to have to be sick before going on, but that came later.)

It was the authentication of an experience I had been living through films and pulp novels and music for probably twenty of my twenty-four years: the chink of ice, the clink of glasses, the syncopation of American conversation (it was a language that climbed on the table and danced its energy), the marimba motion of drinks being made, the tinkling of a cocktail piano.

Heroically-scaled paintings in shades of green-black glowed dimly at the backs of the bigger seating recesses – pictures of fir groves or charging horses or medieval armies or moonlight ripply bowers: their surfaces seemed to form and reform by the minute, and refused to settle down to a single subject or interpretation.

'Energy without depth.' 'Sensation without commitment.' Those were the standard European criticism of the American experience – of 'Yank style' – in the fifties.

But together they represented the American formula for success and were preferable every time (so it seemed to me) to depth without energy, and commitment combined with censoriousness and fire-iron solemnity (the British Way).

I visited many falling-about stations with Sammy in the next weeks (and, in fact, over the next twenty-five years).

Jilly Rizzo's bar near Madison Square Garden, Tony's bar on 52nd Street, Jan Walman's Duplex in the Village, Joe's Elbow Room in New Jersey; the Crystal Caverns in Washington; the Chez Paree and the Club De-Liza in Chicago; the Society in Jermyn Street, and Pal Joey's at the Angel were some of them.

'I think I need three inches of money,' Sammy would tell whoever was holding for him, and we were off for 'a little see and be seen'.

A place we went to on my first visit that became an established favourite was the bar in the back of the old sleazeball America Hotel on West 47th Street, where Will Mastin, Sammy's uncle, Lenny Bruce and others kept small efficiency apartments.

The America Hotel was a notorious couch-camp for prostitutes, and more often than not it was being raided. To gain admission you would have to duck under the 'These premises raided' sign hanging on a chain that stretched across the doorway.

There was a recording studio on the ground floor, in the back of what had once been an old dining-room. The control room was probably the old kitchen. The bar, which had no name, only a slogan – 'Open every day 7.00 to unconscious time' – was fitted into the other half of the dining-room, next to the studio.

It was nothing special – pressed-tin ceiling, granita floor, Formica tables, semi-circular booths, high stools along the long bar where the darkness thinned. There were prawn crackers and peanuts and ketchup squirt tomatoes on the tables, and advertising clocks around the place all giving different times. Overhead in the gloom was a single twenty-two watt circlet bulb of the sort known in the New York of the day as the Landlord's Halo. El Morocco it wasn't. On the contrary, it was its low-rent, semi-secret nature and the interplay between the people who washed up there – stellar talent, as it used to be known in those days – Sinatras, Ava Gardners, Garlands, Bogarts, Lena Hornes, tossed into the usual stir-fry of mob people, rag-traders, fight promoters, and Fifth Avenue hookers working their Chanel – that made the bar at the America Hotel hum. A certain electricity permeated the air; a magnetism that went in higher revolutions than anywhere else I could name, then or now.

'Doctor, let me say this,' Sammy cautioned me on our first visit. 'I got one eye, and that eye sees a lot of things that my brain tells me I shouldn't talk about. Because my brain says that if I do, my one eye might not be seeing anything after a while.'

Over the years I made the acquaintance of a stream of men called Julie and Cleo and Lulu and Connie and Ruby and Tammi – tough guys with big girls' names. They wore conservatively-cut suits with *tuono e lampi* linings and convincing black hair pieces and made each other presents of – *gifted each other with* – Cartier lighters, medals, name bracelets, tie-clips, watches, cuff-links, sweaters, suits, girls, luggage, movie projectors, cases of Chivas, wallets full of money, Charvet ties, tips on the stockmarket, new hangover cures, and bulbous circumferentially-inscribed friendship rings.

The warning I was given once about one of them – 'He's the

132

most fascinating person, but don't stick your hand in the cage' – held good for them all.

Sammy and the performer clientele stole licks from the street characters, while the street characters picked up shtick from Sammy and his circle and wrote it into their act. It was a two-way traffic of mannerisms, postures, gestures and jokes. New fashions in clothes and ways of talking started there and, by way of records, films, television, etcetera, gradually filtered out into the bigger world.

The one occasion I briefly met the President and Mrs Kennedy was at the America Hotel – not in the bar, but in the studio next door. The 'These premises raided' sign was up across the entrance, Sammy was recording inside, a buffet supper of wine, cheese, cold meat-ball and corned-beef sandwiches was set out in the control room, and every exit had an armed guard.

The Kennedys were there perhaps four or five minutes. They met everyone, smiled, chatted, and everybody shook the President's hand.

A week later I saw Jackie Kennedy on Fifth Avenue ringed by secret service people when I was just a face in the crowd. A few months later the President was dead.

But my strongest memory of the America Hotel is not of being glamoured by the Kennedy presence. It's not even the scenes in the bar after the President's departure, involving Sammy and Jackie's secretary and her sister, the princess, when the three of them were all touching and dirty dancing and darting tongues.

What impressed me was the speed with which the bar closed over the occasion like quicksand, baffled the excitement surrounding the President's visit, and quickly returned people to themselves; before long it was just another night being soaked up into the dark mahogany counters and tarry sepia patinas, taking its shape from the shifting volumes of Billy May's and Nelson Riddle's arrangements – these were played all night, every night, from first shout to last knockings, under some unspoken but generally accepted ordinance – for Sinatra.

133

The night moved back into itself, moment by boozy moment, and the valuable sense of being part of the uncalibrated flow of experience, of all being headed for the high-jump together, returned.

The idea that similar conditions could be consciously contrived only occurred to me in my second or third year here, when a parcel arrived containing what, to anybody else who might have opened it, would have seemed worthless bits and pieces, useless junk.

The International (never known as anything but the 'Nash') was a basement bar in a narrow lane joining St Giles High Street to Denmark Street/Tin Pan Alley. Its heyday was in the days when the Alley was a warren of broom cupboard studios cutting demo discs (some days you would swear you could see the pavement tossing and buckling, like a cartoon carpet with Tom and Jerry under it), and the Nash was the haunt of songwriters, publishers, pluggers, disc jockeys and 'talent' – people like me, looking for a hit.

Because it stayed the same when everything around it was being blown out of the water, the Nash became a refuge for the old guard. Eventually it turned into a period piece, popular for promotional parties and fashion shoots.

There was a rustle of media interest (he sent me the clippings) when Beatty, whose roost it had been for thirty-five years, retired in '81 or '82. By that time it had been taken over by cobwebby goths and punks and the art school crowd.

'Dear Alma,' Beatty wrote in the note which accompanied his parcel, 'a few things which I hope may stir memories of happy times. If not, you don't need me tell you what to do. Trust I will raise an elbow with you sometime in Imazaz (Imazaz the pub next door).'

In individually wrapped newspaper bundles, I found the following: a Watney's Red barrel-shaped lamp base and a Furstenberg lager shade; a cardboard advertising plaque

('Columbus discovered it/Don Juan loved it/Ron Davies drinks it') for San Miguel beer; a bullfight poster with a blue bandarilla and ribbon attached; a charity collecting box with the picture of an emaciated child and the words 'What is this child's health worth to you?'; a gold plastic statue of a body-builder flexing his pecs but looking as if he's holding his nose; a framed black-and-white photo of Mr Acker Bilk playing darts; a 'straw' boater with a red band reading 'Packaging News'; two signs that hung for years behind the bar at the International ('Warning – I may make mistakes, but being wrong isn't one of them'; 'The impossible we do today – miracles take a little longer'); and a faded photocopy of a Louis MacNeice poem in a deep nicotine-coloured (it was the feature all the items had in common) plastic frame:

> The same tunes hang on pegs
> > in the cloakroom of the mind
> That fitted us ten or twenty or thirty years ago
> On occasions of love or grief; tin pan alley or folk
> Or Lieder or nursery rhyme,
> > when we open the door we find
> The same tunes hanging in wait

These days, what I listen to, like what I read, mainly depends on chance, randomness, unintention – something sneaking up out of the jukebox being played in the pub as I pass, the radio playing as a background in the village shops or by gardeners in the village or tree-trimmers in the woods, or the audio systems of cars descending the hill at the rear of the house or parked up in the official parking areas or on the quay (a confirmation that cars now are engineered for optimum acoustic output).

I was woken up before eight this morning by car doors slamming and a modern remix – phased, synthed, lots of variable lag, the trebly trumpet riff blanked completely – of Tom Jones' *It's Not Unusual*.

Conversion work on the old marine yard that shares the quay with Kiln Cottage started at the end of the summer. Since then the days have had an unbroken backing track of chartbusters and golden oldies whose hooks and catchy choruses have become a murmuring subconscious.

It's music which feels laid on like the gas; an on-tap amenity. This is not the case with the fifties cabinet radio in the cottage, whose signal comes two ways: choked and very choked.

It is whiney, and strangled with static and interference, and as a consequence carries a sense of technological complexity and *distance* – radio waves fighting their way through the crowded sky and around natural barriers into the valley, like salmon swimming upstream to spawn.

I only switch on in the late evenings for the news, which I have learned to take spliced with plainchant and Javanese gamelan music, or underlaid with sing-song Dutch or glottal Spanish or a jazz ballad's poignant seventh chords going out on the American Forces Network.

The equipment in the improvised bar in the lumber room which is put through its paces for an hour or so about this time every evening is compatibly lo-fi: a portable record-player of the stacking type (monophonic) and a cassette machine which occasionally chews up the tape.

I can't ever remember liking more than a handful of records at the same time. Like clothes and shoes, I tend to remain faithful to the same few pieces and play them into the ground.

For *Desert Island Discs* I found it difficult getting the selections up to the required eight: the four or five tracks I was hooked on at that point were, in an absolute, literal sense, all I wanted to hear. (In the end I threw in a Brahms symphony and a Love Duet by Verdi which I had to bluff my way around.)

I tend to play the same few tracks night after night, week after week sometimes, with a Mexican Mary or a Buñueloni or a slayer G and T to put me over the horizon.

I mentioned this (rather drunkenly) once to a friendly face in a crowded room – a volatilely-complexioned young man sipping un-iced water and practising tantric breathing. He said he must send me something about Philip V of Spain and the *castrato*, Farinelli; and, most improbably (he scribbled my address in the back of the copy of Salinger's *Franny and Zooey* he had in his pocket) he did.

In 1737 (he wrote) Farinelli, a *castrato* and one of the most celebrated voices in Europe, was invited to the comparative obscurity of the Spanish court. King Philip V was in a state of nervous breakdown, unable to cope with the least responsibility: the court was in despair.

Every possible cure had been tried for the royal melancholy. At last it was arranged that Farinelli would come and sing, unseen, in an adjacent room. The doctors watched for the right moment. As evening descended and the air grew calm, the order was given: Farinelli intoned his sweetest, most touching songs.

But nothing happened. The king, unshaved, sullen, distraught, remained sunk in a gloomy dejection behind drawn drapes and closed door. The effort was renewed every evening. Then, after some time, Philip V was suddenly aware of his surroundings. He was attentive and seemed to expect the hour.

And when the voice of the artist filled the air in his dark room, it was as if the songs had seeped into the innermost depths of his heart. The servants who arranged the bedroom, and the doctors who came to check the state of the royal patient at bedtime found him absorbed in the music while tears welled up in his eyes and streamed down his cheeks. The next day he opened his door, and shortly thereafter regained his spirits.

But Philip's repose remained dependent on his therapy, and every night until the king's death ten years later, Farinelli would sing the same four songs that had first broken the spell.

He added, 'The belief in its mood-altering properties was rooted in ancient narratives of the miraculous effects of music: Homer recounting that his warriors' choral singing could stave off the plague; Varro claiming that flute pieces relieved the pain of gout; the biblical David, on the testimony of the Scriptures, employing his musical ability to cure Saul's mental derangement by playing the harp.'

My present listening – I'm listening to it now – consists of four versions of the Fields-Kern evergreen, 'The Way You Look Tonight' – two vocal (by Fred Astaire, 1936 vintage, and Peggy Lee), two meandering jazz instrumentals.

I once had the difference between pop and jazz set out for me by a jazzman at whose feet I was prepared to sit in those days: 'It's as if you had two roads, both going in the same direction, but one of them was straight with no scenery around it, and the other twisted and turned and had a lot of beautiful trees on all sides.'

It put me on the defensive for a long time. But I've been around long enough now to stand my ground. There are times when you don't want the scenic route; you want the road that gets you where you're going fastest and is featureless only to those who are on it for the first time: for the regular user, its bald verges and concrete uprights are as loaded with meaning as the sayings of Einstein or the essays of Sartre.

I happen to find 'The Way You Look . . .' in the straight, no detours versions resonant enough.

But the way the melody unravels like string on the extended improvised tracks does take the mind for a different kind of walk – to a place where your whole life becomes suspended in time and you can feel immune, beyond calamity.

But it's not happening tonight. Tonight I'm feeling unsettled and loosely wrapped. My thoughts keep lurching in a morbid direction – to photoelectric eyes guarding bedroom doors, and electric circuit sensors leading to the nearest police station.

When I explain what I found waiting for me here on my return from London, perhaps you'll understand why.

I got back two days ago to find the cottage eerily as I'd left it, as if Ruth, Staff's sister, and her children hadn't been here at all. The kitchen window had been blacked out with mud thrown up by passing traffic, but that wasn't surprising, given how close it is to the road.

When I finally got round to having a go at it this afternoon, however, rushing with a rag and a bucket before the dark set in, I discovered that it wasn't mud at all but dogshit, daubed in a nauseatingly neat way that missed the glazing bars and reached far into the corners of the loosening elderly panes.

I noticed the letters last – two rows of four letters, one per pane:

P I G W
O R L D

They had been scratched in with a stick or other pointed object in faint, barely legible lines that quivered with drivenness and compacted human rage.

For the last few minutes I have been watching a piece of lemon pith rising and falling, falling then rising like the bubble in a spirit-level in my glass.

In addition to the souvenirs of the International – the advertising kitsch, the Red Barrel lamp (wired and lit) and the rest – there are rainyday pastimes, mounds of children's things stored in here: a table-tennis net with clamps, pimpled bats, game boards, plastic shuttlecocks, plimsolls, wellingtons with frogs' eyes, old-fashioned lead farm animals, learner fishing rods, rubber flippers, rainbow-soled flip-flops still lightly dusted with sand, snorkels with ping-pong ball breathing valves, a red plastic horse on springs, tiny plastic sandals, strap-on roller skates, a skateboard with the name 'Lesley' on Dymo-tape and cloudy blue nylon wheels.

Someday, when I'm awfully low, when the world is cold

'We're going to leave her room just as it was the morning she walked out of here . . .'
'He just ran round to the shop to buy crisps and pop . . .'

I will feel a glow just thinking of you

'It wasn't late. She just went round her nan's to show her her new watch . . .'
'Please. *Please*. Just give us something to let us know she's safe . . .'

The many faces have become one face – swollen, distraught, raw with grief and alarm, the scratchy halo of guilt just beginning to form.

Photographed in a raking light to emphasise the diagonal stress cracks, it is the face at the centre of the formal disposition of the police press conference, the focus of attention but wildly out-of-focus (tight on the eyes, camera-3) in the context of the silvery-roseate deputy chief-constable, the suited-up detective leading the hunt, the police PR flaks and human interest scribblers, the pretty WPC with French-rolled hair, a clearing skin problem, and easeful, telegenic body language.

It is a formation as easily readable as the ragged wave of police, friends, neighbours, tourist volunteers lapping slowly across the area of outstanding natural beauty, scouring the snicket popular with local courting couples, sudsing across the open terrain: another child disappeared off the street.

Oh but you're lovely, with your smile so warm and your cheek so
soft
  There is nothing for me but to love you

'Please, Mum . . .'

  With each word your tenderness grows
  Tearing my fear apart
  And that laugh that wrinkles your nose
  Touches my foolish heart

'There's no need to worry, Mum. I got a bit wet but I'm quite dry now . . .'

  Lovely – never never change
  Keep that breathless charm
  Won't you please arrange it, 'cause I love you
  Just the way you look tonight

'I'm being treated very well. Okay? Please, Mum . . .'

Then later (sometimes so much later that the portrait on the evening news rings only distant bells): the figure under the prison blanket with the hand hovering over its head to protect it (the cranial bones and meninges; the cerebro-spinal fluid, the vagus nerve) from the door arch all instinct is to smash it against.

And the companion piece to this: the hawking feeding-time noises of electric shutters directed at arms-length into the

accelerating inky glass on the off-chance that something anything – something syndicable – might stick to the film.

Victory Marine had ended its active life before I arrived here. I
watched the paint of the sign gradually flake and peel; fat wax-
headed weeds come up between the cobbles in the building-yard;
the woodwork become waterlogged and spongy; carpets of blue
algae breed on the broad concrete slipway.

Now this picturesque dilapidation has gone into sharp reverse.
The main boatyard building is being converted into individual
residential units – an 'off-the-shelf nautical environment of one-
bedroom cabin-size flats', according to the literature, 'where the
home is almost an extension of the leisure pursuit.'

A developer's board went up soon after work started, showing
Spanish pantiles, inverted dormers, iroko decking, Sindy-doll
families at picnic tables, a herringboned car-parking area.

The heavy work involving bulldozers and dumpers and
hydraulic cranes had been done. Now work has moved inside
and is continually serviced by vehicles whose skeletal codes –
'Alcoa', '3M', 'dBase', 'Z88', 'Hudevad', 'DR-Dos' – are like a
micro-jargon intelligible only to those who have advanced
beyond some brave new frontier.

The core of the regular workforce arrive a few minutes early,
and sit smoking in their cars until eight. At ten, and then at
regular intervals, they troop back to their flasks and their papers
and individually reclaim their own space.

One man, however, consistently arrives ahead of the others in
the mornings and drinks his way through a four-pack of Special
Brew before starting work.

The first time I saw him I had been woken by the dog reacting
to the unusual pattern of activity on the quay. There had been a

storm overnight and the light was forest green. He was sitting at the wheel with a can raised and a cigarette going in the same fist, floating in a river mist as dense as the fog he was trying to disappear into.

He buries the empties in a carrier-bag pushed under the passenger seat, then bins them along with the rest of the day's intake before setting off for home at night.

The concern with personal privacy has been unexpected. It doesn't square with my experience of how men generally behave in groups in public. Some time ago I had my way blocked on a pavement in London by a building worker: he slid in front of me on his knees and, with a broom handle for a microphone, started singing 'You've Lost That Loving Feeling' while his mates whooped and whistled and egged him on. 'Top man!' they shouted as he swaggered back to rejoin them. 'Top man!'

I've followed the progress of the work on the boathouse with interest – seen the fabric heave and shift, grow a turreted addition here, a premium river-view there, until the exterior now more or less conforms to the clean, lightweight lines of the airbrushed brochure drawing.

But, as is usually the case, I have found what has been going on behind the scenes even more absorbing. It has given me the opportunity to trespass on a world which has always been blocked off to me until now.

I never thought of investigating what was happening inside the building until I followed the dog across the small shingle beach and beyond the utility lights on to the site one night.

The similarity to being backstage in the theatre was pronounced. What is usually concealed and tidied away was exposed and available for inspection. I played the flashlight on a jungle of loose wires through which a current would soon be running. I tried unsuccessfully to follow a complex network of plastic pipes through the foundations and up into the rafters to their source.

Bags of cement. U bends. Planes, power saws, wood in vices,

plugs plugged into unmade walls. Flora. Sunburst. Westphalian Mortadella (a packet featuring a stylised burgher with thumbs hooked into waistcoat pockets and piebald pale meat for a shirt).

Familiar things looked unfamiliar, like game-show prizes, isolated in the beam of bright light.

Nescafé. Half a loaf, a teaspoon, a knife and a bag of sugar standing on a square of cardboard. A mug: 'If you can't be good be *real* bad'. A set of trowels and other tools lined up scraped and cleaned on a newspaper.

> He's A Hunk page 19
> She's A Tease page 7
> He's A Hero page 5
> She's A Bore page 14

In Timbuktu, I read somewhere once, the houses are built of grey mud. Many of the walls are covered in graffiti, written in the neatest of copybook hands.

Customs and procedures. The underwalls on the boathouse site are covered in pencilled doodles, diagrams, telephone numbers, pricings, elementary additions, dimensions and personalised hieroglyphs.

They lie concealed now, along with the bodgings and rough improvisations (matchstick levers, milk carton wedges, cataracts of custardy glue) behind plasterboard partitions whose own pencilled-in marks and gestures are starting to disappear under coats of paint.

Again what is unexpected is the properness, the propriety – no lewd drawings, swear words, scatalogical humour; as though they suspect that it is on this evidence, designed to outlast them, that they may one day come to be judged.

Work has advanced. The walls are flush and skimmed. The latest refinements of the wipe aesthetic are in the process of being installed. Tassels of coloured wire await connection, to activate manufacturers' warranties of de luxe superfry, easy defrost, logic creaseguard, audio cancel, crystaljet.

The water rushing over the weir is as loud as motorway traffic. A pipe leaks drips into a saw-edged can.

Silk Cut. Fisco Unimatic. A ball-headed hammer with insulated handle. A Stanley knife. A scraped-down spade.

There's a radio with bare wires poking into the wall which, when I begin to apply pressure to the on-off button – it gives me pleasure to feel the tension between resistance and give, to play out the moment between off and on – kicks into life in an unanticipated but welcome way.

The noise that comes out of the radio on this occasion is as abstract as the surrounding night-time outdoor sounds – a barrage of loud *click* and *clack* that rattles the plaster and hits me like a rush of reminiscence.

It's a sound that could be being beamed direct from the days when footballers wore leather studs and baggy bloomers – the sound of wooden counters being shaken in a canvas bag by officials with scaly build-up on the arms of their glasses and grease across the shoulders of their aldermanly suits, making the draw for the next round of the FA Cup.

Newcastle United and Wolverhampton Wanderers. Brighton and Bradford. West Bromwich Albion and Portsmouth. Gillingham and Darlington. Leyton Orient and Middlesbrough. Everton and Port Vale.

The *click* and *clack*. And in every rattling a distant crowd-echo, the irradiation of light from webbed lighting stacks silhouetting brick factories and refineries and tanks against the partial darkness of a winter afternoon.

It's like doodling the beam on the freshly rendered walls and coming across a friendly message or something you scored into the wall yourself very many years before.

Instead of that though, what I see when I play the flashlight in an arc around me is: a Page Three girl with a large-mouthed and

145

brassy vulgarity of expression and her nipples burned out in the picture by the tip of a cigarette.

Then oboe nails scattered in sawdust. Psyche cleaning out the last smearings of a Flora carton. A coffee jar containing viscous black oil. A double-page feature stained with whorls and drips of coffee and headlined (as I see when I remove a plastic sack) THE STOLEN YEARS.

The piece is illustrated with what are clearly victim pictures – pictures uncontaminated by news values or documentary purpose when they were taken, and informed by nothing more than childhood notions of ways of presenting the self.

Pauline Reade was sixteen when she was murdered by Myra Hindley and Ian Brady in 1963, although she appears younger in the picture. She is wearing what is almost certainly her communion dress and a white lace (or possibly crocheted or knitted) mantilla, and dark shoulder-length hair.

Keith Bennett was twelve when he was murdered, also in Manchester, in 1964. He has a basin cut, skewey wire glasses and a disarming gap-toothed grin.

Hindley and Brady denied responsibility for these murders for more than twenty years. The bodies were never found. Now, on the basis of new information provided by Myra Hindley, and using pictures of Hindley and Brady picnicking on or near the graves as a guide to the topography, it is Pauline Reade's and Keith Bennett's remains they have reopened the search for on Saddleworth Moor.

But the victim pictures are not the main graphic element of the story: repeated reproduction has stripped them of their pathos and therefore their power to stir the emotions; instructions for a fresh angle have been sent down; money has been spent.

Most of the space has been given over to what look like television images rescreened in newsprint – images with opalescent shirring around the main features; pictures full of temporal-screech and -skid. But pictures with something superadded; something inauthentic.

146

They are 'photohoroscopes'; computer composites of what Pauline Reade and Keith Bennett might look like if they were still alive, and aged thirty-nine and thirty-four respectively.

The method, as I understand it, has been to take the pictures of them as they were when they disappeared and 'age' them using photographs of the family members who most resemble them physically.

All the features are converted into video images and imposed one on the other on a screen before the electronic moulding and pummelling and detailed manipulation ('warping') takes place. The putting down of a 'wrinkle mask' is the final stage.

Unlike a typical photograph that draws meaning from its connection to a real person's living hair and skin and clothes, the result is ghost-like accretions of information referring to nothing; phantasms with no organic presence; forms without substance; shadings on a computer memory.

The two sets of pictures are patched on to the page in such a way as to suggest a natural progression, a trajectory: from the innocence of faces that don't know they're going to die, to discarnate beings built up from encoded rays and glazes of numerical light.

And in between? The decomposition, the decay, the mulch-down they are trying to pin-point on the vastness of the Moors. Mud in the caves of the eyes; silt and mud in the tunnels of the nose; sheep dung, hoar grass and bracken commemorating the spot where a named individual lies.

Eight

A story, possibly apocryphal (one of hundreds), about Mae West:

She was approached once by an intense young girl, who announced, 'I saw *Diamond Lil* last week; it was wonderful.'

'Didja honey? Wheredja see it?'

'At the museum. The Modern Museum.'

And a dismayed Mae, seeking shelter in the sassy drawl of her film persona, inquired: 'Just whaddya mean, honey? A *museum*?'

I thought of the story this morning as I drifted through the connected but separate climate systems of the galleries at the Tate, looking for the portrait Peter Blake painted of me nearly a quarter of a century ago and that I haven't seen for almost that long.

I could have asked for directions at the information desk just as you come in, but I was hoping to come across myself without warning, to take myself unawares, even if it did mean denying a constant urge to run to the toilet and a banging in my chest like the Derry Apprentice Boys' parade.

It was early. I was among the first in. There was still the feeling of overhang from the previous day. In addition to dollars and yen and layers of small change, the glass donation boxes were choked with messages posted by school parties – 'Jo 4 Stuart', 'Sharon 4 Cookie', 'Homefucking is killing prostitution', 'What are you looking at DICKHEAD', 'If I wanted to listen to somebody talking out of his arse, I would've farted'.

148

There was the sound of banged metal and spilled cutlery and conversations in iron-curtain accents coming from the kitchens. The attendants were assembled in a group under the rotunda, being assigned their areas of responsibility for the shift – room 10, Rural Naturalism and Social Realism, 1870–1900; room 14, Bloomsbury and Vorticism, 1910–20 – where they would sit and watch the day stack up and listen to the humidity and temperature stabilisers ticking through their programmes.

(Room 28, the chapel-like space containing Rothko's looming soft-edged stacks of rectangles for the Seagram Building is where I would angle to get placed. It must be the equivalent of a diplomatic posting to Paris or Washington.)

In some galleries it was like being the first to walk on a new snowfall; the air hadn't been displaced. Room 23, Abstract Expressionism, was like this. The only sign of any life was in the paintings, which were humming with the urgency of mark-making and 'the liberated unconscious'.

I stood in front of one of de Kooning's 'Women' for at least a minute before I got a bead on the figure embedded in the loops and slashings of paint. Before I lost it again, it reminded me of something I had seen a million times in the mirror: make-up being smeared into waxy swipes and lurid skirls of colour by the application of theatrical remover cream.

Among the information given on the card on the wall was a quotation from the artist: 'Flesh was the reason why oil painting was invented'.

A few galleries on, I stood at the edge of a tour group and listened while the guide filled them in on the background to Stanley Spencer's 'The Resurrection, Cookham'. 'You can see the artist sandwiched between the two book-like tombstones at the bottom right-hand corner . . . You can also see him naked in the centre of the painting . . . "I don't want to lose sight of myself," Spencer once admitted, "for an instant." '

The students – they were a mature group – wrote this down on their pads. They kept their hands free by wearing the collapsible stools they were carrying over their shoulders or – in the case of most of the men – transversely across the chest, like armour.

The Spencer wasn't hanging on the wall. It was standing on rubber blocks on the floor, with gallery staff going backwards and forwards with ladders and lengths of wood in front of it as if they were among the resurrected and had just stepped out of the painting.

I continued wandering haphazardly, following no particular plan. Once or twice I thought I saw the picture Peter Blake did of me in the palaeolithic era out of the corner of my eye – something about the scale as I remembered it, the composition, the colour. But when I edged nearer it would turn out to be a still-life of Shelf with Objects, or View of Hackney with Dalston Lane, Evening.

In the end I had to admit defeat and backtracked to Information, where I asked the person on duty if she could point me in the direction of the Peter Blake painting titled *Alma Cogan*, dated, I thought, 1961–63.

She was an interesting combination of half-prim (cashmere cardigan, pearls) and half-punkette (high-shaved side-panels, gold wire ring in her nose). Acid-green letters started dancing in her tiny glasses as her fingers ran over the keys. Behind and above her, meanwhile, a second display panel spooled out slogans in liquid crystal letters of peony and tangerine.

DISGUST IS THE APPROPRIATE RESPONSE TO MOST SITUATIONS . . . DYING AND COMING BACK GIVES YOU CONSIDERABLE PERSPECTIVE . . . LOVING ANIMALS IS A SUBSTITUTE ACTIVITY . . . THE HAPPINESS OF BEING ENVIED IS GLAMOUR . . . PUBLICITY IS THE LIFE OF THIS CULTURE . . . NOSTALGIA IS A PRODUCT OF DISSATISFACTION AND RAGE . . . On and on they rolled. Around and around.

'I'm afraid I can't access that information,' the girl said. '*Alma Cogan* is currently on-loan to the VIP Lounge at Heathrow.' Then a signal from the screen started throbbing in her eye like a nerve. She keyed in another code which supplied her with the information that the painting had recently been returned. I could make an appointment to come in and see it in storage at a later date.

'Name?'

It occurred to me to quickly make something up. But 'Cogan,' I said. 'A.'

There was a pause, as if the 'search' function of the console in front of her was flying through its documents and folders making another match. 'The . . . the subject of the work?' I nodded. She walked to the back of the information area and picked up a phone.

CHASING THE NEW IS DANGEROUS TO SOCIETY . . . RECLUSES GET WEAK EVEN IF STRONG ORIGINALLY . . . MURDER HAS ITS SEXUAL SIDE . . . LACK OF CHARISMA CAN BE FATAL . . . The words trickled over the jagged surface of her isolated island of hair. When she came back I half expected to see the neon colour combed in.

Somebody from conservation would be up to collect me in a few minutes, she said, if I would care to wait. And meanwhile if I would fill in the form, taking care to make sure that the information registered on the carbon duplicates underneath . . .

The first time I met Peter Blake was when he had just stopped being a student. It was at the all-night party Mike Todd gave at the Battersea Festival Gardens after the London opening of *Around the World in 80 Days*, which would date it as 1956.

He was working on one of the amusements – rifle-range, coconut shy, tombola, dodgems (they were all free that night of course, along with everything else). He was wearing the bottom half of a boiler suit, the closest you could get at that time in England to American jeans, and a similarly improvised jean jacket.

But what I remember most vividly about him are the seams of blue puckered scars that extended from his mouth to his nose on one side of his face like a hinge and were emphasised rather than hidden by his attempt at a straggly student beard. (Since the

151

mauling I'd witnessed just two years earlier, I had taken a more-than-usual interest in the movement of people's mouths, the wetness and glitter and the shape of the mouth and the teeth.)

He reminded me of this first meeting the second time we met, at one of my parties, when he was coming into his first fame and I was just starting to be aware of the calm that was waiting round the corner. (It was a phrase Billy Eckstine used, which had caught on. 'All of a sudden,' he said, 'it gets calm.')

It was on this occasion I think he said he would like to do a painting. I was flattered, of course, but slightly nonplussed when he said he would prefer to use a magazine picture (he seemed to already know which one) than have me come to the studio and sit for him.

But we did have lunch – at Cunningham's, the champagne and oyster bar then at the height of its fashionability, in Curzon Street. The owner, Owen Cunningham's, mother had been a maid in the 1920s in a Shepherd's Market laundry, earning a pittance from scrubbing the mountain of soiled linen sent out from the great Mayfair mansions.   ·

Owney enjoyed a kind of social revenge by screwing the titles and blue-bloods among his regulars, who included the Gerald Legges, the Dockers, Anthony Armstrong-Jones and Olga Deterding, the Shell heiress who eventually threw it all in to go and work for Albert Schweitzer in Africa, while at the same time making sure that his showbusiness customers always got good value for money.

It was a lively lunch, with few of the longueurs that occur when two people are sitting alone at a table together for the first time. We were almost exactly the same age; Peter Blake had seen me perform on several occasions at the Chiswick Empire and the Chelsea Palace, and had a fan's knowledge of all departments of the wonderful business we call show.

Most of what we talked about went the way of the champagne and the oysters. The only thing that is fixed in my memory is our shared enthusiasm for fairs and in particular the way a field looks after a fair has moved on, with its circles and scars and mysterious relief patterns of raised and flattened grass.

He gave me a Betjeman quote, to the effect that there is nothing more empty than a deserted fairground, which encouraged me to try and put into words something which had been only the shadow of a notion until then.

'I love the way the wagons you see bowling along under their own steam on the road disappear inside the rides when they're set up,' I told him (as nearly as I can remember). 'The way the wheels are locked and jacked up on wooden blocks; how the overhead spokes and duckboards of the carousel are added; then the painted and mirrored panels, then the chairs or horses . . . Something in it seems to correspond to my own situation on the road, disappearing every night into the apparatus of sequins and wigs and spreading ostrich feathers . . .'

I saw him filing this away as a mental reference – the rims of his ears glowed momentarily – to use in whatever he might paint.

Some time later I received a souvenir – a small framed collaged piece, built up from that 1960 menu at Cunningham's, which would itself I suppose now be worth several thousand pounds in the salerooms. But it is gone, as far as I know, along with everything else.

'Miss Cogan?'

'Conservation' had suggested chemicals and white lab coats of the kind worn by the technicians in the EMI studios at Abbey Road as late as the mid-sixties. Facing me, though, and giving me a discreet once-over to see what twenty-five years had done to 'the subject of the work', was a person dressed in unremarkable civilian smart-casualwear – Kickers, newish jeans, cheesecloth-type shirt.

'If you'd like to come with me.'

I followed him past a piece of art splashed with whitewash on the ground like some primitive trail, and then round a tree decorated with small paintings of Christmas bells and decorations instead of the real thing, down some stairs.

At the bottom of the stairs I saw that the love notes and teenage obscenities had been removed from the donation box set into the wall and foreign notes in the higher denominations (the trick of lavatory attendants and cloakroom personnel) fluffed up on the surface like thinning hair.

We proceeded past a barrier spooled out of a plastic post and then, courtesy of a combination-lock, through a door marked 'SECURE AREA – Passes must be worn'. On the other side it was like a public swimming bath – fresh after the recycled air of the gallery, with that kind of echoey no-noise and vaulted unsourced light.

A concrete ramp led down to the long sub-basement corridor, at the end of which Steenhuis, Peter flashed his identity tag at a man sitting in an oak box of the kind cashiers sit in at the few remaining old-style butchers. 'SECURITY STATE OF VIGILANCE – BLACK SPECIAL' it said on a print-out strip inside the box where you weren't supposed to see.

Another combination-lock. Another door with another message – 'Under *no circumstances* must this door be left open'. Another mini-climate of crackling air filtered through Mylex and Ticene gills, but with that metallic edge or imbalance that can strip the sinuses if breathed in too long.

'You can't get in here hardly in the summer,' Peter Steenhuis said in his Dutch-inflected American-English accent, 'especially in the lunch break, everybody trying to chill out.'

I went on being popular in the Netherlands and Scandinavia – also Iceland and Japan – long after my star had waned at home. I spent years singing phonetically in languages of which I barely understood a word. Being no older than thirty, though, Peter Steenhuis was too young to remember.

'You can get all the English TV programmes in Holland now. Satellite, cable. My parents are big fans of the two Ronnies,' he said, consulting a piece of paper with the painting's acquisition number on it, as if he hadn't already sneaked a look before coming upstairs to collect me.

The pictures were hung on steel-mesh partitions which rolled soundlessly out into the sieved and bounced light like mortuary drawers. They radiated a second field of cold into the already part-refrigerated room.

When we got to the appropriate stack, he kicked a chuck which released the wheels and hauled out the frame containing a number of paintings by the British Pop artists of the early sixties.

Among them were four by Peter Blake: *The Masked Zebra Kid* of 1965; *Tuesday* (a portrait of Tuesday Weld), 1961, which prompted Peter Steenhuis to remark that he thought she was Melanie Griffith's mother ('Isn't Melanie Griffith married to that *Miami Vice* guy for the second time?'); *The Meeting, or Have A Nice Day, Mr Hockney*, 1981–5 – and T. 02285, *Alma Cogan*.

I don't know what I had been expecting. Of course I know what I had been expecting: to look down the dark tunnel of time and see myself preserved as I would choose to be in my best memory – unflawed, retouched; all minuses turned to plus, all sins forgiven, 'the fundamental rightness of the nature in question laid uppermost' (an inspiriting phrase plucked from one of the gallery walls during my morning's wandering).

But my first impression was that, unlike the elaborate gilt-wood frame, which seemed as timeless and solid as the Edwardian theatre interiors it echoed, the picture seemed to have aged with me, as if we had kept a parallel course.

It was as if the reverses of the intervening years, as well as the uncertainty of my present situation, had been able to paint themselves in; as if the pigment had been invaded by air sadness.

Its guardian and protector stepped forward and released the painting and carried it to a velvet-curtained area where he set it down carefully on a table packed and triple-packed with bubble paper whose bubbles you could burst if you pressed very hard, in the way that always drives Psyche up the wall.

'Nice painting,' Peter Steenhuis said, removing an invisible film of dust from the surface with delicate puffs of air from a rubber bulb. 'I like the restraint. None of that see-me-dance-the-polka brushwork.'

Then he withdrew to a diplomatic distance, thoughtfully removing a large-scale nude of a bodybuilder with a semi-erect penis out of my sight-line on the way.

The Tate Gallery Illustrated Catalogue of Acquisitions, 1974–76, pp. 54–6:

T.02285 Alma Cogan 1961–63

> Not inscribed
> Oil on panel, 17½ × 14½ × 1½ (44.5 × 36.8 × 3.8cm)
> Presented by E. J. Power through the Friends of the Tate Gallery 1974

Coll: Arthur Tooth and Sons Ltd.; bt E. J. Power 1962
Lit: Robert Melville, 'The Durable Expendables of Peter Blake', *Motif*, x, Winter 1962–3, pp. 20–22, repr.p. 20

Known as 'the girl with a chuckle in her voice' and for her large wardrobe of extravagant, self-designed dresses, the subject of T.02285 was one of Britain's most popular recording stars in the fifties.

Her string of twenty hits, more than any female vocalist of the era, included 'Bell Bottom Blues' (a cover of Teresa Brewer's 1953 American hit); 'I Can't Tell A Waltz From A Tango' (a cover of Patti Page's hit) in 1954; 'Dreamboat', the only No. 1 by a British female singer in the fifties; 'Twenty Tiny Fingers' (1955); a cover of Vaughn Monroe's 'In The Middle Of The House' (1956); and a cover of The Maguire

Sisters' 'Sugartime' (1958). Her last hit was 'Cowboy Jimmy Joe' (1961).

Alma Cogan was one of the large generation of immediately pre-beat boom stars whose style went out of public fashion after the emergence of the Beatles and other 'Merseysound' groups in the 1960s.

The sixties saw her moving into cabaret, overseas touring, and even a brief stint in TV commercial work – a detergent ad – while continuing to record without success for HMV, then Columbia. Her active career as a performer ceased c. 1970.

Peter Blake saw Alma Cogan on various variety bills in London in the mid-to-late fifties. He considered her to be one of the last remaining links with a music hall tradition that was on the point of disappearing (letter from the artist to the compiler, dated 11.10.74; Tate Gallery Archive TAV 503A) and that, in British art, had direct links with, *inter alia*, Sickert, Gore, Ginner and the painters of the Camden Town Group (see Gore T.02260; Sickert T.02039).

Peter Blake shares with Sickert an extended and profound understanding of the world of show business and a fascination with its glamour and lively vulgarity.

'Marriage did not interfere with his . . . habit of attending the halls, and he would even absent himself from a dinner party in his own home in order to go to a performance' (D. Sutton, *Sickert*, London, 1974, p. 235). 'His eagerness to capture the correct rendering of the tights worn by Emily Lyndale led him to follow her from hall to hall'.

Blake's interest in painting T.02285, however, was not primarily reminiscential or nostalgic, but the combination in one work of the nostalgic impulse with extreme mass-circulation-linked contemporaneity. In its transposition of pre-existing ready-made source material, the painting shares and, to some extent, pre-dates, the concerns of Lichtenstein, Warhol and other American Pop artists.

Blake started work on the painting in 1961. The source of the image was probably, though not certainly, a photograph of Alma Cogan in performance reproduced in *Fans' Library*, a monthly periodical of the fifties which featured a single entertainer in each issue and constituted a kind of early part-work.

Peter Blake purchased copies of the magazine as they were published, partly for pleasure, in his capacity as a 'fan', and partly because of his life-long interest in the images, significance and meaning of mass culture.

In his work of this period, Blake was drawn towards significant personalities as often as to the quality of the performance. Of Elvis Presley, for example, who figures in a large variety of Blakeian imagery, the artist said that he himself did not particularly respond to Presley's music: 'I have always been a fan of the legend rather than the person,' he told the compiler in a taped conversation, 3.10.74 (Archive TAV 499A).

'I wasn't ever particularly a fan of Alma Cogan, but I was very *aware* of her.' (Alma Cogan was the first female singer to have her own major TV series in the UK, 1959–61, ITV. Though her chart hits ceased, her chirpy personality guaranteed her regular British tours and TV appearances throughout the early sixties.) 'She was very much a presence on a national scale, and seemed to represent *something* – the innocence of the decade immediately following the war, old-fashioned glamour.'

Peter Blake chose the photograph of Alma Cogan on which T.02285 is based for a number of reasons. Although it was supposedly taken during a theatre performance, it looked posed. It was also printed on the same paper, in the same pocket-size format (and almost certainly by the same publisher) as *Spic*, *Span*, *Jem*, *Monsieur* and other 'girlie' magazines of the period which were later to form the basis of his *Pin-Ups* and *Strippers* series of works.

158

The disposition of the arms and hands seemed to echo for Blake the arms and hands in Francis Bacon's *Study After Velasquez's Portrait of Pope Innocent X* (1953); while the open mouth also recalled the human scream that has been a preoccupation of Bacon's throughout his career.

Blake also believed that Alma Cogan had lost the use of her voice for a period in the early part of her career and was attracted to this particular shot of the singer because of 'the soundless "O" of the mouth'. (She suffered hysterical aphonia, an affliction that strangles the vocal cords, in c. 1953, and was ordered not to sing for six months. It was subsequent to this illness that she developed her famous laugh-in-the-voice style.)

The curtains against which the figure is painted also invoke a device often used by Bacon in the years 1949–55. ('I've always wanted to paint curtains. I love rooms that are hung all around with just curtains hung in even folds' – David Sylvester, *Interviews With Francis Bacon*, London 1975, p. 112.)

Peter Blake's description of the colour of the curtains in T.02285 – 'spinach green' – derives from a postcard in his possession, sent to him from America by a friend and captioned, 'Alma, Alabama, Spinach capital of the world'. (He considered calling the painting *Alma Alabama* at one point.)

T.02285 evidences Blake's interest, stronger in 1961 than it has since become, in animation of surface texture. The retention of originally unintentional rough paint passages was deliberate. The most open assertion of the value of spontaneous gesture and of inflected handling is to be found, characteristically of Blake at this time, in the rendering of the diaphanous fabric of the dress, and in the areas around the eyes and mouth.

The scumbling, glazing and scraffito techniques suggest

signs of age, wear and damage and are evidence of the preoccupation running through all Blake's work with the obsolescence inherent in the popular images thrown up by a culture one of whose chief activities is producing and consuming images.

Peter Blake was completing work on *Alma Cogan* when he began his portrait *The Beatles* in 1963. One painting shows a performer approaching the end of her period of celebrity; the other shows four musicians on the threshold of overwhelming global fame.

But the emotional climate is not noticeably different: both works are equally wistful and equally solemn. He seems to see both past and present at the same nostalgic distance, so that the young Beatles seem to have as much period charm as a fading variety performer, a publicity still as an engraving. No image is so brashly contemporary that he cannot see it in this way.

This entry has been corrected and approved by the artist.

(The compiler is indebted to Miss Christine Bowles, Curator, the Pop Collection, the Victoria and Albert Museum, London, and to F.McL.)

Chilblains. Impetigo. It seems a world ago that people used to get chilblains, scaly red ripple marks on their legs, from sitting too close to the fire. Or went round with purple ink painted on the sores on their faces. Poverty-related ailments that you don't see now.

But chilblains and impetigo are what the fleshy parts of my body reminded me of when I studied them through a magnifying glass (actually a flexible strip of magnifying plastic, grooved like a thumb-print, made in Japan) in the meat-safe sub-basement at the Tate.

Areas of colour which in reproduction or viewed from a distance looked flat and uncorrupted, close-to turned out to be shot and broken and exquisitely damaged with legions of tiny nicks and lacerations. The flesh tones broke down into chance blots and controlled mergings which ranged in colour from oyster grey to angry red.

Passages of greasy lustre, reminiscent of real skin, were blotted up by matt or coarse passages where the trails of thin paint lost their legibility. The texture of chest and shoulder was particularly enlivened with trace lines, tones, shadows and local colour, swirling together like smoke in a bottle.

The whiteness of the scalp was visible in patches through the mass of dense dark hair, and through that, other marks – corrections, counter-images, outlines painted over, chappings and abrasions soothed with transparent glazes – could also be clearly detected.

Under magnification, the face looked like a valuable urn which had been painstakingly reconstructed. The surface had been painted in a way that seemed to contain evidence of its bloatings and shrinkages and rebloatings over the years, as well as ghostly intimations of how it was going to change with age.

Looking into the painting was like looking at a lifetime's reflections fixed in a mirror – at bits of yourself that had found a place to go when they died.

The longer I looked, the more I saw several kinds of history smudgily superimposed; former selves which floated to the surface like memories, only to become submerged again.

The curtain behind the figure is stained with tide-lines, rejected versions, spectres of myself which are not visible on the postcard reproduction, out of print for some time, which Peter Steenhuis gave me as I was preparing to leave.

IT'S BETTER TO BE LONELY THAN TO BE WITH INFERIOR PEOPLE

161

. . . IT'S BETTER TO BE NAIVE THAN JADED . . . MEDIA IMAGES
ONLY SHOW US WHAT WE ALREADY KNOW the sign was saying as I
stepped into the damp, fungus-forming air and quickly headed
off in the direction of London's rich shabbiness.

When I got back I started going through drawers and cupboards
trying to find a photographic reminder of the life locked into the
underlayers of the painting, but soon gave up. Everything I
opened had the death smell of camphor and old clothes that have
never been worn and ashy drifts of insect corpses.

Interleaved among my mother's personal belongings, her
underwear and stockings and nightclothes, hidden as if in a game
and never detected, was a collection of items which, as Bob
Brotherhood would say, were not very eyeful.

Blown lightbulbs, nibbled squares of chocolate, razor blades, a
packet of CrackerBarrel, stale biscuits, a dog chew, greying
dentures, sardine-tin keys, an obsessive number of Vick inhalers,
and a years-old piece of meat in a tissue were among the things I'd
unearthed when I decided to stop before I came across something
I would really regret finding.

The whole flat smells of neglect, decay, staleness. Dirt is
ingrained in the windows, the curtains are heavy with dust, the
plastic covers on the sofa where I'm sitting are scored and urine-
coloured. Even after so many years, the cushions still hold the
shape of my mother's broad back and tired old buttocks.

The Moors is again at the top of the news. Tuesday, December
16. Hindley has been back on the Moors, trying to help police
pinpoint the graves where Pauline Reade and Keith Bennett lie
buried.

The first part of the report is to camera, against an establishing
backdrop of snowy moorland dotted with operations vehicles,
transit vans and police Range Rovers.

'A massive security operation involving armed policemen was

mounted and the area sealed off by a cordon of roadblocks as Hindley arrived on Saddleworth Moor by helicopter shortly after dawn this morning. She spent over seven hours with senior detectives' – cut to overhead shots of vehicles speeding in convoy along the glassy ribbon of road across the Moor – 'retracing places she had visited with her former lover Ian Brady. While Hindley walked the Moor, head bowed against driving rain and heavy winds, she was watched by police marksmen.'

A red circle hovers around the head of one of a party of tadpole figures slithering across the lunar landscape of snow. It encloses a black hood worn over a black balaclava which, when they blow it up, pushing as far as it will go, hovers on the edge of disclosing who or what is in there, but in the end dissolves into dots of primary colours.

That she has an existence independent of the image that has represented her for twenty-one years – the trowel nose, the defiant eyes, the peroxide hair – is a mystery that seems hard to get to grips with. Hindley was twenty-three when she was arrested. Now she's forty-four. It is as if by changing her appearance, and keeping her current identity secret, she has effected some form of escape.

'The senior detective leading the investigation said that Hindley's recollection of bleak moorland she has not visited for over twenty years was surprisingly vivid. It had led police to a new search area where she believes more young bodies may be buried, and where digging may begin tomorrow.'

The wind-burned face of one of the searchers (filmed from above, probably from a ladder, over the heads of the other camera crews and reporters) now fills the screen. 'We will be using the new digging techniques we have been taught by experts in buried body detection, removing the topsoil and then using a trowel and a hoe to identify the different layers of soil and looking for signs that the natural layering has been disturbed,' he says.

Extract from **Tate Gallery Archive Tape TAV 499A**, recorded 3.10.74:

COMPILER: I sense a certain sexual ambivalence in the figure of Alma Cogan as you have portrayed her in the painting. The hands, for instance, are very big. This could be a woman imitating a man imitating a woman.

PETER BLAKE: That was intentional. On the occasion when we met to discuss the painting, I remember her saying something along the lines of her learning all her make-up tricks from drag queens – what kind of mascara lasts longest, how to apply eyeshadow, 'all the important decisions'.

Later, some years after the portrait was finished, in the mid-sixties, I believe there was a drag act who billed himself as '. . . in the gowns of Alma Cogan', which is very strange.

A thing I realised many years ago is that nobody believes what they read in the papers more than the people who write for them.

Similarly, the biggest suckers for the old 'roar of the greasepaint / no people like show people' routine are performers themselves. The bigger they get, the more they buy it. Sammy Davis has always been particularly susceptible. 'Sammy, dear boy, don't be so blasted gauche,' Larry Harvey was always telling him. 'It doesn't suit you.'

But Sammy has gone on building up his collection anyway. John Wayne's stetson from *Stagecoach*, James Dean's jacket from *Rebel Without a Cause*, the bullfighter Dominguin's suit of lights, a 'Grecian-style' lamé dress belonging to Marilyn Monroe, Judy Garland's dancing shoes . . . They've all been given places of honour in the house in Beverly Hills.

The market in showbiz tat and memorabilia has boomed in the last few years. It used to be that they were content with an autograph and a snap. Now they're prepared to bid for your family albums, contracts, letters, old clothes and bed-linen. Once or twice a year I get a letter asking me to authenticate the latest piece of my past that has found its way into the saleroom.

'Life is a bridge. Cross over it, but build no house on it.': Indian proverb. I've tried to make that my philosophy in the past decade: I had been there, but now it looked as though I had never been. I had made a deeper and apparently more permanent mark than most, but all the signs had been obliterated, swept away. 'As soon as you leave the room you are forgotten': something we used to tell each other in our cups.

But it seems now that this is not the case. What's happening is like a real-life enactment of those television title sequences where an atomised image shinily reassembles itself, like an explosion in reverse.

I'm finding out that a lot of what I thought had been bonfired, Oxfam-ed, used for land-fill, has in fact been tidied away in sound archives, stills libraries, image banks, memorabilia mausoleums, tat troves, mug morgues.

It's an odd experience to find yourself catalogued, card-indexed, museumised, a speck of data for the information professionals to bounce around.

It seems that as long as you're in print or on film or a name on a buff envelope in an archive somewhere, you're never truly dead now. You can be electronically colourised, emulsified, embellished, enhanced, coaxed towards some state of virtual reality.

You can be reactivated or reëmbodied; simulated and holo-grammed. In just the last two years my voice has been artificially reprocessed for stereo effect and reincarnated in half-speed remasterings and on digital compact disc.

The spare-parts that make this possible are housed in a proliferating number of noninvasive environments in London, where they may be viewed (fingered, sniffed, listened to) by appointment.

The basement door at the rear of the Theatre Museum in Covent Garden clicks open without me having to lift a finger. There's a TV monitor in the security man's cubicle and he has seen me coming. I sign the visitors' book. He slaps an identity sticker on my jacket. Security Heightened Awareness it says on a sign next to his electric kettle.

'Please ensure that your hands are clean. Washbasins are situated on the back staircase', a sign says at the door to the Research Room. 'No fountain, ball-point, felt tip or any other sort of pen. Pencils only.'

The work surfaces are dark and polished, the lighting indirect, the walls lined in green baize.

'C' is for 'Cogan'. I pull open one of the catalogue drawers and run a finger over the coloured cards indicating the main categories.

Cakes
Calypso Music
Cartoons
Cassettes
Chart rigging
Charts
China and Rock
Clubs
Competitions
Computers
Concerts for Causes
    (Red Wedge,
    Apartheid / Sun City,
    Prince's Trust, etc.
    – see individual entries)
Copyright
Country Music Hall of Fame
C & W Rock

A reading of the 'How to use this resource' notice tells

me I'm fishing in the wrong pond. Personal Files is where I should be looking.

> Cochran Eddie
> Cocker Joe
> Cockney Rejects
> Cocteau Twins
> Cogan Alma
> Cohen Leonard
> Cole Lloyd

> 'Cogan Alma: See 'H' – 'Has Beens, Whatever Happened To . . . articles etc.'

> 'Has Beens – Cogan Alma – See 'P', Pop Personal Effects Index'

Chastened, my heart hammering behind my ribs by now, I approach the Personal Effects Index anti-alphabetically.

> Vaughan Frankie
> > Cane. Black painted wood with silver coloured metal top. 36″. Used on-stage by Frankie Vaughan. Purchased from Christie's South Kensington, 'Stars' Memorabilia' sale, December 1985

> Stardust Alvin
> > Part of black leather glove
> > worn at Birmingham Cresta nightclub,
> > June 7, 1975.
> > Champagne cork from same occasion.

> Presley Elvis
> > Ornate custom-made stage belt designed for Elvis Presley by Bill Belew, the white leather belt 4in. wide, decorated with brass eagles, enamel 'stars and stripes', and two layers of brass 'rope work' chain looped from lower edge, the

inside signed and inscribed by designer 'Elvis sample of belt Bill Belew' and initialled by Presley 'E.P.' (p. Sotheby's 1985)

Moon Keith

Two-piece denim suit in 'western' style, the jacket trimmed with brass and chrome studs and decorated with leather and sable tails attached by Buffalo and Indian-head nickels on the sleeves, the flared trousers trimmed with leather to simulate chaps, similarly decorated with sable tails attached by nickel heads. (p. Christie's, 1982)

Harrison George

Letter and cards to a fan Doreen comprising a letter from the Star Club, Hamburg . . . 'Did I tell you your hair was looking good at the Majestic?' dated December 1962, four publicity photographs signed by George, a Mersey Beat card at the Cavern, George's novelty handkerchief made as a miniature pair of French knickers and a hazelnut signed from George, 1962. (p. Sotheby's 1984)

Bolan Marc

Gold lamé suit held together with safety pins. Made circa 1967/68 but a favourite suit of Bolan's and worn on his penultimate TV show, in its held together state to appeal to 'punk' tastes. (Donated by estate of Marc Bolan, 1979)

I dawdle back towards my own entry, which I have caught a glimpse of in passing, via David Bowie, Elkie Brooks, Bucks Fizz, Kate Bush and The Carpenters. There are two cards.

Cogan Alma

Décolleté full-length stage dress from the 1950s of opulent duchesse satin, pearl trompe-l'oeil,

sapphire cornucopia and silver abstract glitter,
gathered at the bust, the front draped over
a-symmetrical fastening. With matching cape of
grass-green faille, weighted at hem. (Extended
loan, collection F.McL.)

Cogan Alma
Two-piece outfit comprising bell-shaped dress
of ivory coloured silk crêpe, embroidered with
silver gilt thread and decorated with vermicelli
beadwork, with shoestring straps and cropped
jacket of exotic osprey and paradise plumes and
matching feather fan with tortoiseshell sticks.
(Extended loan, collection F.McL.)

Our cleaning woman for many years was a man – Ricci Howe,
a veteran of the all-male 'Soldiers In Skirts'-type touring revues
that were popular with provincial theatre audiences immediately
after the war. It wasn't unusual to see him wearing something
from my wardrobe, a pair of shoes belonging to my mother and a
fluffy platinum wig while he pushed a Hoover around.

'Her face is the sort of face that looks as if the rest of the body is
making love,' he'd croon while he worked, quoting imaginary
reviews. 'She just laps you up with her eyes and lips and tongue.'

'She has the equipment of a bitch in the long shot. And yet
when you look in her eyes in close-up,' he'd tell the mirror, 'she's
like a baby. You can't tell if she's an angel or a bitch.'

In the mid sixties, when I was often out of the country for long
periods and had anyway abandoned my old style, he took an act
on the road in which he billed himself as 'Mr Ricci Howe,
appearing in the gowns of Miss Alma Cogan'.

I only went to see him once, at a large pub called the Four
Chimneys close to the power station and the dogs' home in
Battersea. I understood, as he had told me, that it was meant to be
an affectionate take-off, 'a way of keeping the legend alive'. But I
probably don't have to explain the confusion I felt seeing a man

on a stage in my clothes, moving his lips to the sound of my voice.

I felt disembodied. I felt as if some strange voodoo was going on.

He did well for a time. He was making a better living out of being me than I was. Then eventually the audience for even the camp version melted away and he went back to working for the cleaning agency. I have assumed that the relics that have been coming on to the market in the last few years are from his collection (nobody else had any), earning him a modest pension.

Now, courtesy of their current owner, 'F.McL.', a couple of characteristic examples have been made available for serious students of showbiz in the Crypt, the name given by the people who work here to the below-ground storage area at the Theatre Museum.

We're not far from the river, and the barrel-ceilinged tunnels where the reserve stock is stored give the sense of interconnected culverts or drains. It is cobbled underfoot with here and there heavy cast-iron grates through which it seems it is possible to hear the sound of distant running water.

When the uniformed minder who has accompanied me asks for the code written on the inevitable form, his voice echoes and a trace of his breath lingers on the air.

The smaller parts of the collection are stored in brown box files, rubber-stamped 'Supplied for the public service' and stacked on crude industrial shelves. The clothes are hung on hangers on long metal racks which, in some instances, sag under the weight.

They are protected by bin-liners, which emphasises the no-man's-land they occupy, somewhere between treasures and refuse, or (and this is the case with my old threads) zippered plastic bags.

Half the trick of getting a dress to live on stage lay in the lights and the lighting-plots – getting the beads and heaped-on glitter to catch the light streaming from the gantry in a way that broke it up and sent it flying around like tracer fire.

Off-stage, out of the lights, the dresses always had something forlorn about them. They were so solidly constructed they stood up unaided when you took them off. Tony Hancock once poked his head into an empty room and saw one standing on its own and said he found it as disturbing as the occasion he glimpsed Peter Brough's dummy, 'Archie Andrews', hanging on a hook behind a door. Both experiences gave him occasional nightmares for months afterwards.

I was expecting the tinsel to have tarnished, the sequins to have sloughed off like cells, the fabric to be distressed to some degree. What I wasn't prepared for was the total deadness; the lack of human imprint. What I am holding in my hands don't feel like clothes emptied of their owner, at least not if I think of the owner being me.

Ricci Howe had a slight build and the slender hips of a dancer, and both dresses have been cut down to fit this shape. The discrepancy – the grotesque shrinkage – is obvious when I measure them against my body, in a gesture that for a second revives memories of Wednesday afternoons and taking turns dancing with my father and my mother in a pre-war dancehall near the sea.

I leave by way of the museum proper, with its doomy showcases of dummies in famous dead people's clothes. The only visitors are a party of schoolchildren who are rough-housing it, acting out how they got the fake black-eyes and cuts and fat-lips that are the obvious highlight of a dreary outing.

The make-up girl responsible for the effects is leaning into a mirror fixing her own eyes, preparing for home. 'What is it with kids and scars?' she says, a droplet of black glop poised in mid-air. 'They've all got to have one.'

171

In the clippings libraries of some newspapers, I know there are A4-size brown envelopes with my name on them and the information: Obituary Available.

The contents have been subtracted from, rather than added to, the further I have drifted away from my celebrity. I would guess that I now merit three paragraphs, bottom of the page, plus, depending on whether it's a slow day, a one-column head-and-shoulders and a sub-head that says something like 'A significant practitioner of the amusement trade'.

Those old enough to remember will be surprised to learn that I am not dead already. When you stop appearing on television, the assumption, natural enough I suppose, is that you've died.

I have in front of me a collection of pictures which the obits editor, if it is a day when they need filler, will be able to select from. Some of them are already marked up from past use, with ruled lines in red biro round my head, cropping me out from the other people in the photograph.

In this one, for example, taken at the Beatles MBE party at Brian Epstein's house in Belgravia, I am standing next to Brian in a group which also includes George Harrison, Judy Garland, Mick Jagger and Brian's mother and grandmother. In this one, taken three or four years earlier, I'm performing the opening ceremony at the second Epstein family business in Whitechapel in Liverpool.

There are a number of early publicity pictures – period pieces of me posing at home with LP records, a dog, a flamenco guitar. There's a dressing-room shot of me and Danny Kaye, another with members of the Crazy Gang, a third with Princess Margaret and Cliff Richard.

One of Sammy Davis's collecting enthusiasms was Hammer horror – bits of scenery, props, even masks and fangs from the films. Often they would be delivered to his suite at the Mayfair hotel direct from the set by members of the cast still costumed as vampires, sexy witches and ghouls. It was always an excuse for an instant party. In this shot I'm squeezed in between what could be Ken Connor in Latex and a boffin wig and a bimbette wearing not much more than body powder and gauze.

And here I am with Cary Grant, pondering, as the caption writers would say, the menu at the Ivy. ('Cary Grant's Secrets – His Wild Temper, His Male Lovers, How He Dressed in Women's Underwear' one paper ran as a front-page flash following his death last month. It was all news to me. We'd just come from a matinée performance of *Humpty Dumpty* at the Palladium when this picture was taken.)

In the end, I have to say, it wouldn't matter which picture they settled on. I'm wearing the same expression, giving the same value, striking the same attitude in all of them.

This was before the fashion for violent and unflattering lighting; before fish-eye lenses and unnatural angles. The smudgers of those days touched out wrinkles, spots, heat rashes (tell-tale hands, overflowing glasses) without waiting to be asked. They weren't looking for the 'real' you. They weren't looking for the real *anybody*. They wore Tootal scarves and trilbies; carried rolled umbrellas.

Cut out and set down alongside each other, the images of me in the photographs I have here would show as little variety of expression as the faces in an Andy Warhol 'repeater' painting of Mao or Marilyn.

Only two pictures stand outside the formula. One because it isn't, no matter what the labelling says, a picture of me at all but of Ricci Howe in full drag: he's too eager – you can see him coming on to the camera in the parodying way he came on to the mirrors during the hoovering, rather than holding back.

The second stands out because it records the only sign of slippage; the only hint that the official personality may not also be the real one.

It was taken at the beginning of a short autumn season at Blackpool aimed at the Illuminations trade – all those people coming into town to drive up and down the front and look at Bugs Bunny and moving-leg can-can dancers and *The King And I* recreated in tableaux of jerky lights.

It shows me posing with one of the fortune-tellers off the Golden Mile, the old crones who, with their brassy rings, ratty furs, crimson lips and yellow beach-donkey teeth filled me with a deep, instinctive childhood apprehension (rats in the toilet, spiders in the sink).

I'd only agreed to the picture under duress from the management, who claimed the publicity would be good for business, but whose real motive I suspected stemmed from a superstition that a refusal might result in Gypsy Rosalee or Gypsy Petulengro putting a jinx on the season.

She arrived backstage, I was wheeled out, and as the shot was being set up she looked at me the way I had always dreaded and told me (had she been tipped off I was a reluctant subject? merely picked up on the negative vibrations?) that she saw death in my aura. 'I see death in your aura,' she said in a matter-of-fact way through lips whose colour bled in tiny tributaries towards her nose and her chin.

At which point she prised open my palm with her jemmy-like fingers and the flash-gun released its acrid memorialising puff of smoke.

If they're right, and the whole of a life may be summed up in a momentary appearance, then perhaps this is the definitive shot of me here: a state of upheaval struggling to disguise itself not quite successfully behind a happy smile and a mask of impassivity.

To be the owner of a famous face, even in the days when mine was famous, in an age when the advertising and publicity industries were in their infancy, was an enlivening thing. You felt invigorated, extra-alive, knowing that you were out there somewhere, circulating, multiplying, reproducing, like a spore in the world, even when you were sleeping.

I recognised it this way once when a train in which I was

travelling creaked to a halt unexpectedly. I was in the toilet at the time, and when I looked out through the clear oval in the frosted window to see what was happening, I saw a girl with two young dogs on leads walking in a field of half grass and half mud of the kind that you get on the sumpy industrial edge of towns, close to the railway lines.

The field was bounded by a metal fence and, beyond that on three sides, by allotments, pigeon sheds, a row of run-down houses, some small factories. The girl bent and let the dogs off the leads and then, for as long as I watched, remained absolutely still as they reeled and boxed and tripped over each other, racing back to her occasionally for reassurance and to show their pleasure, burning off their energy.

When Cary Grant was in London filming *Indiscreet* with Stanley Donen in the late fifties, he used the time to go round the archives and newspaper libraries and, with a razor, personally removed all references to his former existence.

I have thought of him often in recent days as I lurked in the lairs of the information professionals, listening to the squeak of rubber on parquet, the trill of a distant phone, the murmur of a discreet enquiry, waiting for an assistant to resurface with the anorexic envelopes and whippy folder-files bearing my name.

The pictures I have fanned out in front of me aren't much to show for the thousands of exposures that were made. But they tell me something I was curious to establish: they tell me how dedicated 'F.McL.' has been in his scavenging; how thoroughly he has picked the bones clean.

F.McL. – my taxonomist, my taxidermist, *sammler*, embalmer, stasher and storer, considerer of trifles, tireless tender of the flame.

Francis McLaren. Biografiend. Fetishiser. Jealous hoarder of my life.

175

Nine

The scenery keeps going by like a sentence read a dozen times and never taken in. Most people seem to have given up trying.

They are hemmed in by presents that, when they carried them on to the train, made them walk like fat people. The presents are wrapped in ways that speak of the full, well-paid lives they have made for themselves in the city, and explain their flushed, glassy-eyed exhaustion. They are travelling north to spend Christmas with their families.

The man in the seat next to me is trying to ground himself by listening to the Elgar Cello Concerto played by Jacqueline du Pré. I have identified it from the tsk-ing and buzzing that is the fall-out from the detonations happening in his brain.

I have the perfect anecdote teed-up ready and waiting in case we have to get into conversation, which I hope we won't.

I saw Jacqueline du Pré from the upper deck of a bus in Knightsbridge about a year ago. She was wearing high black polished boots and a sleek deep-pile black fur coat and sitting in a wheelchair waiting for the lights to change.

When they did, she was tipped backwards at a furious angle by the woman with her, who repeated the procedure at the other side to get the wheelchair up on to the pavement again.

I pressed my face against the window and looked towards the sky to try to see what she might have seen: it looked like sand pounded solid by the surf, but there was no way of telling how it might look at the end of a backwards-falling movement through nearly ninety-degrees and with bodies surging by on either side.

Her cheeks were inflated like bladders as a result of the drugs she was taking, and brightly veined. The hands which produced the growls and runs and sweeping cello chords I can hear pounding into the head of the man who happens to be sitting next to me lay uselessly in her lap.

Every record I put out in the fifties carried HMV's 'Dog and Trumpet' trademark, adapted, so it was said, from a painting showing Nipper the fox-terrier listening to the voice of his dead owner, and sitting (so it was further said) on the lid of his master's coffin.

The message of the drawing now seems obvious: death-in-life, life-in-death, phonographic magic; record listening as a seance where you choose your own ghosts.

(In 1950, half a century after Nipper himself had died, EMI organised an exhumation at the site in Kingston-upon-Thames where he was thought to have been buried. A few bones were found, but it couldn't be claimed with any certainty that they were Nipper's.)

At the time, though, it never occurred to me to ever wonder how the sounds that came out when I opened my throat ended up embedded in acetate and vinyl. It certainly never occurred to me that they were going to be entombed there for ever and always, time immemorial, world without end.

The records were breakable and therefore disposable. They were as short-lived as the careers of the people who performed them: the obsolescence was built in.

And yet yesterday I was able to sit at a study cubicle in a wood-panelled room with a brass-and-crystal chandelier and have my self played back to me, moment for moment, bum note for bum note, breath for breath. The quality of reproduction was so advanced I imagined I could hear my heart pounding between phrases, my lungs tightening, gathering their strength; I could almost hear the threads of saliva breaking in that moment thirty years ago as I parted my lips to sing.

The room was laid out like a language laboratory, with individual control panels, headsets and table-top partitions. There were two or three other people doing research in addition to myself. The technicians, who remained out of sight, on the end of a phone, provided a one-to-one service: you only had to say the word and you could have the strings separated from the bass, or the vocal mixed up or mixed down or even isolated from the backing track completely.

When I had this done I experienced an odd sensation of my voice being poured back where it had come from; of something returning to its source; of a cycle being completed.

Everything had been transferred to tape. The next person to play this would hear only dead air, tape hiss, only the fleck of a human presence woven into the pattern of interference.

It was overcast and raining beyond the big ground-level bay window, with sudden flurries of rain and the odd pedestrian running to find shelter. The rain whipped around the telephone box opposite, which I could see was plastered with stickers offering services of sexual degradation and humiliation.

'For security reasons this room is patrolled periodically. We are sorry if this causes any distraction', a sign said high on a wall close to where I was sitting.

I don't know how long I had been there when I was startled – I did literally jump; something fell from my lap to the floor – by a hand touching my shoulder.

I was listening to my 1954 cover of Kitty Kallen's 'Little Things Mean a Lot', cranked up so high it should have been physically painful, and apparently I could be heard some distance away, in other parts of the building, double-tracking, singing at the top of my lungs and intruding on the study environment like a Saturday-night drunk.

A modern structure of red metal and perspex has been erected inside the old Victorian shell of the station, in line, I take it, with British Rail's current 'We're getting there' slogan. They are playing seasonal muzak, as they were three hours ago in Euston. It swims around in the space between the old roof and the new like some kind of orchestral insulation. 'It Came Upon the Midnight Clear' changes to 'Jolly Saint Nicholas' just as I reach the barrier.

I apparently met Francis McLaren more than once, many years ago, when he was still in short trousers. But nothing about the figure stepping away from the newsagent's hole-in-the-wall and making a bee-line for me strikes me as in any way familiar.

Who looking at him now would guess he was the slave of a secret passion? Or identify me (more accurately, 'me') as the object of it?

The car-coat is beige, the shoes sensible, the trousers just perceptibly flared and hoisted an inch or two above the ankle. The pink of the shirt he is wearing gives some colour to his face, which has adapted to the Arctic-blue lighting of the modern office the way lower life-forms adapt to deserts and tropical swamps, and has sickly sick-building-syndrome circles under the eyes. His tie is fluttering excitedly over his shoulder and he has his left hand pressed to his right temple, chimp-fashion, to prevent the ropes of hair unpeeling to make a second streaming pennant, as he comes.

Sight. Smell. Sound. I see him before I smell him. I smell him before he speaks. What the bottle probably describes as 'a masculine fragrance' is coming off him in wavy concentric lines, like cartoon shorthand for extreme ponginess or heat.

But before he even speaks he slips an Instamatic from the

179

plastic pod hanging from his shoulder and snaps off a single frame. 'Well. Who ever would have believed it. You. I mean . . .' – he wants to correct this to 'Alma Cogan', but doesn't – 'Here. After all these years.'

When I sensed weakness, my instinct was always to bore in, grind down. I can see I'm going to have to fight it in the hours ahead.

Travelling by train in order not to disappoint his expectations is a concession I resent. Ditto the metallic green puffa jacket (I feel like a misplaced present in it) and dated comin'-atya make-up I sensed the role demanded.

When he goes to pick up my overnight bag I tell him I'm capable of carrying it myself. With both our hands gripping the handle, though, I get a sense of the shivering and shaking and old knee-knocking heebie-jeebies and let him have his way.

In the car-park, a lot of the first pleasure of being reunited is already evaporating into irritability and apprehension. For all their best efforts and good intentions, the members of various parties are quickly reverting to their old roles. From several family saloons come the sounds of peevishness and bickering. A woman slaps a small girl across the back of the legs as we pass, producing ear-piercing screams. There's some Christmas paper with a bow still attached on top of the litter-bin closest to where F.McL., as I can't help thinking of him, is parked.

When he opens the tailgate of the car, the rear shelf rises dinkily with it, like a music box. He puts my bag in next to a pair of heavy-weather boots and a golf umbrella, then holds the passenger door open for me in a display of old-world manners. ('Miss Cogan says she prefers considerate fellows with good manners to the Adonis type and has dark thoughts concerning the "Hiya, babe" variety of male.' I don't know where or to whom I said this, but naturally he would be able to tell me.)

Inside, the car is anonymous, clean. The smell of plastics and laminates and disinfectant competes with his own artificial odour. There are no distinguishing features.

180

When he switches on the ignition, the radio comes on with it – a news report of a smash-and-grab at a local building society, which he hears to its conclusion before turning it off, in the way of somebody used to always riding alone.

He pulls on a pair of open-weave gloves as we take our place in the stream of home-bound traffic, and it occurs to me, not for the first time, that nobody knows I'm here.

Women start to become visible in bright, well-lighted kitchens, preparing evening meals while half-watching television, going through the same small repertory of gestures, as we draw clear of the town centre.

The driver of a car cruising alongside us opens his window just enough to let a chewing gum wrapper float out on to the air. Something in my expression must suggest disapproval, because he gives me the finger. F.McL. appears not to notice.

'Twenty-eight years,' he says, carefully avoiding any contact between his gloved hand on the gear-shift and my thigh, calmer now that we're moving. 'November 15th, 1959. A Tuesday. I was only about eleven. That was the first time I met her. You.' (He doesn't like the sound of this.) 'Alma. My mother booked in for me to see her at the Manchester Palace. Billy Daintie was the support. I have the poster of course. And the programme. And – although I can't be categorical; I wouldn't want to swear to this – I think the dress she had on that night.'

I ask him how he managed to get backstage; it was never easy. But he's overtaking and so doesn't immediately answer. He hikes himself forward so that his face is within inches of the rear-view mirror and continues rocking agitatedly until he's safely back in lane.

'My letter of introduction from the fan club. On the door they said: She's having a bath between shows. Then you can imagine the trepidation, a child going down the corridor to this big door and knocking, and then the husky voice saying "Come in" . . . I wasn't by myself. There were others. She saw a few of us at once.

181

I mean, she never made much of a fuss of me. I was just one of the many.'

Now there are fewer kitchen windows, the distance between them is greater, the darkness more intense. Out of the darkness looms the business park where Francis McLaren is a paperpusher for the Inland Revenue, Customs and Excise, the Equal Opportunities Commission, I can't remember.

Membranous buildings with wigwam roofs and curtain walls and abstract facings of lime-green and peach and pink rise out of a landscape of pig breeders and car breakers and humpy ploughed fields.

He seems increased in definition, less battened-down, being close to his place of work. 'We'll have everything in there when they've finished. Swimming pool, squash courts, restaurant, wine bar, cycleway, equestrian centre, pub, a trim trail, *nursery* would you believe . . . Built on a hundred acres of Lancashire rubbish,' he says, with an air of triumphalism. 'Three point five million cubic metres of earth was rearranged, with the older rubbish being turned over the newer, more unstable stuff to compress and control it.'

This new landmark dissolves like an apparition and the stench of slurry starts oozing through the ventilators. He squirts water onto the windscreen, as if there was some connection. He does it in the deft, almost sly, way that television weather forecasters move seamlessly through their sequence of maps and satellite pictures.

We turn right on to an unlighted road, and drive for what I estimate is three or four miles until we come to a village with a fish-and-chip shop and an '8 'Til Late' with pre-packed fuel heaped like anti-flood defences outside it and a SlushPuppy beaker revolving lopsidedly in the window.

We pass a school and a mill, then start climbing towards a group of farm buildings which open directly on to the road: the big sliding doors of one of them are parted to provide a glimpse into a high dark space which suggests dungheat and bodyheat and the passivity of dumb animals.

A short distance further on, we turn between a pair of concrete pillars that must have once held the estate gates, into a semi-concealed cut or snicket. The road is pitted and cobbled and at the end of it, illuminated in the headlights, a gate opens into a field.

'Be it ever so humble,' he says when he switches off the ignition, but makes no attempt to move.

'One thing I'd like to say to you, I meant to say over the phone, so as to avoid offence.' I see a curtain move at a window. Somebody, possibly in the nearby field, calls to their dog. 'You haven't come to ask if you can borrow anything, have you? Because I'm sorry, but I've had a bad experience, as you know from my letters. I'm a very poor judge of character; I take everybody on face value. Now I never, *never*, never let anything of Alma go from the house.'

As I duck into the cold, I do something I haven't done for years: I go to bunch my clothes to my body the way I had to do to get in and out of doors, and up and down stairs when I was, as they used to say, gowned. It's something I found myself doing involuntarily in off-stage life as a tic, a kind of neurotic mannerism (I was constantly afraid I was going to send glasses flying, sweep things off tables; that my body mass was several times greater than it was). It was something I had to learn to train myself out of.

He calls his cottage '. . . this ole house . . .'. Written this way in his letters, but spelled conventionally in wrought-iron, as I now see, by his front door. The roof and outside walls are corrugated, like a temporary building converted for living. There is a porch made of trellis with bare branches twisted through it.

' "This Ole House". HMV B-series catalogue number 10717. Alma accompanied by Felix King, his piano and orchestra,' he says in the mechanistic manner of the fact-fattened tour guide, as he fishes in his pocket for the key. 'Released 8th of October,

1954, and squeezed out of the chart action by Rosemary Clooney of course, and also, surprisingly, by Billie Anthony, who chalked up her only ever hit with it, I believe.'

The cottage smells of cold and damp and paraffin from the heater whose blue flame putters weakly in a corner. He leaves me by the door, which opens straight into the room, and goes to put a match to a gas log fire which lights with a small boomy blowback explosion.

He has to edge through the gap between two massive pieces of furniture. Flush with the wall directly opposite the fire and close to where I am standing is a Chinese cherrywood table with a lapis and mother-of-pearl inlay top. It is perhaps four feet wide and rises to chest-level – a desk, perhaps, rather than a table, and designed for leaning on rather than sitting at (your eyes would be parallel with the surface).

The equation it makes with the surrounding bowed walls and low false ceiling is reminiscent of that between the new and old station buildings.

The wallpaper on this side of the room is of bamboo poles. But any oriental 'theme' element is almost certainly accidental. There is a feeling of things having drifted together. The carpet, for example – oatmeal, with a lumpy three-dimensional pattern; and the skimped curtains, drooping from their rail – have the unmistakable air of inherited fixtures and fittings.

Occupying the area between the Chinese table and the fire is a sofa of pseudo-Hollywood dimensions. It makes a three-quarters circle which can only be entered from the fireplace side.

To the left of it is a television with a video machine, and a stack of stereo equipment. To the right, a drop-leaf table set for two and on it a Christmas log with a spiral red candle and a half-pint mug with snowman-and-holly paper napkins fanned out in it.

On each wall are brackets containing what I have seen advertised as 'Pickwick' bulbs: unshaded pink phalluses that are supposed to recreate the Dickensian candle glow of poorhouse, debtors' prison and tavern.

184

An overhead dish light spills a harsher pool of light that shows up the dark stains and grease-spots on the carpet and the mossy fine-wale velour of the sofa. I sit as much out of it as possible, among the fake-fur cushions.

'It won't take long to get a fug up,' McLaren says and disappears into the kitchen. A couple of seconds later he's back with a plate covered in discs of processed meat. 'There's a shop I go to does wonderful cut-offs. There's, let's see . . . spam; pressed tongue; brisket; turkey. We'll eat again later on, but I thought I'd make us some sandwiches to have with our tea. That fire can go up a bit if you want.'

The gas logs are in a sealed stone surround, and above and to either side of that is wallpaper with a grey stone pattern. A reproduction of swans on a lake hangs in a frame above the fireplace. On the mantelpiece there's a large ceramic swan with a hollowed-out body containing a spider plant whose satellites fall within inches of the back-lit logs and pale humming fire.

'I'm sorry. It's only just occurred to me. If you'd like to use the facilities, you'll find them upstairs.'

He has stepped out of the kitchen into the white light like somebody stepping into a baby spot. And it's true, with a captive audience, there's now something theatrical in his performance – the two growing spots of colour like blusher behind the eyes; the tea-towel tucked into the waistband of his trousers; the white cuffs of his rose shirt folded precisely back; the hair disposed on his head just-so.

But if I stepped into a crowded lift with Francis McLaren in it this time next week I'm not sure I would recognise him.

'People who had worked with X found it hard to believe that he was guilty of the crimes, and described him as mild-mannered and intelligent.'

'X had lived in the street for fifteen years, hardly known to his neighbours, who regarded him as a loner.'

'You can't put them together. It's just incomprehensible that

185

he could have done the things he's done, when you know him as we've known him. He was merriment from the word go.'

Dennis Nilsen, the Muswell Hill goulasher, had long conversations with the corpses of his victims. He bathed them, talced them, put them to bed, sat them at the table before laying them under the floorboards in his living-room. Brady and Hindley made frequent trips back to the graves of the children they murdered. They picnicked on them, got drunk, wrestled with the dog, took happy snaps.

Francis McLaren lives alone in this house. With me. With my carcass. My corpse. My earthly remains. With his memory of what I was. I am waiting to have tea brought to me in a museum of myself.

But I can't see the evidence. It has to be behind the sliding doors of the small bookcase which stands next to the cherrywood table, or in the cupboard built into the same wall, which has a keyhole but no key.

Somewhere upstairs, either in his own room or the room where I am going to be sleeping (these arrangements have been finalised on the telephone), there is not only my stagewear, a heavy wardrobe packed full of damask, silk chiffon, gold spatters, crackle nylon and dyed cold spiny feathers; but also my street clothes – suits, skirts, sweaters, underwear, for all I know; stockings. Bun bases; hairpieces; wigs in plastic bags and on biroed-over polystyrene heads.

Under the TV remote I see there is an opened letter address to 'Colin Darren' at this address.

'At last,' McLaren says, setting a tray down between us on the sofa. 'You must be half-starved . . . You look a bit out of the kirk over there. Shall I come to you, or do you want to come to me?'

'It's very good of you to go to all this trouble,' I tell him, not moving. He has taken off the tea-towel and buttoned up his cuffs again. He hands me a plate with a Christmas napkin on it. The

186

sandwiches have been made with unsoftened butter. Small hard lumps of it show through the tears in the bread. 'Do you like any mustard or sauce or anything on your sandwiches? I've got cranberry, if you like cranberry on your turkey . . . No, I *enjoy* it. I love talking about Alma. Apart from when they rob me, of course. I'm very bitter about it . . .'

A saga in his most recent letters (which, in their long history have never, or at least rarely, received replies) has concerned the lifting of some pieces from his collection by a rival at a recent convention or bazaar, Magical Memories swap-shop or nostalgia mart. Solicitor's letters have been fired off. Sotheby's expert in the field has been alerted to the theft and advised not to accept the item(s) for auction.

Networks have been formed to move this stuff around which are as low-key and vendetta-prone in their way as those trafficking in snuff movies, kiddie porn, video nasties.

There are catalogues, contact books, subscription clubs, coded small ads in privately circulated magazines. Audio tapes, videos, rare pressings, private negatives and transparencies, flimsy cyclostyled discographies, filmographies, bibliographies, personal letters and items of clothing pass from hand to hand at small gatherings of like-minded people.

Francis McLaren has secured a monopoly, cornered the market in his own specialised area. By hunting down and gathering together the debris, he has made himself the clearing-house for the minutiae of my life and career: studios, engineers, band personnel, takes accepted and rejected, numbers of records pressed and sold, highest chart position achieved, radio/TV appearances supporting the promotion, theatres visited, dresses worn, fees received, holidays taken . . . He's a statistics gobbler. A relics sniffer. An information junkie.

And now it is time to see the material evidence of his adoration.

'Are you not going to have your sandwich? Or a piece of – '

'I really think it's time to see what I've travelled all this way to see. It's already well after seven.'

With a paper napkin he cleans the tips of his fingers and then the spaces in between them with a piece of the napkin wrapped round a single finger, the way people in public places sometimes pick their nose.

There are keys on the end of a chain attached to a belt loop on his trousers. The key he selects is the old-fashioned kind, with a piece of stepped metal soldered to a hollow core – the key for the cupboard let into the wall behind me.

The booty is stashed in various carrier bags and cardboard boxes and in half a dozen picture albums which couldn't be any fatter if they had spent a month in the rain.

He tips one of the albums towards him with his forefinger and brings it across to where I'm sitting. As I open it a flash explodes in the room so the photographs on the first page, which must be among the first of me ever taken (I'm aged about fifteen months and wearing ankle-socks and a big bow in my just-brushed hair), appear to be mottled with rust spots or discoloured by damp. Another one for the collection.

Turning the pages I find my parents' wedding pictures; my father's death certificate; Jewish aunts, uncles and cousins shot against tall houses in narrow back gardens; school reports, Christmas cards, holiday postcards, good luck telegrams, birthday-party invitations, receipts, invoices, forty-year-old producers' audition reports from the BBC, still in their internal-delivery envelopes. The tangible fragments of a certain kind of lived life.

I am more interested in how far McLaren has gone with this than in taking a trip down memory lane. There's a lot to see and I want to get through it (this part of it) quickly.

Any slackening of pace is his cue to pounce. Even from the kitchen, where he is trying to give the impression of busying himself, he can sense a shift in the level of concentration, hear a change in the rhythm of the browsing. From the doorway, he is able to identify each item from its degree of discoloration, surface foxing, fold-marks, page position or typography, and can't help himself coming in with a verbal caption or commentary.

'Ah yes. BBC audition, 16th July 1947 at the Paris Cinema. The audition went well and she was noted as "Fifteen year old, deep-voiced crooner showing *great* possibilities".'

Or: 'Very interesting that. First appearance on *Gently, Bently* on the radio, at a fee if I've got it right of twelve guineas, rising through the series to fifteen . . . That's "La Dolce Vita" in Newcastle. Oh, just a minute. Do they look Japanese? Oh sorry, that's in Japan. That's the famous tour of Japan. I'll tell you where the "Dolce Vita" is, it isn't that dress at all. There – that's "La Dolce Vita".'

Flash photography is forbidden in galleries because every picture taken apparently jolts loose a particle of pigment. And that's how I have always felt about being on the wrong end of a camera – that some small part of me is flaking off; becoming detached and appropriated.

I was told to think of a photograph being a message from myself in the present to my future self, saying 'I was happy'. But is that the message of these pictures?

They basically divide down the middle: into photographs of private gregariousness (controlled encounters in dressing-rooms, restaurants, my own and other people's parties), and public solitude (PAs, picture-calls, performance shots).

After the age of about ten, there is little or nothing in between. By then I have already acquired a practised air. I have learned to project an outlook for the camera which is unchallenging, passively flirtatious, indirect; an attitude based only on the photographs of other professionals and unconnected to anything in my own life.

'One might think how difficult it is to get a true smile in a single picture of a person we know,' somebody once said. I've found very few here.

'I've got her on video, if you're interested,' McLaren says. 'But I'm taping *Coronation Street* at the minute, so you can't see anything until *Brookside*'s over. *Brookside*'s next.'

He would have to be a soap dope as well. It's another way of living by proxy; under the skin of other people's lives. He probably writes gossipy letters to the actors, calling them by their series' names. He's the sort who sends Valentines and Christmas presents, and wreaths to the 'funerals' of characters who have been killed-off.

'I've got her doing dialects and impressions on a demo disc she cut around 1950 time to show the powers that be at the BBC that she was more than just a singer,' he says, peeling a pair of rubber gloves off his milky-pink fingers. 'I've got it on tape for security reasons. It's a one-off. I know probably half a dozen people who would be prepared to kill to get their hands on this.'

It was a direct-to-disc recording made at one of the many small commercial studios above the HMV shop in Oxford Street. I had worked the script up over many weeks with my parents, whose hopeful fearful faces (I had to get it right first time; there was no overdubbing; any foul-up was going to cost them money) I could see staring at me through a square window set into a wall soundproofed with egg-boxes.

Afterwards, the three of us had lunch at Ross's Kosher Restaurant in Tottenham Court Road, where my mother set the acetate in its plain brown sleeve in full view on the table. There was a small scene when one of the waiters spilled soup on the otherwise pristine white label. 'You spill soup down Sophie Tucker? Bud Flanagan? When my daughter's a star with her face up on the wall here among all these gorgeous people,' she told him, '*then* perhaps you'll be more careful.'

The tension in my voice is evident. My dry mouth and the quaveriness in my breathing are clearer, more pronounced than I remember them. It's like having a third, enlarged organic presence in the room.

'I had it cleaned up by a friend,' McLaren says. 'He took out the background noise, toned down the surface interference, brought the voice forward . . . Her last appearance at the Palladium was on the famous Beatles bill when there was a riot outside the theatre. The 13th of October, 1963. I've got that on audio if you want to hear it.'

'What I would really like,' I tell him, 'is to go for a drink. We passed a lot of pubs on the way here.'

'But I've got all sorts in to cook a meal.'

'I'd be quite happy just to go and have a drink and perhaps another sandwich later, something like that.'

'Really?'

'Really. Don't bother cooking for me.'

'Because we were going to have soup and hunter's stew. I've got the stewing meat and the garlic and I'd just started to do the potatoes and all sorts of things . . . I've got this horror of having a visitor who sort of goes to bed ravenous.'

'Well I won't,' I say, 'because I would speak up if I was hungry. If I am, we can always stop at a fish-and-chip shop after the pub.'

'Oh there's fish-and-chip shops. Any number. There's fish-and-chip shops all *over*. But I wouldn't have insulted a guest by saying I was going to buy fish and chips for them . . . If we went to a place where they do bar meals, then if . . .'

There's only one way to end this: by leaving the room. (I doubt anyway whether it was much more than the excuse for another photo opportunity and the food simply props.)

There are hollows in the floor that haven't been plugged with underlay, so the carpet both sinks and clings to your shoes when you step on it. Something brushes against my hair going upstairs.

I look into the room where I'm going to be spending the night. It is cabin-sized, low and narrow, and dominated by a head and shoulders of Alma Cogan that I don't think I've ever seen before. It has been blown up to perhaps three-times life-size and shows me wearing a fur coat with a stand-away collar and a Cossack fur hat cocked at a gamy angle.

Dangling from a beam at the turn in the stairs, presumably as a reminder to McLaren himself (who else comes here?), is a small rubber duck.

The pub he chooses isn't a homey, end-of-terrace local with worn leather and scrubbed lino and goitered old timers and mangy dogs and the glasses arranged upside-down on the shelves on brewery napkins folded to points. (*Coronation Street* c. 1965).

We drive past several of those to the kind of place popular with business reps and cricket teams and couples still working out how to let go of the other's hand in a way that feels natural and not rejecting. And also, at this time of year of course, with parties of office workers having their annual bash.

'Don't drink and drive – you might spill some' it says on the door into the Public, whose molten-look panes are infused with the red of a real fire. We take the other door into a room full of people in paper party hats eating steakwiches and basket meals and Christmas turkey with all the trimmings.

The only seats we can find are next to a cold-cabinet containing an industrial cheesecake and – hiding in a corner – a half-drunk bottle of milk. McLaren holds his half-pint mug by the handle like a tea-cup and immediately seems crowded by the back of a girl who has thrown herself into what could easily be her boss's lap.

She has a skinny plait growing out of the shingled back of her hair which sweeps against McLaren's neck when she moves. He tugs at the collar of the 'leisure' jacket he is wearing in place of the coat he had on when he collected me at the station (it has semi-fluorescent green and turquoise panels like the modern office block where he works) and irritatedly scrapes his chair forward.

I should probably ask him questions about his own background, but I don't think I really want to know. (I think I already do: elderly parents almost certainly; father who confined his existence to a shed in the garden; mother who kept him in girls' clothes until he started school.)

The noise-level is kept up by a tape of Christmas songs: that one by Slade that comes round every year; 'War Is Over' by John and Yoko; the Phil Spector girl groups . . .

An indisputable fact is that you don't choose your fans. You have no way of knowing what sparks them off.

Joy Prest was a blonde I did the rounds with in the dying days of variety. Her speciality was bending nails with her teeth and tearing up telephone directories. She did this wearing off-the-shoulder leotards, towering stilettos and strawberry fishnet tights.

She'd packed a lot into a short life, sleeping rough in the streets of Soho from the age of thirteen, travelling with a freak show, modelling for Henry Moore and Jacob Epstein among others. And it's true she attracted a certain following.

'Since I'm a child,' she'd say, after the latest dirty raincoat merchant had been seen off by the stage-door keeper, 'things *happen* to me. I'm a magnet for unbalanced minds. A happy hunting ground, actually. If there's a maniac within fifteen miles and I go for a walk, he'll fall on me. Animals, madmen and children. It's always been the same.'

But even she found it hard to laugh off the weirdo who started writing her letters on a daily basis. It was clear he knew where she lived, who her friends were, the details of her movements, etcetera. He said he wanted to marry her and together start the master-race.

She reported it to the police, who said they could do nothing. Soon afterwards the man was found dead in a tiny bedsit complete with the standard sicko paraphernalia: Nazi shrine, guttered candles, volumes on Aleister Crowley, poltergeists, demonology, and a giant blow-up picture of Joy Prest looking down on it all. He was lying on the floor in a leather stormtrooper's coat that had a suicide note addressed to her in the pocket.

I look at Francis McLaren. Searching for some identifying mark, anything to beef up what has so far been a rather pallid description, I can see now that he has what looks like wax floe, far too faint to be called a scar, below the hairline on the right-hand side of his face. It's like the mark made by the soldered seam in the loaf-tin; by a superficial flaw in the mould.

His complexion is like the threadworm fibres in a clean sheet of paper held against the light.

'People say to me: Didn't she sing some tripe, when you think about it?' McLaren is saying. 'And I say, that's only because that's what people *wanted* in 1956. Otherwise obviously she wouldn't have done. I mean, they *sold*. They certainly sell now.

'I'm proud to say she's *enormously* expensive. Thirty pounds, the last I heard, for one of the early albums. Beatles collectors have been known to pay twenty pounds for a 45 from 1964 on which Paul McCartney plays tambourine. In the autograph market she's seventeen-fifty, which I think is incredible for her to be priced at that. You'd pay hundreds for a dress, if you could find one, which you can't any more. But I'm not in it for the mercenary perspective. I've got so many things I've forgotten what I've got.'

'What was it, do you think, that sparked off your interest in Alma Cogan?'

'My *love* for her?' His tone (uncharacteristically bold, bordering on boastful) suggests the terrorist bomber or crack addict opening up for a sympathetic interviewer while having his identity shielded by the dark or, as they do it these days, by computer-blur.

'Maybe I met her at the right time. I only speak from the very humble sort of a fan's viewpoint, but she did have a very, very strange effect on people. When I track down something new of her and know it's in the post on its way, I can't *wait* to get home from work. I spend several minutes just looking at it, not even touching it, drawing out the anticipation, before ripping into the parcel . . . Her mother has let me have a lot of things over the years.'

The girl with the plait is nuzzling the older man's neck, teasing the hair just above his collar with the pointed tip of her tongue. A few minutes ago an iced cake with sparklers in it was delivered to another table, and now the people sitting at it have turned subdued.

Reel Match. Skill Cash. Line Up. Super Two. The lights on the bandit go through their vertical fandango. Another run of lights mimics a stack of silver coins falling. Then everything stops and the orange-yellow central panel flutters for a few seconds like a heart in its syrups and juices.

We have brought fish and chips from a shop that is not the one we saw in the village on the way here: in this one the old sunset-at-sea splashboards had been replaced by stainless steel and you chose from coloured pictures, like in a McDonalds, and was obviously felt by McLaren to be much more suitable.

He has brought fish knives and forks and china plates and lighted the red spiral candle on the table. 'I've been putting it out for . . . This must be its fifth Christmas. I've been saving it for a special occasion.'

We both eat facing the television, which shows fogged pictures of me appearing on various sets constructed of cheap fifties hardboard. He has filled his summer holidays and time off from work sleuthing through film and television vaults and archives and paying to have his finds transferred from sixteen-mil to video cassette.

There is a period innocence to the superficial smoothness, intentional dullness and cheerful banality of the programmes and the way the flying ziggurats and two-dimensional lamp-posts and door-frames quiver perilously in my slipstream.

195

He eats with the remote by his plate on the table beside him and occasionally uses it to move a sequence on or freeze the picture. Because they're black and white, the pictures have a snap-shot quality which disappeared with the increased sophistication of the technology and the coming of colour: you turned a switch and this thing came up like magic in the corner, like an exposure making itself in the darkroom. (We all used to watch television with the lights lowered in those days.)

Run-on like this, the programmes suggest a consistency that is misleading. In the months that sometimes elapsed between TV appearances, my weight, for example, could balloon almost beyond recognition. We were then looking at crash diets, fat farms, polypharmacy and 'miracle' cures that involved being injected with the foetal cells of capuchin monkeys or the urine of pregnant women.

By 1965, as the tape of my last major appearance on television shows, I was svelte, swinging – 'Let there be Ringo, he makes my heart melt' if you can believe; 'Let there be dresses that are more than a belt'; 'Let there be Dylan, and Dudley and Pete . . .' – and on the skids.

I was down to playing toilets in the North of England where you changed in cupboards or behind piles of beer crates at the side of the stage. At the Marimba in Middlesbrough you had to change in the manageress's flat above the club, run down the stairs into the street and make your entrance through an audience that had just climbed out of the trees.

'The last time I saw her, it was rather rock-bottom, I've got to admit,' McLaren says. 'They were gambling in the back, in the same room, and so it was noisy . . . Oh she'd gone down. She wasn't doing good dates right at the end. I couldn't get over it for a long time.'

When we've finished eating, we move to the sofa and start making inroads into the part of the collection where my chief interest lies. His tape-recordings and audio cassettes fill several shoe-boxes whose outsides are obliterated with information relating to running orders, transmission dates if they were taken from the radio, MDs, track times.

He tries to keep his end up, supplying background, quoting chapter-and-verse. But I have timed the visit for a week-night knowing he will be back in the land of rubber bands and holiday rotas and who's-been-using-my-mug in the morning at nine sharp. (Eight-thirty, as it turns out.) And he is already showing signs of flagging. Whole minutes go by without him saying anything, and he looks as though he's about to nod out. He stops trying to stifle his yawns and starts to rub his eyes, putting some red into the circles of oxidised yellow-blue.

Eventually he says: 'Well. I'm sorry. You're welcome to stay down here for as long as you like. But some of us have jobs to go to in the morning. I must away to my bed.' He connects some headphones to the tape machine and pulls on the curly lead until they reach where I'm sitting. The various digital display panels are showing mostly noughts.

For a few minutes I listen to nothing except his footsteps overhead, going from bathroom to bedroom, putting keys and loose change on the bedside table, draping suit-jacket and trousers over the dumb-valet, laying out fresh clothes for tomorrow.

I pick a tape more or less at random – *The Show's The Thing*, recorded 30th January, broadcast on the Light Programme, 3rd February, 1956, the handwritten sticker on the protective perspex box tells me – and shift my position on the perimeter of the sofa so that my back is no longer to the door.

Low noise. High output. Smooth tape running. Excellent high end linearity. Pure crystal gamma haematite magnetic particles. Tapered and flanged seamless guide rollers. Exact tape alignment.

The floor is probably flagged, which accounts for the hollows and dips and why walking across it can suddenly feel like being on wet moorland. But it absorbs sound.

Standing on the bookcase are some flowers in a faceted vase, which itself is standing on a small square of yellowed newspaper. The top shelf is open and lined with books; the lower shelves are concealed behind sliding panel doors.

I open one far enough for a snowstorm paperweight to roll out, followed by an old typewriter ribbon. The paperweight is one of a collection, packed into the shelves along with lengths of flex, place-mats, a box of Christmas tree lights, some bald tennis balls, a toffee tin containing scraps of wool, needles, buttons, cottons . . .

Wedged in the darkened side I can see a cornflakes box which has been crimp-sealed at the top and bound with wide rubber bands. When I take it back to the sofa to inspect it, it turns out to contain a collection of tape-spools, all with miserly amounts of tape on them, and the single cassette to which their contents have obviously been transferred.

When tape recorders came into wide recreational use in the fifties, and could be bought on the never-never, I started to get crank tapes through the post in addition to the usual creepo crank letters.

Most were from men who had developed obsessions about my breastbone, armpits, fingers, leg-hair, ankles. ('I was in the second row, first house at the Alhambra, Bradford on Tuesday, and I came in my trousers when you reached in the air and I got a glimpse of the dark under your arm towards the end of 'Blue Skies'. Now I'm lying here and . . .')

But many were from women (all seemingly in the WAAFs), lying on plastic-headboarded beds in limp-curtained rooms, doing themselves with rolled magazines, the handles of hair-brushes, the heels of shoes, moaning and gasping my name.

You could spot a heavy-breather in the opening seconds from the ambient noise of doors being closed, footsteps crossing floors and the incidental fric-frac of the microphone being set up.

I recognise it now as I clamp the headphones on and substitute

198

the night-time sounds of this room (the whisper of the tape hubs, the noise of my own breathing, the packed silence bearing down from outside) for the sounds of another room committed to tape twenty-odd years ago.

(Sound of door banging.) (Crackling noise.) (Footsteps across room and then recording noise followed by blowing sound into microphone.) (Voice, quiet, unreadable.) (Coughing.) (Throat-clearing.) (A man's voice.) 'Alma you know what I'd like I'd like you to wank me off all over your fat beautiful tits. Then I'd like to put my swollen cock in your mouth, pull the . . .'

Fast-forward. Play. A different man's voice. '. . . twirl your tits around my mouth, bite off both your nipples at the same time. Lick your pubes. Suck . . .'

The liquid crystal figures flicker as if caught in a sharp draught. Overhead, Francis McLaren moves in bed.

I replace the tapes in the Kelloggs packet and put them back where I found them.

Among the books lining the upper shelf are a set of textbooks or encyclopedias with plain brown wrappers and small windows in the spines giving their titles tooled onto burgundy leather. The books are closely packed except for 'Biology' and 'Mathematics', which have something inserted between them that prevents the covers from touching.

Exploring with my fingers, I discover a strip of cheap varnished wood of the kind you find on sale in souvenir shops at the seaside: on one side are four spots of Blu-tack, as smooth and flat as the surface they recently adhered to; on the other, the transfer of a figure in a blue crinoline dress and, in painted letters to the right of it, the words: Alma's Room.

The house where they discovered the mutilated remains of Mrs Crippen (stage name: 'Belle Elmore') was a stone's throw from the Finsbury Park Empire; it was turned into a theatrical digs by Sandy McNab, the Scottish comedian, after Crippen was apprehended and hanged.

When they searched 10 Rillington Place after arresting the necrophiliac murderer Christie, they found, in addition to a number of women's bodies, a tobacco tin containing four lots of pubic hair.

In those instances where the tapes aren't sufficient to fill a shoe-box completely, McLaren has made up the extra volume with tissue paper. The box containing the tapes relating to the year 1964 and, I suspect, the object of my visit, is roughly half and half. I pick out a cassette dated December 26th, 1964, and load it into the machine.

It's a fragment of a Christmas show which went out that evening on Radio Luxembourg. According to the information given on the box, I sing three numbers: 'Happy Days Are Here Again', in the slow-tempo Streisand version; a pretty, schmaltzy song, 'This Time of Year', and 'Little Drummer Boy'.

The tape in fact begins towards the end of 'Happy Days . . .' and proceeds uneventfully until a few lines into the second track. Then the headset communicates a sensation which is like falling through several hundred feet in an air-pocket, with the accompanying drop in air pressure.

It stabilises – 'Evergreens are snowy white/Sleighbells ring through the night/This time of year'; then the same thing again in a less stomach-rolling version.

It continues in this way for the remaining seven minutes – lurching from almost perfect clarity and balance in one passage, to what could be a third- or fourth-generation, or even older, copy in the next.

It's as though dropouts caused by physical damage to the tape, or sections of tape corruption or decay, have been laboriously reconstituted, layer on layer, and the original magnetic impulses boosted back to nearly full strength. There is evidence of dub-editing, splicing, and sophisticated electronic enhancement of the final product.

Yet, for all that, a fluctuating, almost subliminal undercurrent

200

of discords and weird microtones persists; the tracks are punctu-
ated with indistinct muffled cracks and swoops.

There is none of the hyper-reality that characterises even the
oldest of the other tapes. The density of information is low and
resonates with the acoustics of a particular room at a particular
but, as it has proved, infinitely reclaimable moment in time.

It is only since they reopened the search for bodies on the Moors
that it has emerged that Ian Brady bought Myra Hindley a pop
record every time he decided to do another killing.

On the day of Pauline Reade's death it was the theme music
from *The Hill*, a film they had seen together at a cinema in
Oldham. On the day they murdered a twelve-year-old called
John Kilbride it was Gene Pitney singing 'Twenty-four Hours
From Tulsa'. For Keith Bennett it was Roy Orbison's 'It's Over';
and for Edward Evans, whom Brady murdered with a hatchet on
their living-room carpet, it was Joan Baez's version of 'It's All
Over Now, Baby Blue'.

'Girl Don't Come' by Sandie Shaw was Brady's present to
commemorate the murder of Lesley Ann Downey. But 'Little
Red Rooster' by the Rolling Stones is the record that Hindley
would associate with this killing. That's what was playing at the
funfair in Miles Platting in Manchester when they approached
the ten-year-old girl and asked her to help them carry some
shopping back to the car and then to their house.

Like all their child victims, according to Myra Hindley, she
went 'like a lamb to the slaughter'. It was between five and six in
the evening on Boxing Day, December 26th, 1964.

McLaren is sleeping half-propped up in bed with his head tilted
towards the door. He has grown a pale stubble beard in the last
two hours. He's wearing pyjamas and a tweedy dressing gown

201

under the blankets and when he opens his eyes seems unsurprised to see me standing by the bed.

A plastic strip shading the light in the headboard has buckled from the heat. My picture smiles down from a poster for a bill at the Ardwick Empire, with Eddie Arnold, Mr Everybody, Alf Carlson, Continental Contortionist, Devine and King, Professors of Music, Raf and Julian, Two Wrongs Make A Riot, and the Lyn Bahrys, Fast and Furious, in support.

They drove Lesley Ann Downey to where they were living at 16 Wardle Brook Avenue in the Hattersley district of Manchester, where Hindley knew Brady had already set up his camera, tripod and lighting equipment in the upstairs back room. The tape recorder was under the bed, hidden by a sheet.

Brady made the little girl take off her clothes and pose for pornographic pictures on the bed, before raping her and strangling her with a piece of string. Hindley, standing by the window while all – some – of this was going on (the black wig she had worn to the funfair removed or still in place?), tuned the radio to Radio Luxembourg, allowing my voice to bring the message (which is really radio's only message now) that the rest of the world was still there and all right.

She interrupted her reverie to help Brady pack a gag into Lesley Ann's mouth, and to run a bath to get rid of any dog hairs or fibres on her body.

         pa-ruppa-pum-pum . . .

WOMAN   Will you stop it. Stop it.
            (Woman's voice, unreadable)
            (Child whimpering)

MAN	Quick. Put it in now. (Child whimpering) (Retching noise)
MAN	Just put it in now, love. Put it in now. (Retching noise)

I am a poor boy too pa-ruppa-pum-pum . . .

CHILD	Please God. I can't breathe.
CHILD	Can I just tell you summat? Please take your hands off me a minute, please. Please – mummy – please.

So to honour him pa-ruppa-pum-pum . . .

MAN	Why don't you keep it in?
CHILD	Why? What are you going to do with me?

Shall I play for him pa-ruppa-pum-pum . . .

MAN	(Unreadable) . . . some photographs, that's all.
MAN	Put it in.
CHILD	Don't undress me, will you?

And then he smiled at me pa-ruppa-pum-pum . . .

MAN	Put it in your mouth. (Pause.) Right in.
CHILD	I'm not going to do owt.
MAN	Put it in. If you don't keep your hand down I'll slit your neck. (Pause. Woman speaking, unreadable.) Put it in.
CHILD	Won't you let me go? Please.
MAN	No, no. Put it in. Stop talking.

The ox and lamb kept time pa-ruppa-pum-pum . . .

CHILD	I have to get home before eight o'clock. I got to get – (Laboured breathing.) Or I'll get killed if I don't. Honest to God.
MAN	Yes.

I played my drum for him pa-ruppa-pum-pum . . .
                    (Oh yes I did)

> (Quick footsteps of woman leaving room and going
> downstairs; then a click; then sound of door closing;
> then woman's footsteps coming upstairs; then eight
> longer strides)

WOMAN   I've left the light on.
MAN   You have?

I played my best for him pa-ruppa-pum-pum . . .

CHILD   It hurts me neck.
MAN   Hush, put it in your mouth and you'll be all right.
WOMAN   Now listen, shurrup crying.
CHILD   (Crying) It hurts me on me—
WOMAN   (Interrupting) Hush. Shut up. Now put it in. Pull that
         hand away and don't dally and just keep your mouth
         shut, please.

I played my drum for him . . .
I played my best for him . . .

WOMAN   Wait a bit, I'll put this on again. D'you get me?
CHILD   (Whining) No I—
WOMAN   Sh. Hush. Put that in your mouth. And again—
         packed more solid.
CHILD   I want to go home. Honest to God. I'll –(Further
         speech muffled)– before eight o'clock.
WOMAN   No, it's all right.
MAN   Eh!

. . . and my drum
Rat-a-tat-ta . . . Rat-a-tat-ta . . .
Say it! – Me and my drum . . .
You'll never get lonely . . . With me and my drum . . .

204

(Three loud cracks, systematic, even-timed)
(Music goes fainter)
(Footsteps)
(Sounds on tape cease)

Francis McLaren puts the cassette back in its *Ray Conniff: For Sentimental Reasons* box and returns it to the anonymity of the rack. (So many secrets!)

The cord of his dressing-gown ends in tassels with heavy silken domes. The backs of his slippers have been broken under his heels.

'I don't see what the fuss is about,' he says, although this is contradicted by a vein in his temple. 'A few years ago anybody could buy a copy in Manchester. If you went to the right pub. You could buy *pictures* of the girl if you knew the right channels. The people into this area. Distributors. Dealers. Collectors. One of the police from the case was done for selling pictures, for Godsake.

'My only interest was you. The unavailability of those tracks anywhere else. The rarity value. It was a big job getting it up to even the quality it is now.'

What am I going to say?

I read somewhere that no musical vibrations are ever lost: that even though they are dispersed, they will go on vibrating through the cosmos for eternity.

I imagine I hear screams coming from cars when I am standing waiting to cross at the kerb sometimes, but it's only *Orfeo ed Euridice*, Madonna, B. B. King and Lucille or some other electric ghost trapped in the tape shell, the transport mechanism, the spatial dynamics in which two solitudes promiscuously approach one another.

Ten

Laura Ashley in the bedroom. Crabtree and Evelyn in the bathroom (horse-chestnut and hop bath gel; calendula and evening primrose soap; vetiver talcum powder).

And no sign – or just one sign: a used tray of Nurofen caplets at the bottom of the wastebin – of the bodies who have tumbled in the bed, streaked the towels, called down for the special 'Eye-Opener breakfast' of bacon and egg muffin and chilled orange juice, steadied themselves to face the world with a ten-pound spend at the mini-bar.

The paper seal across the toilet reminded me of the tape markers the police wind between lamp-posts and parking meters in bomb-scare areas. The corners of the first sheet of toilet paper had been turned in, the top tissue in the Kleenex dispenser fluffed up. The extractor roars like a DC-10 when the light goes on, with the result that everything is done in the half-dark.

There's blow-drier, mini-safe, electric trouser-press, electric kettle, sachets of hot chocolate, Maxwell House, Sweetex, a caramel wafer, 'everything', according to the wallet of room-service menus and brochures, 'to enable the renaissance businessman or woman to temper effort with relaxation.'

The television has Teletext, a picture-in-picture digital effects system, subscriber porno-channel. At the minute a Welsh collie bitch called Josie is snuffling up and down a row of handkerchiefs trying to find the right one to bring to her owner in a re-run of the obedience trials at this year's Crufts. There's a number '3' in a fluttering green box in the top right-hand corner of the picture whose significance I don't understand.

'This is a non-smoking bedroom in support of the British Lung Foundation' it says beside the symbol of a small red balloon on a string on the door. And yet it smelled of stale smoke when I arrived, which suggests somebody trying to kid themselves that they've kicked the habit, or a heavy smoker in the next room.

There's an adjoining door. The television was on late, and again first thing this morning. When I got up to let some air in around two, there was a line of light running across the carpet and a news report about a Cambridge woman becoming the world's first triple heart, lungs and liver transplant patient.

There was steady traffic on the ring-roads and service roads around the six-lane flyover that curves past the hotel. Turning a map of the local area around in my hands until it becomes aligned with it, I can now identify it as the A627M.

'15 mins Manchester City Centre' it says next to an arrow pointing in one direction. Other arrows point towards Ashton-under-Lyne, Macclesfield, Leeds and the Acorn, West Point and Star industrial estates. Numbered blobs on the map, prepared by the hotel, indicate all-night petrol stations, chemists, cash machines and other essential back-up services for pistol-packing eighties lives lived on the run.

Number twelve is Butterflys Nightclub; thirteen, Mario's Trattoria. Fourteen is the Light of Bengal Indian Restaurant in Waterloo Street, which had disappeared when I tried to find it last night. Waterloo Street was still there, but the Light of Bengal was a water-filled hole in the ground.

I ended up eating the three-nuggets-and-fries special from a box in a Tennessee Chicken where I was the only customer, but it wasn't as desolate as that makes it sound. It was wet outside, which is always a good feeling; and there was a row of shops opposite with interesting sodium-washed displays and fronts, and

207

I could see the boy who had served me reflected in the window reading what looked like a worthwhile book.

Although it's midday there's a queue snaking from the ballroom entrance right across the car park in front of the hotel. The names of the surrounding streets – Union, Foundry, Corporation, Albion – and their still-to-be-developed façades, suggest dole queues, soup kitchens, bread lines.

But the people queueing don't look poor. They have padded shoulders, big hair, stacked heels, tight bright patent surfaces of viscose, polycotton, elastane-enriched nylon, glazed rubber compounds.

'Car radio. Compact disc hi-fi. Deep freeze,' the taxi driver says. 'Walkman. Video recorder. Portable telephone. Answer machine. Household goods. They buy.' He passes me back a flyer. 'Auction sale. Comprehensive stock and assorted merchandise of manufacturers, distributors and others. All items to clear!!'

He's wearing a turban, which makes him a Sikh. A tight strap of grey beard.

Sikhs. Fighting men. Sabres. The Golden Temple at Amritsar. A taboo on cutting hair. I know nothing about their history or what they believe. If I did would I find anything, some ritual or rite or piece of arcana, to rationalise what I'm doing, or at least help throw some light on what it exactly is that has brought me here?

We pass the open market, combining drabness with cheerful displays on vivid plastic grass; then the football ground. Then the close black streets quickly give way to moorland and oppressive black hills.

We are climbing into what I have learned is known locally as 'moor grime' – fog that rolls off the moors and along the terraces of cottage houses, casting a smutty grey-turning light.

The village of Greenfield has a newsagent, a chapel, a baker, a shop specialising in model railways, a hairdresser called 'P'Zazz', and a pub, the Clarence, where Myra Hindley waited in her scarf and black wig on the night Brady killed John Kilbride on the Moor.

A left turn at the Clarence begins the ascent on to Saddleworth Moor. There are terraced gardens on the left for a while, with people pottering; and then fog-coloured sheep with their coats hanging off them in ice-ball clumps; and then – nothing.

The Moor rises like a wall on the left and falls away steeply to the right for several hundred yards, and then this is reversed; it breaks up into ravines and chines and blood-blisters in the middle-distance and is marbled all over with brooks and streams like stewing meat.

It suggests the overview of a city – earthworks and mounds muffling the monumental architecture of a Glasgow or a Leeds. Victorian town halls, public libraries, banks, swimming baths, corn exchanges, railway stations and squares cladded in hoar grass, heather, bracken, gorse and rich dark peaty earth.

Occasional police vehicles pass us travelling in the opposite direction, but that is the only clue that people are out there, excavating, digging, covering the ground.

I get the driver to pull in to a lay-by close to what I estimate is Hollin Brow Knoll, where they found the body of Lesley Ann Downey in 1965. Brady had practised carrying bodies with Hindley at this spot, telling her to make herself as limp as possible and then putting her over his shoulder and walking with her on the Moor.

Lesley Ann Downey's is the only body he had to carry: the others all walked to their deaths, lured there by Myra Hindley, who asked them to help her find a glove she had lost.

The earth looks scorched, not loamy and wet. Pauline Reade stepped on it wearing the white shoes she had bought a few hours earlier for the dance she was on her way to when she was waylaid.

Brady cut her throat with a knife then buried her in her pink dress, her blue coat and her new shoes with the chafing heels and the manufacturer's gold writing still on the curve of the sole.

Half a mile further on we come across a tea wagon with an old man in a white coat at the window and a single customer in the nothingness leaning in. 'Snoopys', a big sign on pink card says. 'As seen on TV. LWT. TVAM. NewsNorthWest. World In Action. BBC Breakfast Time.'

I pay off the driver and arrange for him to collect me near the pub in the village in two hours.

'Reporter?' the old man calls. 'You a reporter? You could be a reporter. What paper?'

It's only the living you have to be scared of, not the dead. Somebody said that to me once. Who, I can't remember. But it's as good a thought as any to hang on to now as I start back on the road to Greenfield through the skirts of rubbing mist and grime.

It's no longer possible to step off the road directly on to the Moor: irrigation ditches have been dug; barbed wire fences have gone up fringed with scraps of wool which give the direction of the wind.

But a gap will open up soon, an opportunity will present itself. And when it does I will slip through it and, with the knife which has grown warm under my hand – a satisfyingly heavy piece of flatware with the name of the hotel stamped in the blade – will cut a small grave for the door plaque with the words 'Alma's Room' and the crinoline lady that I am carrying in my pocket.

I will pack the peat around it with my fingers and close the lid of turf and make certain before I leave it that the Moor has been put back to its original state.

A Selected List of Fiction Available from Minerva

While every effort is made to keep prices low, it is sometimes necessary to increase prices at short notice. Mandarin Paperbacks reserves the right to show new retail prices on covers which may differ from those previously advertised in the text or elsewhere.

The prices shown below were correct at the time of going to press.

☐ 7493 9145 6	**Love and Death on Long Island**		Gilbert Adair	£4.99
☐ 7493 9130 8	**The War of Don Emmanuel's Nether Parts**	Louis de Bernieres		£5.99
☐ 7493 9903 1	**Dirty Faxes**		Andrew Davies	£4.99
☐ 7493 9056 5	**Nothing Natural**		Jenny Diski	£4.99
☐ 7493 9173 1	**The Trick is to Keep Breathing**		Janice Galloway	£4.99
☐ 7493 9124 3	**Honour Thy Father**		Lesley Glaister	£4.99
☐ 7493 9918 X	**Richard's Feet**		Carey Harrison	£6.99
☐ 7493 9028 X	**Not Not While the Giro**		James Kelman	£4.99
☐ 7493 9112 X	**Hopeful Monsters**		Nicholas Mosley	£6.99
☐ 7493 9029 8	**Head to Toe**		Joe Orton	£4.99
☐ 7493 9117 0	**The Good Republic**		William Palmer	£5.99
☐ 7493 9162 6	**Four Bare Legs in a Bed**		Helen Simpson	£4.99
☐ 7493 9134 0	**Rebuilding Coventry**		Sue Townsend	£4.99
☐ 7493 9151 0	**Boating for Beginners**		Jeanette Winterson	£4.99
☐ 7493 9915 5	**Cyrus Cyrus**		Adam Zameenzad	£7.99

All these books are available at your bookshop or newsagent, or can be ordered direct from the publisher. Just tick the titles you want and fill in the form below.

Mandarin Paperbacks, Cash Sales Department, PO Box 11, Falmouth, Cornwall TR10 9EN.

Please send cheque or postal order, no currency, for purchase price quoted and allow the following for postage and packing:

UK including BFPO £1.00 for the first book, 50p for the second and 30p for each additional book ordered to a maximum charge of £3.00.

Overseas including Eire £2 for the first book, £1.00 for the second and 50p for each additional book thereafter.

NAME (Block letters) ....

ADDRESS ....

....

☐ I enclose my remittance for ....

☐ I wish to pay by Access/Visa Card Number

Expiry Date